MEMOIRS OF A GEISHA

Arthur Golden

MEMOIRS OF A
GEISHA

VINTAGE

Published by Vintage 1999

8 10 9

Copyright © Arthur Golden 1997

The right of Arthur Golden to be identified as the author
of this work has been asserted by him in accordance
with the Copyright, Designs and Patents Act, 1988

This book is sold subject to the condition that it shall not, by
way of trade or otherwise, be lent, resold, hired out, or otherwise circulated without the publisher's prior consent in any
form of binding or cover other than in which it is published
and without a similar condition including this condition being
imposed on the subsequent purchaser

First published in Great Britain by
Chatto and Windus 1997

Vintage
Random House, 20 Vauxhall Bridge Road,
London SW1V 2SA

Random House Australia (Pty) Limited
20 Alfred Street, Milsons Point, Sydney,
New South Wales 2061, Australia

Random House New Zealand Limited
18 Poland Road, Glenfield,
Auckland 10, New Zealand

Random House (Pty) Limited
Endulini, 5a Jubilee Road, Parktown 2193,
South Africa

The Random House Group Limited Reg. No. 954009
www.randomhouse.co.uk

A CIP catalogue record for this book
is available from the British Library

ISBN 0 09 928285 2

Papers used by Random House are natural,
recyclable products made from wood grown in sustain-
able forests. The manufacturing processes conform to the
environmental regulations of the country of origin.

Set in 10½/12 Sabon by SX Composing DTP, Rayleigh, Essex
Printed and bound in Denmark by
Nørhaven Paperback A/S, Viborg

TRANSLATOR'S NOTE

ONE EVENING IN the spring of 1936, when I was a boy of fourteen, my father took me to a dance performance in Kyoto. I remember only two things about it. The first is that he and I were the only Westerners in the audience; we had come from our home in the Netherlands only a few weeks earlier, so I had not yet adjusted to the cultural isolation and still felt it acutely. The second is how pleased I was, after months of intensive study of the Japanese language, to find that I could now understand fragments of the conversations I overheard. As for the young Japanese women dancing on the stage before me, I remember nothing of them except a vague impression of brightly colored kimono. I certainly had no way of knowing that in a time and place as far away as New York City nearly fifty years in the future, one among them would become my good friend and would dictate her extraordinary memoirs to me.

As a historian, I have always regarded memoirs as source material. A memoir provides a record not so much of the memoirist as of the memoirist's world. It must differ from biography in that a memoirist can never achieve the perspective that a biographer possesses as a matter of course. Autobiography, if there really is such a thing, is like asking a rabbit to tell us what he looks like hopping through the grasses of the field. How would he know? If we want to hear about the field, on the other hand, no one is in a better circumstance to tell us – so long as we keep in mind that we are missing all those things the rabbit was in no position to observe.

I say this with the certainty of an academician who has based a career on such distinctions. And yet I must confess that the memoirs of my dear friend Nitta Sayuri have impelled me to rethink my views. Yes, she does elucidate for us the very secret world in which she lived – the rabbit's view of the field, if you will. There may well be no better record of the strange life of a geisha than the one Sayuri offers. But she leaves behind as well a record of herself that is far more complete, more accurate, and more compelling than the lengthy chapter examining her life in the book *Glittering Jewels of Japan*, or in the various magazine articles about her that have appeared over the years. It seems that at least in the case of this one unusual subject, no one knew the memoirist as well as the memoirist herself.

That Sayuri should have risen to prominence was largely a matter of chance. Other women have led similar lives. The renowned Kato Yuki – a geisha who captured the heart of George Morgan, nephew of J. Pierpont, and became his bride-in-exile during the first decade of this century – may have lived a life even more unusual in some ways than Sayuri's. But only Sayuri has documented her own saga so completely. For a long while I believed that her choice to do so was a fortuitous accident. If she had remained in Japan, her life would have been too full for her to consider compiling her memoirs. However, in 1956 circumstances in her life led Sayuri to emigrate to the United States. For her remaining forty years, she was a resident of New York City's Waldorf Towers, where she created for herself an elegant Japanese-style suite on the thirty-second floor. Even then her life continued at its frenetic pace. Her suite saw more than its share of Japanese artists, intellectuals, business figures – even cabinet ministers and a gangster or two. I did not meet her until an acquaintance introduced us in 1985. As a scholar of Japan, I had encountered Sayuri's name, though I knew almost nothing about her. Our friendship grew, and she confided in me more and more. One day I asked if she would ever permit her story to be told.

'Well, Jakob-san, I might, if it's you who records it,' she told me.

So it was that we began our task. Sayuri was clear that she wanted to dictate her memoirs rather than write them herself, because, as she explained, she was so accustomed to talking face-to-face that she would hardly know how to proceed with no one in the room to listen. I agreed, and the manuscript was dictated to me over the course of eighteen months. I was never more aware of Sayuri's Kyoto dialect – in which geisha themselves are called *geiko*, and kimono are sometimes known as *obebe* – than when I began to wonder how I would render its nuances in translation. But from the very start I felt myself lost in her world. On all but a few occasions we met in the evening; because of long habit, this was the time when Sayuri's mind was most alive. Usually she preferred to work in her suite at the Waldorf Towers, but from time to time we met in a private room at a Japanese restaurant on Park Avenue, where she was well known. Our sessions generally lasted two or three hours. Although we tape-recorded each session, her secretary was present to transcribe her dictation as well, which she did very faithfully. But Sayuri never spoke to the tape recorder or to the secretary; she spoke always to me. When she had doubts about where to proceed, I was the one who steered her. I regarded myself as the foundation upon which the enterprise was based and felt that her story would never have been told had I not gained her trust. Now I've come to see that the truth may be otherwise. Sayuri chose me as her amanuensis, to be sure, but she may have been waiting all along for the right candidate to present himself.

Which brings us to the central question: Why did Sayuri want her story told? Geisha may not take any formal vow of silence, but their existence is predicated on the singularly Japanese conviction that what goes on during the morning in the office and what goes on during the evening behind closed doors bear no relationship to one another, and must always remain compartmentalized and separate. Geisha simply do not talk for the record about their experiences. Like prostitutes, their lower-class counterparts, geisha are often in the unusual position of knowing whether this or that public figure really does put his pants on one leg at a time like everyone else. Probably it is to their credit that these butterflies of the night regard their roles as a kind of public trust, but in any case, the geisha who violates that trust puts herself in an untenable position. Sayuri's circumstances in telling her story were unusual, in that no one in Japan had power over her any longer. Her ties with her native country had already been severed. This may tell us, at least in part, why she no longer felt constrained to silence, but it does not tell us why she chose to talk. I was afraid to raise the question with her; what if, in examining her own scruples on the subject, she should change her mind? Even when the manuscript was complete, I felt reluctant to ask. Only after she had received her advance from the publisher did I feel it safe to query her: Why had she wanted to document her life?

'What else do I have to do with my time these days?' she replied.

As to whether or not her motives were really as simple as this, I leave the reader to decide.

Though she was eager to have her biography recorded, Sayuri did insist upon several conditions. She wanted the manuscript published only after her death and the deaths of several men who had figured prominently in her life. As it turned out, they all predeceased her. It was a great concern of Sayuri's that no one be embarrassed by her revelations. Whenever possible I have left names unchanged, though Sayuri did hide the identities of certain men even from me through the convention, rather common among geisha, of referring to customers by means of an epithet. When encountering characters such as Mr. Snowshowers – whose moniker suggests itself because of his dandruff – the reader who believes Sayuri is only trying to amuse may have misunderstood her real intent.

When I asked Sayuri's permission to use a tape recorder, I intended it only as a safeguard against any possible errors of transcription on the part of her secretary. Since her death last year, however, I have wondered if I had another motive as well – namely, to preserve her voice, which had a quality of expressiveness I have rarely encountered. Customarily she spoke with a soft tone, as one might expect of a woman who has made a career of entertaining men. But when she wished to bring a scene to life before me, her voice could make me think there were six or eight people in the room. Sometimes still, I play her tapes during the evenings in my study and find it very difficult to believe she is no longer alive.

Jakob Haarhuis
Arnold Rusoff Professor of Japanese History
New York University

I

SUPPOSE THAT YOU and I were sitting in a quiet room overlooking a garden, chatting and sipping at our cups of green tea while we talked about something that had happened a long while ago, and I said to you, 'That afternoon when I met so-and-so . . . was the very best afternoon of my life, and also the very worst afternoon.' I expect you might put down your teacup and say, 'Well, now, which was it? Was it the best or the worst? Because it can't possibly have been both!' Ordinarily I'd have to laugh at myself and agree with you. But the truth is that the afternoon when I met Mr. Tanaka Ichiro really was the best and the worst of my life. He seemed so fascinating to me, even the fish smell on his hands was a kind of perfume. If I had never known him, I'm sure I would not have become a geisha.

I wasn't born and raised to be a Kyoto geisha. I wasn't even born in Kyoto. I'm a fisherman's daughter from a little town called Yoroido on the Sea of Japan. In all my life I've never told more than a handful of people anything at all about Yoroido, or about the house in which I grew up, or about my mother and father, or my older sister – and certainly not about how I became a geisha, or what it was like to be one. Most people would much rather carry on with their fantasies that my mother and grandmother were geisha, and that I began my training in dance when I was weaned from the breast, and so on. As a matter of fact, one day many years ago I was pouring a cup of sake for a man who happened to mention that he had been in Yoroido only the previous week. Well, I felt as a bird must feel when it has flown across the ocean and comes upon a creature that knows its nest. I was so

1

shocked I couldn't stop myself from saying:

'Yoroido! Why, that's where I grew up!'

This poor man! His face went through the most remarkable series of changes. He tried his best to smile, though it didn't come out well because he couldn't get the look of shock off his face.

'Yoroido?' he said. 'You can't mean it.'

I long ago developed a very practiced smile, which I call my 'Noh smile' because it resembles a Noh mask whose features are frozen. Its advantage is that men can interpret it however they want; you can imagine how often I've relied on it. I decided I'd better use it just then, and of course it worked. He let out all his breath and tossed down the cup of sake I'd poured for him before giving an enormous laugh I'm sure was prompted more by relief than anything else.

'The very idea!' he said, with another big laugh. 'You, growing up in a dump like Yoroido. That's like making tea in a bucket!' And when he'd laughed again, he said to me, 'That's why you're so much fun, Sayuri-san. Sometimes you almost make me believe your little jokes are real.'

I don't much like thinking of myself as a cup of tea made in a bucket, but I suppose in a way it must be true. After all, I did grow up in Yoroido, and no one would suggest it's a glamorous spot. Hardly anyone ever visits it. As for the people who live there, they never have occasion to leave. You're probably wondering how I came to leave it myself. That's where my story begins.

In our little fishing village of Yoroido, I lived in what I called a 'tipsy house.' It stood near a cliff where the wind off the ocean was always blowing. As a child it seemed to me as if the ocean had caught a terrible cold, because it was always wheezing and there would be spells when it let out a huge sneeze – which is to say there was a burst of wind with a tremendous spray. I decided our tiny house must have been offended by the ocean sneezing in its face from time to time, and took to leaning back because it wanted to get out of the way. Probably it would have collapsed if my father hadn't cut a timber from a wrecked fishing boat to prop up the eaves, which made the house look like a tipsy old man leaning on his crutch.

Inside this tipsy house I lived something of a lopsided life. Because from my earliest years I was very much like my mother, and hardly at all like my father or older sister. My mother said it was because we were made just the same, she and I – and it was true we both had the same peculiar eyes of a sort you almost never see in Japan. Instead of being dark brown like everyone else's, my mother's eyes were a translucent gray, and mine are just the same. When I was very young, I told my mother I thought someone had poked a hole in her eyes and all the ink had drained out, which she thought very funny. The fortune-tellers said her eyes were so pale because of too much water in her personality, so much that the other four elements were hardly present at all – and this, they explained, was why her features matched so poorly. People in the village often said she ought to have been extremely attractive, because her parents had been. Well, a peach has a lovely taste and so does a mushroom, but you can't put the two together; this was the terrible trick nature had played on her. She had her mother's pouty mouth but her father's angular jaw, which gave the impression of a delicate picture with much too heavy a frame. And her lovely gray eyes were surrounded by thick lashes that must have been striking on her father, but in her case only made her look startled.

My mother always said she'd married my father because she had too much water in her personality and he had too much wood in his. People who knew my father understood right away what she was talking about. Water flows from place to place quickly and always finds a crack to spill through. Wood, on the other hand, holds fast to the earth. In my father's case this was a good thing, for he was a fisherman, and a man with wood in his personality is at ease on the sea. In fact, my father was more at ease on the sea than anywhere else, and never left it far behind him. He smelled like the sea even after he had bathed. When he wasn't fishing, he sat on the floor in our dark front room mending a fishing net. And if a fishing net had been a sleeping creature, he wouldn't even have awakened it, at the speed he worked. He did everything

3

this slowly. Even when he summoned a look of concentration, you could run outside and drain the bath in the time it took him to rearrange his features. His face was very heavily creased, and into each crease he had tucked some worry or other, so that it wasn't really his own face any longer, but more like a tree that had nests of birds in all the branches. He had to struggle constantly to manage it and always looked worn out from the effort.

When I was six or seven, I learned something about my father I'd never known. One day I asked him, 'Daddy, why are you so old?' He hoisted up his eyebrows at this, so that they formed little sagging umbrellas over his eyes. And he let out a long breath, and shook his head and said, 'I don't know.' When I turned to my mother, she gave me a look meaning she would answer the question for me another time. The following day without saying a word, she walked me down the hill toward the village and turned at a path into a graveyard in the woods. She led me to three graves in the corner, with three white marker posts much taller than I was. They had stern-looking black characters written top to bottom on them, but I hadn't attended the school in our little village long enough to know where one ended and the next began. My mother pointed to them and said, 'Natsu, wife of Sakamoto Minoru.' Sakamoto Minoru was the name of my father. 'Died age twenty-four, in the nineteenth year of Meiji.' Then she pointed to the next one: 'Jinichiro, son of Sakamoto Minoru, died age six, in the nineteenth year of Meiji,' and to the next one, which was identical except for the name, Masao, and the age, which was three. It took me a while to understand that my father had been married before, a long time ago, and that his whole family had died. I went back to those graves not long afterward and found as I stood there that sadness was a very heavy thing. My body weighed twice what it had only a moment earlier, as if those graves were pulling me down toward them.

With all this water and all this wood, the two of them ought to have made a good balance and produced children with the proper arrangement of elements. I'm sure it was a surprise to

4

When Mameha mentioned my role on the stage, I thought she was making up a story on the spot to explain why Hatsumomo might lie about me. So you can imagine my surprise the next day when I learned she'd been telling the truth. Or if it wasn't exactly the truth, Mameha felt confident that it would be true before the end of the week.

At that time, in the mid-1930s, probably as many as seven or eight hundred geisha worked in Gion; but because no more than sixty were needed each spring for the production of *Dances of the Old Capital*, the competition for roles destroyed more than a few friendships over the years. Mameha hadn't been truthful when she said that she'd taken a role from Hatsumomo; she was one of the very few geisha in Gion guaranteed a solo role every year. But it was quite true that Hatsumomo had been desperate to see Pumpkin on the stage. I don't know where she got the idea such a thing was possible; Pumpkin may have earned the apprentice's award and received other honors besides, but she never excelled at dance. However, a few days before I presented *ekubo* to the Doctor, a seventeen-year-old apprentice with a solo role had fallen down a flight of stairs and hurt her leg. The poor girl was devastated, but every other apprentice in Gion was happy to take advantage of her misfortune by offering to fill the role. It was this role that in the end went to me. I was only fifteen at the time, and had never danced on the stage before – which isn't to say I wasn't ready to. I'd spent so many evenings in the okiya, rather than going from party to party like most apprentices, and Auntie often played the shamisen so that I could practice dance. This was why I'd already been promoted to the eleventh level by the age of fifteen, even though I probably possessed no more talent as a dancer than anyone else. If Mameha hadn't been so determined to keep me hidden from the public eye because of Hatsumomo, I might even have had a role in the seasonal dances the previous year.

This role was given to me in mid-March, so I had only a month or so to rehearse it. Fortunately my dance teacher was very helpful and often worked with me privately during the afternoons. Mother didn't find out what had happened –

Hatsumomo certainly wasn't going to tell her – until several days afterward, when she heard the rumor during a game of mah-jongg. She came back to the okiya and asked if it was true I'd been given the role. After I told her it was, she walked away with the sort of puzzled look she might have worn if her dog Taku had added up the columns in her account books for her.

Of course, Hatsumomo was furious, but Mameha wasn't concerned about it. The time had come, as she put it, for us to toss Hatsumomo from the ring.

21

LATE ONE AFTERNOON a week or so later, Mameha came up to me during a break in rehearsals, very excited about something. It seemed that on the previous day, the Baron had mentioned to her quite casually that he would be giving a party during the coming weekend for a certain kimono maker named Arashino. The Baron owned one of the best-known collections of kimono in all of Japan. Most of his pieces were antiques, but every so often he bought a very fine work by a living artist. His decision to purchase a piece by Arashino had prompted him to have a party.

'I thought I recognized the name Arashino,' Mameha said to me, 'but when the Baron first mentioned it, I couldn't place it. He's one of Nobu's very closest friends! Don't you see the possibilities? I didn't think of it until today, but I'm going to persuade the Baron to invite both Nobu and the Doctor to his little party. The two of them are certain to dislike each other. When the bidding begins for your *mizuage*, you can be sure that neither will sit still, knowing the prize could be taken by the other.'

I was feeling very tired, but for Mameha's sake I clapped my hands in excitement and said how grateful I was to her for coming up with such a clever plan. And I'm sure it was a clever plan; but the real evidence of her cleverness was that she felt certain she'd have no difficulty persuading the Baron to invite these two men to his party. Clearly they would both be willing to come – in Nobu's case because the Baron was an investor in Iwamura Electric, though I didn't know it at the time; and in Dr. Crab's case because . . . well, because the Doctor considered himself something of an aristocrat, even though he probably had only one obscure ancestor with any aristocratic blood, and would regard it as his duty to attend any function the Baron invited him to. But as to why the Baron would agree to invite either of them, I don't know. He didn't approve of Nobu; very few men did. As for Dr. Crab, the Baron had never met him before and might as well have invited someone off the street,

But Mameha had extraordinary powers of persuasion, as I knew. The party was arranged, and she convinced my dance instructor to release me from rehearsals the following Saturday so I could attend it. The event was to begin in the afternoon and run through dinner – though Mameha and I were to arrive after the party was underway. So it was about three o'clock when we finally climbed into a rickshaw and headed out to the Baron's estate, located at the base of the hills in the northeast of the city. It was my first visit to anyplace so luxurious, and I was quite overwhelmed by what I saw; because if you think of the attention to detail brought to bear in making a kimono, well, that same sort of attention had been brought to the design and care of the entire estate where the Baron lived. The main house dated back to the time of his grandfather, but the gardens, which struck me as a giant brocade of textures, had been designed and built by his father. Apparently the house and gardens never quite fit together until the Baron's older brother – the year before his assassination – had moved the location of the pond, and also created a moss garden with stepping-stones leading from the moon-viewing pavilion on one side of the house. Black swans glided across the pond with a bearing so proud they made me feel ashamed to be such an ungainly creature as a human being.

We were to begin by preparing a tea ceremony the men would join when they were ready; so I was very puzzled when we passed through the main gate and made our way not to an ordinary tea pavilion, but straight toward the edge of the pond to board a small boat. The boat was about the size of a narrow room. Most of it was occupied with wooden seats along the edges, but at one end stood a miniature pavilion with its own roof sheltering a tatami platform. It had actual walls with paper screens slid open for air, and in the very center was a square wooden cavity filled with sand, which served as the brazier where Mameha lit cakes of charcoal to heat the water in a graceful iron teakettle. While she was doing this, I tried to make myself useful by arranging the implements for the ceremony. Already I was feeling quite nervous, and then Mameha turned to me after she had put the kettle on the fire and said:

'You're a clever girl, Sayuri. I don't need to tell you what will become of your future if Dr. Crab or Nobu should lose interest in you. You mustn't let either of them think you're paying too much attention to the other. But of course a certain amount of jealousy won't do any harm. I'm certain you can manage it.'

I wasn't so sure, but I would certainly have to try.

A half hour passed before the Baron and his ten guests strolled out from the house, stopping every so often to admire the view of the hillside from different angles. When they'd boarded the boat, the Baron guided us into the middle of the pond with a pole. Mameha made tea, and I delivered the bowls to each of the guests.

Afterward, we took a stroll through the garden with the men, and soon came to a wooden platform suspended above the water, where several maids in identical kimono were arranging cushions for the men to sit on, and leaving vials of warm sake on trays. I made a point of kneeling beside Dr. Crab, and was just trying to think of something to say when, to my surprise, the Doctor turned to me first.

'Has the laceration on your thigh healed satisfactorily?' he asked.

This was during the month of March, you must understand, and I'd cut my leg way back in November. In the months between, I'd seen Dr. Crab more times than I could count; so I have no idea why he waited until that moment to ask me about it, and in front of so many people. Fortunately, I didn't think anyone had heard, so I kept my voice low when I answered.

'Thank you so much, Doctor. With your help it has healed completely.'

'I hope the injury hasn't left too much of a scar,' he said.

'Oh, no, just a tiny bump, really.'

I might have ended the conversation right there by pouring him more sake, perhaps, or changing the subject; but I happened to notice that he was stroking one of his thumbs with the fingers of his other hand. The Doctor was the sort of man who never wasted a single movement. If he was stroking his thumb in this way while thinking about my leg . . . well, I decided it would be foolish for me to change the subject.

'It isn't much of a scar,' I went on. 'Sometimes when I'm in the bath, I rub my finger across it, and . . . it's just a tiny ridge, really. About like this.'

I rubbed one of my knuckles with my index finger and held it out for the Doctor to do the same. He brought his hand up; but then he hesitated. I saw his eyes jump toward mine. In a moment he drew his hand back and felt his own knuckle instead.

'A cut of that sort should have healed smoothly,' he told me.

'Perhaps it isn't as big as I've said. After all, my leg is very . . . well, sensitive, you see. Even just a drop of rain falling onto it is enough to make me shudder!'

I'm not going to pretend any of this made sense. A bump wouldn't seem bigger just because my leg was sensitive; and anyway when was the last time I'd felt a drop of rain on my bare leg? But now that I understood why Dr. Crab was really interested in me, I suppose I was half-disgusted and half-fascinated as I tried to imagine what was going on in his mind. In any case, the Doctor cleared his throat and leaned toward me.

'And . . . have you been practicing?'

'Practicing?'

'You sustained the injury when you lost your balance while you were . . . well, you see what I mean. You don't want that to happen again. So I expect you've been practicing. But how does one practice such a thing?'

After this, he leaned back and closed his eyes. It was clear to me he expected to hear an answer longer than simply a word or two.

'Well, you'll think me very silly, but every night . . .' I

began; and then I had to think for a moment. The silence dragged on, but the Doctor never opened his eyes. He seemed to me like a baby bird just waiting for the mother's beak. 'Every night,' I went on, 'just before I step into the bath, I practice balancing in a variety of positions. Sometimes I have to shiver from the cold air against my bare skin; but I spend five or ten minutes that way.'

The Doctor cleared his throat, which I took as a good sign.

'First I try balancing on one foot, and then the other. But the trouble is . . .'

Up until this point, the Baron, on the opposite side of the platform from me, had been talking with his other guests; but now he ended his story. The next words I spoke were as clear as if I'd stood at a podium and announced them.

'. . . when I don't have any clothing on –'

I clapped a hand over my mouth, but before I could think of what to do, the Baron spoke up. 'My goodness!' he said. 'Whatever you two are talking about over there, it certainly sounds more interesting than what we've been saying!'

The men laughed when they heard this. Afterward the Doctor was kind enough to offer an explanation.

'Sayuri-san came to me late last year with a leg injury,' he said. 'She sustained it when she fell. As a result, I suggested she work at improving her balance.'

'She's been working at it very hard,' Mameha added. 'Those robes are more awkward than they look.'

'Let's have her take them off, then!' said one of the men – though of course, it was only a joke, and everyone laughed.

'Yes, I agree!' the Baron said. 'I never understand why women bother wearing kimono in the first place. Nothing is as beautiful as a woman without an item of clothing on her body.'

'That isn't true when the kimono has been made by my good friend Arashino,' Nobu said.

'Not even Arashino's kimono are as lovely as what they cover up,' the Baron said, and tried to put his sake cup onto the platform, though it ended up spilling. He wasn't drunk, exactly – though he was certainly much further along in his drinking than I'd ever imagined him. 'Don't misunderstand me,' he went on. 'I think Arashino's robes are lovely. Otherwise he wouldn't be sitting here beside me, now would he? But if you ask me whether I'd rather look at a kimono or a naked woman . . . well!'

'No one's asking,' said Nobu. 'I myself am interested to hear what sort of work Arashino has been up to lately.'

But Arashino didn't have a chance to answer; because the Baron, who was taking a last slurp of sake, nearly choked in his hurry to interrupt.

'Mmm . . . just a minute,' he said. 'Isn't it true that every man on this earth likes to see a naked woman? I mean, is that what you're saying, Nobu, that the naked female form doesn't interest you?'

'That isn't what I'm saying,' Nobu said. 'What I'm saying is, I think it's time for us to hear from Arashino exactly what sort of work he's been up to lately.'

'Oh, yes, I'm certainly interested too,' the Baron said. 'But you know, I do find it fascinating that no matter how different we men may seem, underneath it all we're exactly the same. You can't pretend you're above it, Nobu-san. We know the truth, don't we? There isn't a man here who wouldn't pay quite a bit of money just for the chance to watch Sayuri take a bath. Eh? That's a particular fantasy of mine, I'll admit. Now come on! Don't pretend you don't feel the same way I do.'

'Poor Sayuri is only an apprentice,' said Mameha. 'Perhaps we ought to spare her this conversation.'

'Certainly not!' the Baron answered. 'The sooner she sees the world as it really is, the better. Plenty of men act as if they don't chase women just for the chance to get underneath all those robes, but you listen to me, Sayuri; there's only one kind of man! And while we're on this subject, here's something for you to keep in mind. Every man seated here has at some point this afternoon thought of how much he would enjoy seeing you naked. What do you think of that?'

I was sitting with my hands in my lap, gazing down at the wooden platform and trying to seem demure. I had to respond in some way to what the Baron had said, particularly since everyone else was completely silent; but before I could think of what to say Nobu did something very kind. He put his sake cup down onto the platform and stood up to excuse himself.

'I'm sorry Baron, but I don't know the way to the toilet,' he said. Of course, this was my cue to escort him.

I didn't know the way to the toilet any better than Nobu; but I wasn't going to miss the opportunity to remove myself from the gathering. As I rose to my feet, a maid offered to show me the way, and led me around the pond, with Nobu following along behind.

In the house, we walked down a long hallway of blond wood with windows on one side. On the other side, brilliantly lit in the sunshine, stood display cases with glass tops. I was about to lead Nobu down to the end, but he stopped at a case containing a collection of antique swords. He seemed to be looking at the display, but mostly he drummed the fingers of his one hand, on the glass and blew air out his nose again and again, for he was still very angry. I felt troubled by what had happened as well. But I was also grateful to him for rescuing me, and I wasn't sure how to express this. At the next case – a display of tiny netsuke figures carved in ivory – I asked him if he liked antiques.

'Antiques like the Baron, you mean? Certainly not.'

The Baron wasn't a particularly old man – much younger than Nobu, in fact. But I knew what he meant; he thought of the Baron as a relic of the feudal age.

'I'm so sorry,' I said, 'I was thinking of the antiques here in the case.'

'When I look at the swords over there, they make me think of the Baron. When I look at the netsuke here, they make me think of the Baron. He's been a supporter of our company, and I owe him a great debt. But I don't like to waste my time thinking about him when I don't have to. Does that answer your question?'

I bowed to him in reply, and he strode off down the hallway to the toilet, so quickly that I couldn't reach the door first to open it for him.

Later, when we returned to the water's edge, I was pleased to see that the party was beginning to break up. Only a few of the men would remain for dinner. Mameha and I ushered the others up the path to the main gate, where their drivers were waiting for them on the side street. We bowed farewell to the last man, and I turned to find one of the Baron's servants ready to show us into the house.

Mameha and I spent the next hour in the servants' quarters, eating a lovely dinner that included *tai no usugiri* – paper-thin slices of sea bream, fanned out on a leaf-shaped ceramic plate and served with *ponzu* sauce. I would certainly have enjoyed myself if Mameha hadn't been so moody. She ate only a few bites of her sea bream and sat staring out the window at the dusk. Something about her expression made me think she would have liked to go back down to the pond and sit, biting her lip, perhaps, and peering in anger at the darkening sky.

We rejoined the Baron and his guests already partway through their dinner, in what the Baron called the 'small banquet room.' Actually, the small banquet room could have accommodated probably twenty or twenty-five people; and now that the party had shrunk in size, only Mr. Arashino, Nobu, and Dr. Crab remained. When we entered, they were eating in complete silence. The Baron was so drunk his eyes seemed to slosh around in their sockets.

Just as Mameha was beginning a conversation, Dr. Crab stroked a napkin down his mustache twice and then excused himself to use the toilet. I led him to the same hallway Nobu and I had visited earlier. Now that evening had come, I could hardly see the objects because of overhead lights reflected in the glass of the display cases. But Dr. Crab stopped at the case containing the swords and moved his head around until he could see them.

'You certainly know your way around the Baron's house,' he said.

'Oh, no, sir, I'm quite lost in such a grand place. The only reason I can find my way is because I led Nobu-san along this hallway earlier.'

'I'm sure he rushed right through,' the Doctor said. 'A man like Nobu has a poor sensibility for appreciating the items in these cases.'

I didn't know what to say to this, but the Doctor looked at me pointedly.

'You haven't seen much of the world,' he went on, 'but in time you'll learn to be careful of anyone with the arrogance to accept an invitation from a man like the Baron, and then speak to him rudely in his own house, as Nobu did this afternoon.'

I bowed at this, and when it was clear that Dr. Crab had nothing further to say, led him down the hallway to the toilet.

By the time we returned to the small banquet room, the men had fallen into conversation, thanks to the quiet skills of Mameha, who now sat in the background pouring sake. She often said the role of a geisha was sometimes just to stir the soup. If you've ever noticed the way miso settles into a cloud at the bottom of the bowl but mixes quickly with a few whisks of the chopsticks, this is what she meant.

Soon the conversation turned to the subject of kimono, and we all proceeded downstairs to the Baron's underground museum. Along the walls were huge panels that opened to reveal kimono suspended on sliding rods. The Baron sat on a stool in the middle of the room with his elbows on his knees – bleary-eyed still – and didn't speak a word while Mameha guided us through the collection. The most spectacular robe, we all agreed, was one designed to mimic the landscape of the city of Kobe, which is located on the side of a steep hill falling away to the ocean. The design began at the shoulders with blue sky and clouds; the knees represented the hillside; below that, the gown swept back into a long train showing the blue-green of the sea dotted with beautiful gold waves and tiny ships.

'Mameha,' the Baron said, 'I think you ought to wear that one to my blossom-viewing party in Hakone next week. That would be quite something, wouldn't it?'

'I'd certainly like to,' Mameha replied. 'But as I mentioned the other day, I'm afraid I won't be able to attend the party this year.'

I could see that the Baron was displeased, for his eyebrows closed down like two windows being shut. 'What do you mean? Who has booked an engagement with you that you can't break?'

'I'd like nothing more than to be there, Baron. But just this one year, I'm afraid it won't be possible. I have a medical appointment that conflicts with the party.'

'A medical appointment? What on earth does that mean? These doctors can change times around. Change it tomorrow, and be at my party next week just like you always are.'

'I do apologize,' Mameha said, 'but with the Baron's consent, I scheduled a medical appointment some weeks ago and won't be able to change it.'

'I don't recall giving you any consent! Anyway, it's not as if you need to have an abortion, or some such thing . . .'

A long, embarrassed silence followed. Mameha only adjusted her sleeves while the rest of us stood so quietly that the only sound was Mr. Arashino's wheezy breathing. I noticed that Nobu, who'd been paying no attention, turned to observe the Baron's reaction.

'Well,' the Baron said at last. 'I suppose I'd forgotten, now that you mention it . . . We certainly can't have any little barons running around, now can we? But really, Mameha, I don't see why you couldn't have reminded me about this in private . . .'

'I am sorry, Baron.'

'Anyway, if you can't come to Hakone, well, you can't! But what about the rest of you? It's a lovely party, at my estate in Hakone next weekend. You must all come! I do it every year at the height of the cherry blossoms.'

The Doctor and Arashino were both unable to attend. Nobu didn't reply; but when the Baron pressed him, he said, 'Baron, you don't honestly think I'd go all the way to Hakone to look at cherry blossoms.'

'Oh, the blossoms are just an excuse to have a party,' said the Baron. 'Anyway, it doesn't matter. We'll have that Chairman of yours. He comes every year.'

I was surprised to feel flustered at the mention of the Chairman, for I'd been thinking of him on and off throughout the afternoon. I felt for a moment as if my secret had been exposed.

'It troubles me that none of you will come,' the Baron went on. 'We were having such a nice evening until Mameha started talking about things she ought to have kept private. Well, Mameha, I have the proper punishment for you. You're no longer invited to my party this year. What's more, I want you to send Sayuri in your place.'

I thought the Baron was making a joke; but I must confess, I thought at once how lovely it would be to stroll with the Chairman through the grounds of a magnificent estate, without Nobu or Dr. Crab, or even Mameha nearby.

'It's a fine idea, Baron,' said Mameha, 'but sadly, Sayuri is busy with rehearsals.'

'Nonsense,' said the Baron. 'I expect to see her there. Why do you have to defy me every single time I ask something of you?'

He really did look angry; and unfortunately, because he was so drunk, a good deal of saliva came spilling out of his mouth. He tried to wipe it away with the back of his hand, but ended up smearing it into the long black hairs of his beard.

'Isn't there one thing I can ask of you that you won't disregard?' he went on. 'I want to see Sayuri in Hakone. You could just reply, "Yes, Baron," and be done with it.'

'Yes, Baron.'

'Fine,' said the Baron. He leaned back on his stool again, and took a handkerchief from his pocket to wipe his face clean.

I was very sorry for Mameha. But it would be an understatement to say I felt excited at the prospect of attending the Baron's party. Every time I thought of it in the rickshaw back to Gion, I think my ears turned red. I was terribly afraid Mameha would notice, but she just stared out to the side, and never spoke a word until the end of our ride, when she turned to me and said, 'Sayuri, you must be very careful in Hakone.'

'Yes, ma'am, I will,' I replied.

'Keep in mind that an apprentice on the point of having her *mizuage* is like a meal served on the table. No man will wish to eat it, if he hears a suggestion that some other man has taken a bite.'

I couldn't quite look her in the eye after she said this. I knew perfectly well she was talking about the Baron.

22

AT THIS TIME in my life I didn't even know where Hakone was – though I soon learned that it was in eastern Japan, quite some distance from Kyoto. But I had a most agreeable feeling of importance the rest of that week, reminding myself that a man as prominent as the Baron had invited me to travel from Kyoto to attend a party. In fact, I had trouble keeping my excitement from showing when at last I took my seat in a lovely second-class compartment – with Mr. Itchoda, Mameha's dresser, seated on the aisle to discourage anyone from trying to talk with me. I pretended to pass the time by reading a magazine, but in fact I was only turning the pages, for I was occupied instead with watching out of the corner of my eye as people who passed down the aisle slowed to look at me. I found myself enjoying the attention; but when we reached Shizuoka shortly after noon and I stood awaiting the train to Hakone, all at once I could feel something unpleasant welling up inside me. I'd spent the day keeping it veiled from my awareness, but now I saw in my mind much too clearly the image of myself at another time, standing on another plat-form, taking another train trip – this one with Mr. Bekku – on the day my sister and I were taken from our home. I'm ashamed to admit how hard I'd worked over the years to keep from thinking about Satsu, and my father and mother, and our tipsy house on the sea cliffs. I'd been like a child with my head in a bag. All I'd seen day after day was Gion, so much so that I'd come to think Gion was everything, and that the only thing that mattered in the world was Gion. But now that I was outside Kyoto, I could see that for most people life had nothing to do with Gion at all; and of course, I couldn't stop from thinking of the other life I'd once led. Grief is a most peculiar thing; we're so helpless in the face of it. It's like a window that will simply open of its own accord. The room grows cold, and we can do nothing but shiver. But it opens a little less each time, and a little less; and one day we wonder what has become of it.

Late the following morning I was picked up at the little inn overlooking Mount Fuji, and taken by one of the Baron's motorcars to his summer house amid lovely woods at the edge of a lake. When we pulled into a circular drive and I stepped out wearing the full regalia of an apprentice geisha from Kyoto, many of the Baron's guests turned to stare at me. Among them I spotted a number of women, some in kimono and some in Western-style dresses. Later I came to realize they were mostly Tokyo geisha – for we were only a few hours from Tokyo by train. Then the Baron himself appeared, striding up a path from the woods with several other men.

'Now, *this* is what we've all been waiting for!' he said. 'This lovely thing is Sayuri from Gion, who will probably one day be 'the great Sayuri from Gion.' You'll never see eyes like hers again, I can assure you. And just wait until you see the way she moves . . . I invited you here, Sayuri, so all the men could have a chance to look at you; so you have an important job. You must wander all around – inside the house, down by the lake, all through the woods, everywhere! Now go along and get working!'

I began to wander around the estate as the Baron had asked, past the cherry trees heavy with their blossoms, bowing here and there to the guests and trying not to seem too obvious about looking around for the Chairman. I made little headway, because every few steps some man or other would stop me and say something like, 'My heavens! An apprentice geisha from Kyoto!' And then he would take out his camera and have someone snap a picture of us standing together, or else walk me along the lake to the little moon-viewing pavilion, or wherever, so his friends could have a look at me – just as he might have done with some prehistoric creature he'd captured in a net. Mameha had warned me that everyone would be fascinated with my appearance; because there's nothing quite like an apprentice geisha from Gion. It's true that in the better geisha districts of Tokyo, such as Shimbashi and Akasaka, a girl must master the arts if she expects to make her debut. But many of the Tokyo geisha at that time were very modern in their sensibilities, which is why some were walking around the Baron's estate in Western-style clothing.

The Baron's party seemed to go on and on. By mid-afternoon I'd practically given up any hope of finding the Chairman. I went into the house to look for a place to rest, but the very moment I stepped up into the entrance hall, I felt myself go numb. There he was, emerging from a tatami room in conversation with another man. They said good-bye to each other, and then the Chairman turned to me.

'Sayuri!' he said. 'Now how did the Baron lure you here all the way from Kyoto? I didn't even realize you were acquainted with him.'

I knew I ought to take my eyes off the Chairman, but it was like pulling nails from the wall. When I finally managed to do it, I gave him a bow and said:

'Mameha-san sent me in her place. I'm so pleased to have the honor of seeing the Chairman.'

'Yes, and I'm pleased to see you too; you can give me your opinion about something. Come have a look at the present I've brought for the Baron. I'm tempted to leave without giving it to him.'

I followed him into a tatami room, feeling like a kite pulled by a string. Here I was in Hakone so far from anything I'd ever known, spending a few moments with the man I'd thought about more constantly than anyone, and it amazed me to think of it. While he walked ahead of me I had to admire how he moved so easily within his tailored wool suit. I could make out the swell of his calves, and even the hollow of his back like a cleft where the roots of a tree divide. He took something from the table and held it out for me to see. At first I thought it was an ornamented block of gold, but it turned out to be an antique cosmetics box for the Baron. This one, as the Chairman told me, was by an Edo period artist named Arata Gonroku. It was a pillow-shaped box in gold lacquer, with soft black images of flying cranes and leaping rabbits. When he put it into my hands, it was so dazzling I had to hold my breath as I looked at it.

'Do you think the Baron will be pleased?' he said. 'I found it last week and thought of him at once, but –'

'Chairman, how can you even imagine that the Baron might not feel pleased?'

'Oh, that man has collections of everything. He'll probably see this as third-rate.'

I assured the Chairman that no one could ever think such a thing; and when I gave him back the box, he tied it up in a silk cloth again and nodded toward the door for me to follow. In the entryway I helped him with his shoes. While I guided his foot with my fingertips, I found myself imagining that we'd spent the afternoon together and that a long evening lay ahead of us. This thought transported me into such a state, I don't know how much time passed before I became aware of myself again. The Chairman showed no signs of impatience, but I felt terribly self-conscious as I tried to slip my feet into my *okobo* and ended up taking much longer than I should have.

He led me down a path toward the lake, where we found the Baron sitting on a mat beneath a cherry tree with three Tokyo geisha. They all rose to their feet, though the Baron had a bit of trouble. His face had red splotches all over it from drink, so that it looked as if someone had swatted him again and again with a stick.

'Chairman!' the Baron said. 'I'm so happy you came to my party. I always enjoy having you here, do you know that? That corporation of yours just won't stop growing, will it? Did Sayuri tell you Nobu came to my party in Kyoto last week?'

'I heard all about it from Nobu, who I'm sure was his usual self.'

'He certainly was,' said the Baron. 'A peculiar little man, isn't he?'

I don't know what the Baron was thinking, for he himself was littler than Nobu. The Chairman didn't seem to like this comment, and narrowed his eyes.

'I mean to say,' the Baron began, but the Chairman cut him off.

'I have come to thank you and say good-bye, but first I have something to give you.' And here he handed over the cosmetics box. The Baron was too drunk to untie the silk cloth around it, but he gave it to one of the geisha, who did it for him.

'What a beautiful thing!' the Baron said. 'Doesn't everybody think so? Look at it. Why, it might be even lovelier than the exquisite creature standing beside you, Chairman. Do you know Sayuri? If not, let me introduce you.'

'Oh, we're well acquainted, Sayuri and I,' the Chairman said.

'How well acquainted, Chairman? Enough for me to envy you?' The Baron laughed at his own joke, but no one else did. 'Anyway, this generous gift reminds me that I have something for you, Sayuri. But I can't give it to you until these other geisha have departed, because they'll start wanting one themselves. So you'll have to stay around until everyone has gone home.'

'The Baron is too kind,' I said, 'but really, I don't wish to make a nuisance of myself.'

'I see you've learned a good deal from Mameha about how to say no to everything. Just meet me in the front entrance hall after my guests have left. You'll persuade her for me, Chairman, while she walks you to your car.'

If the Baron hadn't been so drunk, I'm sure it would have occurred to him to walk the Chairman out himself. But the two men said good-bye, and I followed the Chairman back to the house. While his driver held the door for him, I bowed and thanked him for all his kindness. He was about to get into the car, but he stopped.

'Sayuri,' he began, and then seemed uncertain how to proceed. 'What has Mameha told you about the Baron?'

'Not very much, sir. Or at least . . . well, I'm not sure what the Chairman means.'

'Is Mameha a good older sister to you? Does she tell you the things you need to know?'

'Oh, yes, Chairman. Mameha has helped me more than I can say.'

'Well,' he said, 'I'd watch out, if I were you, when a man like the Baron decides he has something to give you.'

I couldn't think of how to respond to this, so I said something about the Baron being kind to have thought of me at all.

'Yes, very kind, I'm sure. Just take care of yourself,' he said, looking at me intently for a moment, and then getting into his car.

I spent the next hour strolling among the few remaining guests, remembering again and again all the things the Chairman had said to me during our encounter. Rather than feeling concerned about the warning he had given me, I felt elated that he had spoken with me for so long. In fact, I had no space in my mind at all to think about my meeting with the Baron, until at last I found myself standing alone in the entrance hall in the fading afternoon light. I took the liberty of going to kneel in a nearby tatami room, where I gazed out at the grounds through a plate-glass window.

Ten or fifteen minutes passed; finally the Baron came striding into the entrance hall. I felt myself go sick with worry the moment I saw him, for he wore nothing but a cotton dressing robe. He had a towel in one hand, which he rubbed against the long black hairs on his face that were supposed to be a beard. Clearly he'd just stepped out of the bath. I stood and bowed to him.

'Sayuri, do you know what a fool I am!' he said to me. 'I've had too much to drink.' That part was certainly true. 'I forgot you were waiting for me! I hope you'll forgive me when you see what I've put aside for you.'

The Baron walked down the hallway toward the interior of the house, expecting me to follow him. But I remained where I was, thinking of what Mameha had said to me, that an apprentice on the point of having her *mizuage* was like a meal served on the table.

The Baron stopped. 'Come along!' he said to me.

'Oh, Baron. I really mustn't. Please permit me to wait here.'

'I have something I'd like to give you. Just come back into my quarters and sit down, and don't be a silly girl.'

'Why, Baron,' I said, 'I can't help but be a silly girl; for that's what I am!'

'Tomorrow you'll be back under the watchful eyes of Mameha, eh? But there's no one watching you here.'

If I'd had the least common sense at that moment, I would have thanked the Baron for inviting me to his lovely party and told him how much I regretted having to impose on him for the use of his motorcar to take me back to the inn. But everything had such a dream-like quality . . . I suppose I'd gone into a state of shock. All I knew for certain was how afraid I felt.

'Come back with me while I dress,' said the Baron. 'Did you drink much sake this afternoon?'

A long moment passed. I was very aware that my face felt as though it had no expression on it at all, but simply hung from my head.

'No, sir,' I managed to say at last.

'I don't suppose you would have. I'll give you as much as you like. Come along.'

'Baron,' I said, 'please, I'm quite sure I'm expected back at the inn.'

'Expected? Who is expecting you?'

I didn't answer this.

'I said, who is expecting you? I don't see why you have to behave this way. I have something to give you. Would you rather I went and fetched it?'

'I'm very sorry,' I said.

The Baron just stared at me. 'Wait here,' he said at last, and walked back into the interior of the house. A short time later he emerged holding something flat, wrapped in linen paper. I didn't have to look closely to know it was a kimono.

'Now then,' he said to me, 'since you insist on being a silly girl, I've gone and fetched your present. Does this make you feel better?'

I told the Baron I was sorry once again.

'I saw how much you admired this robe the other day. I'd like you to have it,' he said.

The Baron set the package down on the table and untied the strings to open it. I thought the kimono would be the one showing a landscape of Kobe; and to tell the truth, I felt as worried as I did hopeful, for I had no idea what I'd do with such a magnificent thing, or how I would explain to Mameha that the Baron had given it to me. But what I saw instead, when the Baron opened the wrapping, was a magnificent dark fabric with lacquered threads and embroidery in silver. He took the robe out and held it up by the shoulders. It was a kimono that belonged in a museum – made in the 1860s, as the Baron told me, for the niece of the very last shogun, Tokugawa Yoshinobu. The design on the robe was of silver birds flying against a night sky, with a mysterious landscape of dark trees and rocks rising up from the hem.

'You must come back with me and try it on,' he said. 'Now don't be a silly girl! I have a great deal of experience tying an obi with my own hands. We'll put you back into your kimono so that no one will ever know.'

I would gladly have exchanged the robe the Baron was offering me for some way out of the situation. But he was a man with so much authority that even Mameha couldn't disobey him. If she had no way of refusing his wishes, how could I? I could sense that he was losing patience; heaven knows he'd certainly been kind in the months since I'd made my debut, permitting me to attend to him while he ate lunch and allowing Mameha to bring me to the party at his Kyoto estate. And here he was being kind once again, offering me a stunning kimono.

I suppose I finally came to the conclusion that I had no choice but to obey him and pay the consequences, whatever they might be. I lowered my eyes to the mats in shame; and in this same dreamlike state I'd been feeling all along, I became aware of the Baron taking my hand and guiding me through the corridors toward the back of his house. A servant stepped into the hallway at one point, but bowed and went back the moment he caught sight of us. The Baron never spoke a word, but led me along until we came to a spacious tatami room, lined along one wall with mirrors. It was his dressing room. Along the opposite wall were closets with all their doors closed.

My hands trembled with fear, but if the Baron noticed he

made no comment. He stood me before the mirrors and raised my hand to his lips; I thought he was going to kiss it, but he only held the back of my hand against the bristles on his face and did something I found peculiar; he drew my sleeve above my wrist and took in the scent of my skin. His beard tickled my arm, but somehow I didn't feel it. I didn't seem to feel anything at all; it was as if I were buried beneath layers of fear, and confusion, and dread . . . And then the Baron woke me from my shock by stepping behind me and reaching around my chest to untie my *obijime*. This was the cord that held my obi in place.

I experienced a moment of panic now that I knew the Baron really intended to undress me. I tried saying something, but my mouth moved so clumsily I couldn't control it; and anyway, the Baron only made noises to shush me. I kept trying to stop him with my hands, but he pushed them away and finally succeeded in removing my *obijime*. After this he stepped back and struggled a long while with the knot of the obi between my shoulderblades. I pleaded with him not to take it off – though my throat was so dry that several times when I tried to speak, nothing came out – but he didn't listen to me and soon began to unwind the broad obi, wrapping and unwrapping his arms around my waist. I saw the Chairman's handkerchief dislodge itself from the fabric and flutter to the ground. In a moment the Baron let the obi fall in a pile to the floor, and then unfastened the *datejime* – the waistband underneath. I felt the sickening sensation of my kimono releasing itself from around my waist. I clutched it shut with my arms, but the Baron pulled them apart. I could no longer bear to watch in the mirror. The last thing I recall as I closed my eyes was the heavy robe being lifted from around my shoulders with a rustle of fabric.

The Baron seemed to have accomplished what he'd set out to do; or at least, he went no further for the moment. I felt his hands at my waist, caressing the fabric of my underrobe. When at last I opened my eyes again, he stood behind me still, taking in the scent of my hair and my neck. His eyes were fixed on the mirror – fixed, it seemed to me, on the waistband that held my underrobe shut. Every time his fingers moved, I

298

tried with the power of my mind to keep them away, but all too soon they began creeping like spiders across my belly and in another moment had tangled themselves in my waistband and begun to pull. I tried to stop him several times, but the Baron pushed my hands away as he'd done earlier. Finally the waistband came undone; the Baron let it slip from his fingers and fall to the floor. My legs were trembling, and the room was nothing more than a blur to me as he took the seams of my underrobe in his hands and started to draw them open. I couldn't stop myself from grabbing at his hands once again.

'Don't be so worried, Sayuri!' the Baron whispered to me. 'For heaven's sake, I'm not going to do anything to you I shouldn't do. I only want to have a look, don't you understand? There's nothing wrong in that. Any man would do the same.'

A shiny bristle from his face tickled against my ear as he said this, so that I had to turn my head to one side. I think he must have interpreted this as a kind of consent, because now his hands began to move with more urgency. He pulled my robe open. I felt his fingers on my ribs, almost tickling me as he struggled to untie the strings holding my kimono undershirt closed. A moment later he'd succeeded. I couldn't bear the thought of what the Baron might see; so even while I kept my face turned away, I strained my eyes to look in the mirror. My kimono undershirt hung open, exposing a long strip of skin down the center of my chest.

By now the Baron's hands had moved to my hips, where they were busy with my *koshimaki*. Earlier that day, when I had wrapped the *koshimaki* several times around me, I'd tucked it more tightly at the waist than I probably needed to. The Baron was having trouble finding the seam, but after several tugs he loosened the fabric, so that with one long pull he was able to draw the entire length of it out from beneath my underrobe. As the silk slid against my skin, I heard a noise coming out of my throat, something like a sob. My hands grabbed for the *koshimaki*, but the Baron pulled it from my reach and dropped it to the floor. Then as slowly as a man might peel the cover from a sleeping child, he drew open my underrobe in a long breathless gesture, as though he were

299

unveiling something magnificent. I felt a burning in my throat that told me I was on the point of crying; but I couldn't bear the thought that the Baron would see my nakedness and also see me cry. I held my tears back somehow, at the very edge of my vision, and watched the mirror so intently that for a long moment I felt as though time had stopped. I'd certainly never seen myself so utterly naked before. It was true that I still wore buttoned socks on my feet; but I felt more exposed now with the seams of my robe held wide apart than I'd ever felt even in a bathhouse while completely unclothed. I watched the Baron's eyes linger here and there on my reflection in the mirror. First he drew the robe still farther open to take in the outline of my waist. Then he lowered his eyes to the darkness that had bloomed on me in the years since I'd come to Kyoto. His eyes remained there a long while; but at length they rose up slowly, passing over my stomach, along my ribs, to the two plum-colored circles – first on one side, and then on the other. Now the Baron took away one of his hands, so that my under-robe settled against me on that side. What he did with his hand I can't say, but I never saw it again. At one point I felt a moment of panic when I saw a naked shoulder protruding from his bathrobe. I don't know what he was doing – and even though I could probably make an accurate guess about it now, I much prefer not to think about it. All I know is that I became very aware of his breath warming my neck. After that, I saw nothing more. The mirror became a blur of silver; I was no longer able to hold back my tears.

At a certain point the Baron's breathing slowed again. My skin was hot and quite damp from fear, so that when he released my robe at last and let it fall, I felt the puff of air against my side almost as a breeze. Soon I was alone in the room; the Baron had walked out without my even realizing it. Now that he was gone, I rushed to dress myself with such desperation that while I knelt on the floor to gather up my undergarments, I kept seeing in my mind an image of a starving child grabbing at scraps of food.

I dressed again as best I could, with my hands trembling. But until I had help, I could go no further than to close my underrobe and secure it with the waistband. I waited in front of the mirror, looking with some concern at the smeared makeup on my face. I was prepared to wait there a full hour if I had to. But only a few minutes passed before the Baron came back with the sash of his bathrobe tight around his plump belly. He helped me into my kimono without a word, and secured it with my *datejime* just as Mr. Itchoda would have done. While he was holding my great, long obi in his arms, measuring it out in loops as he prepared to tie it around me, I began to feel a terrible feeling. I couldn't make sense of it at first; but it seeped its way through me just as a stain seeps across cloth, and soon I understood. It was the feeling that I'd done something terribly wrong. I didn't want to cry in front of the Baron, but I couldn't help it – and anyway, he hadn't looked me in the eye since coming back into the room. I tried to imagine I was simply a house standing in the rain with the water washing down the front of me. But the Baron must have seen, for he left the room and came back a moment later with a handkerchief bearing his monogram. He instructed me to keep it, but after I used it, I left it there on a table.

Soon he led me to the front of the house and went away without speaking a word. In time a servant came, holding the antique kimono wrapped once again in linen paper. He presented it to me with a bow and then escorted me to the Baron's motorcar. I cried quietly in the backseat on the way to the inn, but the driver pretended to take no notice. I was no longer crying about what had happened to me. Something much more frightful was on my mind – namely what would happen when Mr. Itchoda saw my smeared makeup, and then helped me undress and saw the poorly tied knot in my obi, and then opened the package and saw the expensive gift I'd received. Before leaving the car I wiped my face with the Chairman's handkerchief, but it did me little good. Mr. Itchoda took one look at me and then scratched his chin as though he understood everything that had happened. While he was untying my obi in the room upstairs, he said:

'Did the Baron undress you?'

'I'm sorry,' I said.

'He undressed you and looked at you in the mirror. But he

didn't enjoy himself with you. He didn't touch you, or lie on top of you, did he?'

'No, sir.'

'That's fine, then,' Mr. Itchoda said, staring straight ahead. Not another word was spoken between us.

23

I WON'T SAY MY emotions had settled themselves by the time the train pulled into Kyoto Station early the following morning. After all, when a stone is dropped into a pond, the water continues quivering even after the stone has sunk to the bottom. But when I descended the wooden stairs carrying us from the platform, with Mr. Itchoda one step behind me, I came upon such a shock that for a time I forgot everything else.

There in a glass case was the new poster for that season's *Dances of the Old Capital*, and I stopped to have a look at it. Two weeks remained before the event. The poster had been distributed just the previous day, probably while I was strolling around the Baron's estate hoping to meet up with the Chairman. The dance every year has a theme, such as 'Colors of the Four Seasons in Kyoto,' or 'Famous Places from *Tale of the Heike*.' This year the theme was 'The Gleaming Light of the Morning Sun.' The poster, which of course was drawn by Uchida Kosaburo – who'd created nearly every poster since 1919 – showed an apprentice geisha in a lovely green and orange kimono standing on an arched wooden bridge. I was exhausted after my long trip and had slept badly on the train; so I stood for a while before the poster in a sort of daze, taking in the lovely greens and golds of the background, before I turned my attention to the girl in the kimono. She was gazing directly into the bright light of the sunrise, and her eyes were a startling blue-gray. I had to put a hand on the railing to steady myself. I was the girl Uchida had drawn there on that bridge!

On the way back from the train station, Mr. Itchoda

pointed out every poster we passed, and even asked the rickshaw driver to go out of his way so we could see an entire wall of them on the old Daimaru Department Store building. Seeing myself all over the city this way wasn't quite as thrilling as I would have imagined; I kept thinking of the poor girl in the poster standing before a mirror as her obi was untied by an older man. In any case, I expected to hear all sorts of congratulations over the course of the following few days, but I soon learned that an honor like this one never comes without costs. Ever since Mameha had arranged for me to take a role in the seasonal dances, I'd heard any number of unpleasant comments about myself. After the poster, things only grew worse. The next morning, for example, a young apprentice who'd been friendly the week before now looked away when I gave a bow to greet her.

As for Mameha, I went to visit her in her apartment, where she was recovering, and found that she was as proud as if she herself had been the one in the poster. She certainly wasn't pleased that I'd taken the trip to Hakone, but she seemed as devoted to my success as ever – strangely, perhaps even more so. For a while I worried she would view my horrible encounter with the Baron as a betrayal of her. I imagined Mr. Itchoda must have told her about it . . . but if he did, she never raised the subject between us. Neither did I.

Two weeks later the seasonal dances opened. On that first day in the dressing room at the Kaburenjo Theater, I felt myself almost overflowing with excitement, for Mameha had told me the Chairman and Nobu would be in the audience. While putting on my makeup, I tucked the Chairman's handkerchief beneath my dressing robe, against my bare skin. My hair was bound closely to my head with a silk strip, because of the wigs I would be wearing, and when I saw myself in the mirror without the familiar frame of hair surrounding my face, I found angles in my cheeks and around my eyes that I'd never before seen. It may seem odd, but when I realized that the shape of my own face was a surprise to me, I had the sudden insight that nothing in life is ever as simple as we imagine.

An hour later I was standing with the other apprentices in

the wings of the theater, ready for the opening dance. We wore identical kimono of yellow and red, with obis of orange and gold – so that we looked, each of us, like shimmering images of sunlight. When the music began, with that first thump of the drums and the twang of all the shamisens, and we danced out together like a string of beads – our arms outstretched, our folding fans open in our hands – I had never before felt so much a part of something.

After the opening piece, I rushed upstairs to change my kimono. The dance in which I was to appear as a solo performer was called 'The Morning Sun on the Waves,' about a maiden who takes a morning swim in the ocean and falls in love with an enchanted dolphin. My costume was a magnificent pink kimono with a water design in gray, and I held blue silk strips to symbolize the rippling water behind me. The enchanted dolphin prince was played by a geisha named Umiyo; in addition, there were roles for geisha portraying wind, sunlight, and sprays of water – as well as a few apprentices in charcoal and blue kimono at the far reaches of the stage, playing dolphins calling their prince back to them.

My costume change went so quickly that I found myself with a few minutes to peek out at the audience. I followed the sound of occasional drumbeats to a narrow, darkened hallway running behind one of the two orchestra booths at the sides of the theater. A few other apprentices and geisha were already peering out through carved slits in the sliding doors. I joined them and managed to find the Chairman and Nobu sitting together – though it seemed to me the Chairman had given Nobu the better seat. Nobu was peering at the stage intently, but I was surprised to see that the Chairman seemed to be falling asleep. From the music I realized that it was the beginning of Mameha's dance, and went to the end of the hallway where the slits in the doors gave a view of the stage.

I watched Mameha no more than a few minutes; and yet the impression her dance made on me has never been erased. Most dances of the Inoue School tell a story of one kind or another, and the story of this dance – called 'A Courtier Returns to His Wife' – was based on a Chinese poem about a courtier who carries on a long affair with a lady in the

Imperial palace. One night the courtier's wife hides on the outskirts of the palace to find out where her husband has been spending his time. Finally, at dawn, she watches from the bushes as her husband takes leave of his mistress – but by this time she has fallen ill from the terrible cold and dies soon afterward.

For our spring dances, the story was changed to Japan instead of China; but otherwise, the tale was the same. Mameha played the wife who dies of cold and heartbreak, while the geisha Kanako played the role of her husband, the courtier. I watched the dance from the moment the courtier bids good-bye to his mistress. Already the setting was inspiringly beautiful, with the soft light of dawn and the slow rhythm of the shamisen music like a heartbeat in the background. The courtier performed a lovely dance of thanks to his mistress for their night together, and then moved toward the light of rising sun to capture its warmth for her. This was the moment when Mameha began to dance her lament of terrible sadness, hidden to one side of the stage out of view of the husband and mistress. Whether it was the beauty of Mameha's dance or of the story, I cannot say; but I found myself feeling such sorrow as I watched her, I felt as if I myself had been the victim of that terrible betrayal. At the end of the dance, sunlight filled the stage. Mameha crossed to a grove of trees to dance her simple death scene. I cannot tell you what happened after that. I was too overcome to watch any further; and in any case, I had to return backstage to prepare for my own entrance.

While I waited in the wings, I had the peculiar feeling that the weight of the entire building was pressing down on me – because of course, sadness has always seemed to me an oddly heavy thing. A good dancer often wears her white, buttoned socks a size too small, so she can sense the seams in the wooden stage with her feet. But as I stood there trying to find the strength within myself to perform, I had the impression of so much weight upon me that I felt not only the seams in the stage, but even the fibers in the socks themselves. At last I heard the music of the drums and shamisen, and the whisking noise of the clothing as the other dancers moved quickly past me onto the stage; but it's very hard for me to remember anything afterward. I'm sure I raised my arms with my folding fan closed and my knees bent – for this was the position in which I made my entrance. I heard no suggestion afterward that I'd missed my cue, but all I remember clearly is watching my own arms with amazement at the sureness and evenness with which they moved. I'd practiced this dance any number of times; I suppose that must have been enough. Because although my mind had shut down completely, I performed my role without any difficulty or nervousness.

At every performance for the rest of that month, I prepared for my entrance in the same way, by concentrating on 'The Courtier Returns to His Wife,' until I could feel the sadness laying itself over me. We human beings have a remarkable way of growing accustomed to things; but when I pictured Mameha dancing her slow lament, hidden from the eyes of her husband and his mistress, I could no more have stopped myself from feeling that sadness than you could stop yourself from smelling an apple that has been cut open on the table before you.

One day in the final week of performances, Mameha and I stayed late in the dressing room, talking with another geisha. When we left the theater we expected to find no one outside – and indeed the crowd had gone. But as we reached the street, a driver in uniform stepped out of a car and opened the rear door. Mameha and I were on the point of walking right past when Nobu emerged.

'Why, Nobu-san,' Mameha said, 'I was beginning to worry that you no longer cared for Sayuri's company! Every day this past month, we've hoped to hear something from you . . .'

'Who are you to complain about being kept waiting? I've been outside this theater nearly an hour.'

'Have you just come from seeing the dances again?' Mameha said. 'Sayuri is quite a star.'

'I haven't *just* come from anything,' Nobu said. 'I've come from the dances a full hour ago. Enough time has passed for me to make a phone call and send my driver downtown to pick something up for me.'

Nobu banged on the window of the car with his one hand, and startled the poor driver so badly his cap fell off. The driver rolled down the window and gave Nobu a tiny shopping bag in the Western style, made of what looked like silver foil. Nobu turned to me, and I gave him a deep bow and told him how happy I was to see him.

'You're a very talented dancer, Sayuri. I don't give gifts for no reason,' he said, though I don't think this was in any way true. 'Probably that's why Mameha and others in Gion don't like me as much as other men.'

'Nobu-san!' said Mameha. 'Who has ever suggested such a thing?'

'I know perfectly well what you geisha like. So long as a man gives you presents you'll put up with any sort of nonsense.'

Nobu held out the small package in his hand for me to take.

'Why, Nobu-san,' I said, 'what nonsense is it that *you* are asking me to put up with?' I meant this as a joke, of course; but Nobu didn't see it that way.

'Haven't I just said I'm not like other men?' he growled. 'Why don't you geisha ever believe anything told to you? If you want this package, you'd better take it before I change my mind.'

I thanked Nobu and accepted the package, and he banged on the window of the car once again. The driver jumped out to hold the door for him.

We bowed until the car had turned the corner and then Mameha led me back into the garden of the Kaburenjo Theater, where we took a seat on a stone bench overlooking the carp pond and peered into the bag Nobu had given me. It contained only a tiny box, wrapped in gold-colored paper embossed with the name of a famous jewelry store and tied with a red ribbon. I opened it to find a simple jewel, a ruby as big as a peach pit. It was like a giant drop of blood sparkling in the sunlight over the pond. When I turned it in my fingers, the glimmer jumped from one face to another. I could feel each of the jumps in my chest.

'I can see how thrilled you are,' Mameha said, 'and I'm very happy for you. But don't enjoy it too much. You'll have other jewels in your life, Sayuri – plenty of them, I should think. But you'll never have this opportunity again. Take this ruby back to your okiya, and give it to Mother.'

To see this beautiful jewel, and the light that seeped out of it painting my hand pink, and to think of Mother with her sickly yellow eyes and their meat-colored rims . . . well, it seemed to me that giving this jewel to her would be like dressing up a badger in silk. But of course, I had to obey Mameha.

'When you give it to her,' she went on, 'you must be especially sweet and say, 'Mother, I really have no need for a jewel like this and would be honored if you'd accept it. I've caused you so much trouble over the years.' But don't say more, or she'll think you're being sarcastic.'

When I sat in my room later, grinding an ink stick to write a note of thanks to Nobu, my mood grew darker and darker. If Mameha herself had asked me for the ruby, I could have given it to her cheerfully . . . but to give it to Mother! I'd grown fond of Nobu, and was sorry that his expensive gift would go to such a woman. I knew perfectly well that if the ruby had been from the Chairman, I couldn't have given it up at all. In any case, I finished the note and went to Mother's room to speak with her. She was sitting in the dim light, petting her dog and smoking.

'What do you want?' she said to me. 'I'm about to send for a pot of tea.'

'I'm sorry to disturb you, Mother. This afternoon when Mameha and I left the theater, President Nobu Toshikazu was waiting for me –'

'Waiting for Mameha-san, you mean.'

'I don't know, Mother. But he gave me a gift. It's a lovely thing, but I have no use for it.'

I wanted to say that I would be honored if she would take it, but Mother wasn't listening to me. She put her pipe down onto the table and took the box from my hand before I could even offer it to her. I tried again to explain things, but Mother just turned over the box to dump the ruby into her oily fingers.

'What is this?' she asked.

'It's the gift President Nobu gave me. Nobu Toshikazu, of Iwamura Electric, I mean.'

'Don't you think I know who Nobu Toshikazu is?'

She got up from the table to walk over to the window, where she slid back the paper screen and held the ruby into the stream of late-afternoon sunlight. She was doing what I had done on the street, turning the gem around and watching the sparkle move from face to face. Finally she closed the screen again and came back.

'You must have misunderstood. Did he ask you to give it to Mameha?'

'Well, Mameha was with me at the time.'

I could see that Mother's mind was like an intersection with too much traffic in it. She put the ruby onto the table and began to puff on her pipe. I saw every cloud of smoke as a little confused thought released into the air. Finally she said to me, 'So, Nobu Toshikazu has an interest in you, does he?'

'I've been honored by his attention for some time now.'

At this, she put the pipe down onto the table, as if to say that the conversation was about to grow much more serious. 'I haven't watched you as closely as I should have,' she said. 'If you've had any boyfriends, now is the time to tell me.'

'I've never had a single boyfriend, Mother.'

I don't know whether she believed what I'd said or not, but she dismissed me just the same. I hadn't yet offered her the ruby to keep, as Mameha had instructed me to do. I was trying to think of how to raise the subject. But when I glanced at the table where the gem lay on its side, she must have thought I wanted to ask for it back. I had no time to say anything further before she reached out and swallowed it up in her hand.

Finally it happened, one afternoon only a few days later. Mameha came to the okiya and took me into the reception room to tell me that the bidding for my *mizuage* had begun. She'd received a message from the mistress of the Ichiriki that very morning.

'I couldn't be more disappointed at the timing,' Mameha said, 'because I have to leave for Tokyo this afternoon. But you won't need me. You'll know if the bidding goes high, because things will start to happen.'

'I don't understand,' I said. 'What sorts of things?'

'All sorts of things,' she said, and then left without even taking a cup of tea.

She was gone three days. At first my heart raced every time I heard one of the maids approaching. But two days passed without any news. Then on the third day, Auntie came to me in the hallway to say that Mother wanted me upstairs.

I'd just put my foot onto the first step when I heard a door slide open, and all at once Pumpkin came rushing down. She came like water poured from a bucket, so fast her feet scarcely touched the steps, and midway down she twisted her finger on the banister. It must have hurt, because she let out a cry and stopped at the bottom to hold it.

'Where is Hatsumomo?' she said, clearly in pain. 'I have to find her!'

'It looks to me as if you've hurt yourself badly enough,' Auntie said. 'You have to go find Hatsumomo so she can hurt you more?'

Pumpkin looked terribly upset, and not only about her finger; but when I asked her what was the matter, she just rushed to the entryway and left.

Mother was sitting at the table when I entered her room. She began to pack her pipe with tobacco, but soon thought better of it and put it away. On top of the shelves holding the account books stood a beautiful European-style clock in a glass case. Mother looked at it every so often, but a few long minutes passed and still she said nothing to me. Finally I spoke up. 'I'm sorry to disturb you, Mother, but I was told you wanted to see me.'

'The doctor is late,' she said. 'We'll wait for him.'

I imagined she was referring to Dr. Crab, that he was coming to the okiya to talk about arrangements for my *mizuage*. I hadn't expected such a thing and began to feel a tingling in my belly. Mother passed the time by patting Taku, who quickly grew tired of her attentions and made little growling noises.

At length I heard the maids greeting someone in the front

entrance hall below, and Mother went down the stairs. When she came back a few minutes later she wasn't escorting Dr. Crab at all, but a much younger man with smooth silver hair, carrying a leather bag.

'This is the girl,' Mother said to him.

I bowed to the young doctor, who bowed back to me.

'Ma'am,' he said to Mother, 'where shall we . . .?'

Mother told him the room we were in would be fine. The way she closed the door, I knew something unpleasant was about to happen. She began by untying my obi and folding it on the table. Then she slipped the kimono from my shoulders and hung it on a stand in the corner. I stood in my yellow underrobe as calmly as I knew how, but in a moment Mother began to untie the waistband that held my underrobe shut. I couldn't quite stop myself from putting my arms in her way – though she pushed them aside just as the Baron had done, which gave me a sick feeling. After she'd removed the waistband, she reached inside and pulled out my *koshimaki* – once again, just as it had happened in Hakone. I didn't like this a bit, but instead of pulling open my robe as the Baron had, she refolded it around me and told me to lie down on the mats.

The doctor knelt at my feet and, after apologizing, peeled open my underrobe to expose my legs. Mameha had told me a little about *mizuage*, but it seemed to me I was about to learn more. Had the bidding ended, and this young doctor emerged the winner? What about Dr. Crab and Nobu? It even crossed my mind that Mother might be intentionally sabotaging Mameha's plans. The young doctor adjusted my legs and reached between them with his hand, which I had noticed was smooth and graceful like the Chairman's. I felt so humiliated and exposed that I had to cover my face. I wanted to draw my legs together, but I was afraid anything that made his task more difficult would only prolong the encounter. So I lay with my eyes pinched shut, holding my breath. I felt as little Taku must have felt the time he choked on a needle, and Auntie held his jaws open while Mother put her fingers down his throat. At one point I think the doctor had both of his hands between my legs; but at last he took them away, and folded my robe shut. When I opened my eyes, I saw him wiping his hands on a cloth.

'The girl is intact,' he said.

'Well, that's fine news!' Mother replied. 'And will there be much blood?'

'There shouldn't be any blood at all. I only examined her visually.'

'No, I mean during *mizuage*.'

'I couldn't say. The usual amount, I should expect.'

When the young silver-haired doctor had taken his leave, Mother helped me dress and instructed me to sit at the table. Then without any warning, she grabbed my earlobe and pulled it so hard I cried out. She held me like that, with my head close to hers, while she said:

'You're a very expensive commodity, little girl. I underestimated you. I'm lucky nothing has happened. But you may be very sure I'm going to watch you more closely in the future. What a man wants from you, a man will pay dearly to get. Do you follow me?'

'Yes, ma'am!' I said. Of course, I would have said yes to anything, considering how hard she was pulling on my ear.

'If you give a man freely what he ought to pay for, you'll be cheating this okiya. You'll owe money, and I'll take it from you. And I'm not just talking about this!' Here Mother made a gruesome noise with her free hand – rubbing her fingers against her palm to make a squishing sound.

'Men will pay for that,' she went on. 'But they'll pay just to chat with you too. If I find you sneaking off to meet a man, even if it's just for a little talk . . .' And here she finished her thought by giving another sharp tug on my earlobe before letting it go.

I had to work hard to catch my breath. When I felt I could speak again, I said, 'Mother . . . I've done nothing to make you angry!'

'Not yet, you haven't. If you're a sensible girl, you never will.'

I tried to excuse myself, but Mother told me to stay. She tapped out her pipe, even though it was empty; and when she'd filled it and lit it, she said, 'I've come to a decision. Your

313

status here in the okiya is about to change.'

I was alarmed by this and began to say something, but Mother stopped me.

'You and I will perform a ceremony next week. After that, you'll be my daughter just as if you'd been born to me. I've come to the decision to adopt you. One day, the okiya will be yours.'

I couldn't think of what to say, and I don't remember much of what happened next. Mother went on talking, telling me that as the daughter of the okiya I would at some point move into the larger room occupied by Hatsumomo and Pumpkin, who together would share the smaller room where I'd lived up to now. I was listening with only half my mind, until I began slowly to realize that as Mother's daughter, I would no longer have to struggle under Hatsumomo's tyranny. This had been Mameha's plan all along, and yet I'd never really believed it would happen. Mother went on lecturing me. I looked at her drooping lip and her yellowed eyes. She may have been a hateful woman, but as the daughter of this hateful woman, I would be up on a shelf out of Hatsumomo's reach.

In the midst of all of this, the door slid open, and Hatsumomo herself stood there in the hallway.

'What do you want?' Mother said. 'I'm busy.'

'Get out,' she said to me. 'I want to talk with Mother.'

'If you want to talk with me,' Mother said, 'you may ask Sayuri if she'll be kind enough to leave.'

'*Be kind enough to leave, Sayuri,*' Hatsumomo said sarcastically.

And then for the first time in my life, I spoke back to her without the fear that she would punish me for it.

'I'll leave if Mother wants me to,' I told her.

'Mother, would you be kind enough to make Little Miss Stupid leave us alone?' Hatsumomo said.

'Stop making a nuisance of yourself!' Mother told her. 'Come in and tell me what you want.'

Hatsumomo didn't like this, but she came and sat at the table anyway. She was midway between Mother and me, but still so close that I could smell her perfume.

'Poor Pumpkin has just come running to me, very upset,'

314

she began. 'I promised her I'd speak with you. She told me something very strange. She said, "Oh, Hatsumomo! Mother has changed her mind!" But I told her I doubted it was true.'

'I don't know what she was referring to. I certainly haven't changed my mind about anything recently.'

'That's just what I said to her, that you would never go back on your word. But I'm sure she'd feel better, Mother, if you told her yourself.'

'Told her what?'

'That you haven't changed your mind about adopting her.'

'Whatever gave her that idea? I never had the least intention of adopting her in the first place.'

It gave me a terrible pain to hear this, for I couldn't help thinking of how Pumpkin had rushed down the stairs looking so upset . . . and no wonder, for no one could say anymore what would become of her in life. Hatsumomo had been wearing that smile that made her look like an expensive piece of porcelain, but Mother's words struck her like rocks. She looked at me with hatred.

'So it's true! You're planning to adopt *her*. Don't you remember, Mother, when you said you were going to adopt Pumpkin? You asked me to tell her the news!'

'What you may have said to Pumpkin is none of my concern. Besides, you haven't handled Pumpkin's apprenticeship as well as I expected. She was doing well for a time, but lately . . .'

'You promised, Mother,' Hatsumomo said in a tone that frightened me.

'Don't be ridiculous! You know I've had my eye on Sayuri for years. Why would I turn around and adopt Pumpkin?'

I knew perfectly well Mother was lying. Now she went so far as to turn to me and say this:

'Sayuri-san, when was the first time I raised the subject of adopting you? A year ago, perhaps?'

If you've ever seen a mother cat teaching its young to hunt – the way she takes a helpless mouse and rips it apart – well, I felt as though Mother was offering me the chance to learn how I could be just like her. All I had to do was lie as she lied and say, 'Oh, yes, Mother, you mentioned the subject to me

315

many times!' This would be my first step in becoming a yellow-eyed old woman myself one day, living in a gloomy room with my account books. I could no more take Mother's side than Hatsumomo's. I kept my eyes to the mats so I wouldn't have to see either of them, and said that I didn't remember.

Hatsumomo's face was splotched red from anger. She got up and walked to the door, but Mother stopped her.

'Sayuri will be my daughter in one week,' she said. 'Between now and then, you must learn how to treat her with respect. When you go downstairs, ask one of the maids to bring tea for Sayuri and me.'

Hatsumomo gave a little bow, and then she was gone.

'Mother,' I said, 'I'm very sorry to have been the cause of so much trouble. I'm sure Hatsumomo is quite wrong about any plans you may have made for Pumpkin, but . . . may I ask? Wouldn't it be possible to adopt both Pumpkin and me?'

'Oh, so you know something about business now, do you?' she replied. 'You want to try telling me how to run the okiya?'

A few minutes later, a maid arrived bearing a tray with a pot of tea and a cup – not two cups, but only a single one. Mother didn't seem to care. I poured her cup full and she drank from it, staring at me with her red-rimmed eyes.

24

WHEN MAMEHA RETURNED to town the following day and learned that Mother had decided to adopt me, she didn't seem as pleased as I would have expected. She nodded and looked satisfied, to be sure; but she didn't smile. I asked if things hadn't turned out exactly as she'd hoped.

'Oh, no, the bidding between Dr. Crab and Nobu went just as I'd hoped,' she told me, 'and the final figure was a considerable sum. The moment I found out, I knew Mrs. Nitta would certainly adopt you. I couldn't be more pleased!'

This is what she said. But the truth, as I came to understand in stages over the following years, was something quite different. For one thing, the bidding hadn't been a contest between Dr. Crab and Nobu at all. It had ended up a contest between Dr. Crab and the Baron. I can't imagine how Mameha must have felt about this; but I'm sure it accounts for why she was suddenly so cold to me for a short time, and why she kept to herself the story of what had really happened.

I don't mean to suggest that Nobu was never involved. He did bid quite aggressively for my *mizuage*, but only during the first few days, until the figure passed ¥8000. When he ended up dropping out, it probably wasn't because the bidding had gone too high. Mameha knew from the beginning that Nobu could bid against anyone, if he wanted to. The trouble, which Mameha hadn't anticipated, was that Nobu had no more than a vague interest in my *mizuage*. Only a certain kind of man spends his time and money chasing after *mizuage*, and it turned out that Nobu wasn't one of them. Some months earlier, as you may remember, Mameha had suggested that no man would cultivate a relationship with a fifteen-year-old apprentice unless he was interested in her *mizuage*. This was during the same discussion when she told me, 'You can bet it isn't your conversation he's attracted to.' She may have been right about my conversation, I don't know; but whatever attracted Nobu to me, it wasn't my *mizuage* either.

As for Dr. Crab, he was a man who would probably have chosen suicide the old-fashioned way before allowing someone like Nobu to take a *mizuage* away from him. Of course he wasn't really bidding against Nobu after the first few days, but he didn't know that, and the mistress of the Ichiriki made up her mind not to tell him. She wanted the price to go as high as it could. So when she spoke to him on the telephone she said things like, 'Oh, Doctor, I've just received word from Osaka, and an offer has come in for five thousand yen.' She probably had received word from Osaka – though it might have been from her sister, because the mistress never liked to tell outright lies. But when she mentioned Osaka and an offer in the same breath, naturally Dr. Crab assumed the offer was from Nobu, even though it was actually from the Baron.

As for the Baron, he knew perfectly well his adversary was the Doctor, but he didn't care. He wanted the *mizuage* for himself and pouted like a little boy when he began to think he might not win it. Sometime later a geisha told me about a conversation she'd had with him around this time. 'Do you hear what has been happening?' the Baron said to her. 'I'm trying to arrange a *mizuage*, but a certain annoying doctor keeps getting in my way. Only one man can be the explorer of an undiscovered region, and I want to be that man! But what am I to do? This foolish doctor doesn't seem to understand that the numbers he throws about represent real money!'

As the bidding went higher and higher, the Baron began to talk about dropping out. But the figure had already come so close to a new record that the mistress of the Ichiriki made up her mind to push things still higher by misleading the Baron, just as she'd misled the Doctor. On the telephone she told him that the 'other gentleman' had made a very high bid, and then added, 'However, many people believe he's the sort of gentleman who will go no higher.' I'm sure there may have been people who believed such a thing about the Doctor, but

318

the mistress herself wasn't one of them. She knew that when the Baron made his last bid, whatever it was, the Doctor would top it.

In the end, Dr. Crab agreed to pay ¥11,500 for my *mizuage*. Up to that time, this was the highest ever paid for a *mizuage* in Gion, and possibly in any of the geisha districts in Japan. Keep in mind that in those days, one hour of a geisha's time cost about ¥4, and an extravagant kimono might have sold for ¥1500. So it may not sound like a lot, but it's much more than, say, a laborer might have earned in a year.

I have to confess I don't know much about money. Most geisha pride themselves on never carrying cash with them, and are accustomed to charging things wherever they go. Even now in New York City, I live just the same way. I shop at stores that know me by sight, where the clerks are kind enough to write down the items I want. When the bill comes at the end of the month, I have a charming assistant who pays it for me. So you see, I couldn't possibly tell you how much money I spend, or how much more a bottle of perfume costs than a magazine. So I may be one of the worst people on earth to try explaining anything at all about money. However, I want to pass on to you something a close friend once told me – who I'm sure knows what he's talking about, because he was Japan's Deputy Minister of Finance for a time during the 1960s. Cash, he said, is often worth less one year than it was the year before, and because of this, Mameha's *mizuage* in 1929 actually cost more than mine in 1935, even though mine was ¥11,500 while Mameha's was more like ¥7000 or ¥8000.

Of course, none of this mattered back at the time my *mizuage* was sold. As far as everyone was concerned I had set a new record, and it remained until 1951, when Katsumiyo came along – who in my opinion was one of the greatest geisha of the twentieth century. Still, according to my friend the Deputy Minister of Finance, the real record remained Mameha's until the 1960s. But whether the real record belonged to me, or to Katsumiyo, or to Mameha – or even to Mamemitsu back in the 1890s – you can well imagine that Mother's plump little hands began to itch when she heard about a record amount of cash.

It goes without saying that this is why she adopted me. The fee for my *mizuage* was more than enough to repay all my debts to the okiya. If Mother hadn't adopted me, some of that money would have fallen into my hands – and you can imagine how Mother would have felt about this. When I became the daughter of the okiya, my debts ceased to exist because the okiya absorbed them all. But all of my profits went to the okiya as well, not only then, at the time of my *mizuage*, but forever afterward.

The adoption took place the following week. Already my given name had changed to Sayuri; now my family name changed as well. Back in my tipsy house on the sea cliffs, I'd been Sakamoto Chiyo. Now my name was Nitta Sayuri.

Of all the important moments in the life of a geisha, *mizuage* certainly ranks as high as any. Mine occurred in early July of 1935, when I was fifteen years old. It began in the afternoon when Dr. Crab and I drank sake in a ceremony that bound us together. The reason for this ceremony is that even though the *mizuage* itself would be over with quickly, Dr. Crab would remain my *mizuage* patron until the end of his life – not that it gave him any special privileges, you understand. The ceremony was performed at the Ichiriki Teahouse, in the presence of Mother, Auntie, and Mameha. The mistress of the Ichiriki attended as well, and Mr. Bekku, my dresser – because the dresser is always involved in ceremonies of this sort, representing the interests of the geisha. I was dressed in the most formal costume an apprentice wears, a black, five-crested robe and an underrobe of red, which is the color of new beginnings. Mameha instructed me to behave very sternly, as though I had no sense of humor at all. Considering my nervousness, I found it easy to look stern as I walked down the hallway of the Ichiriki Teahouse, with the train of my kimono pooled around my feet.

After the ceremony we all went to a restaurant known as Kitcho for dinner. This was a solemn event too, and I spoke little and ate even less. Sitting there at dinner, Dr. Crab had probably already begun thinking about the moment that would come later, and yet I've never seen a man who looked more bored. I kept my eyes lowered throughout the meal in the interests of acting innocent, but every time I stole a glance in his direction, I found him peering down through his glasses like a man at a business meeting.

When dinner was over, Mr. Bekku escorted me by rickshaw to a beautiful inn on the grounds of the Nanzen-ji Temple. He'd already visited there earlier in the day to arrange my clothing in an adjoining room. He helped me out of my kimono and changed me into a more casual one, with an obi that required no padding for the knot – since padding would be awkward for the Doctor. He tied the knot in such a way that it would come undone quite easily. After I was fully dressed, I felt so nervous that Mr. Bekku had to help me back into my room and arrange me near the door to await the Doctor's arrival. When he left me there, I felt a horrible sense of dread, as if I'd been about to have an operation to remove my kidneys, or my liver, or some such thing.

Soon Dr. Crab arrived and asked that I order him sake while he bathed in the bath attached to the room. I think he may have expected me to help undress him, because he gave me a strange look. But my hands were so cold and awkward, I don't think I could have done it. He emerged a few minutes later wearing a sleeping robe and slid open the doors to the garden, where we sat on a little wooden balcony, sipping sake and listening to the sound of the crickets and the little stream below us. I spilled sake on my kimono, but the Doctor didn't notice. To tell the truth, he didn't seem to notice much of anything, except a fish that splashed in the pond nearby, which he pointed out to me as if I might never have seen such a thing. While we were there, a maid came and laid out both our futons, side by side.

Finally the Doctor left me on the balcony and went inside. I shifted in such a way as to watch him from the corner of my eye. He unpacked two white towels from his suitcase and set them down on the table, arranging them this way and that until they were just so. He did the same with the pillows on one of the futons, and then came and stood at the door until I rose from my knees and followed him.

While I was still standing, he removed my obi and told me

to make myself comfortable on one of the futons. Everything seemed so strange and frightening to me, I couldn't have been comfortable no matter what I'd done. But I lay down on my back and used a pillow stuffed with beans to prop up my neck. The Doctor opened my robe and took a long while to loosen each of the garments beneath it step by step, rubbing his hands over my legs, which I think was supposed to help me relax. This went on for a long time, but at last he fetched the two white towels he'd unpacked earlier. He told me to raise my hips and then spread them out beneath me.

'These will absorb the blood,' he told me.

Of course, a *mizuage* often involves a certain amount of blood, but no one had explained to me exactly why. I'm sure I should have kept quiet or even thanked the Doctor for being so considerate as to put down towels, but instead I blurted out, 'What blood?' My voice squeaked a little as I said it, because my throat was so dry. Dr. Crab began explaining how the 'hymen' – though I didn't know what that could possibly be – frequently bled when torn . . . and this, that, and the other . . . I think I became so anxious hearing it all that I rose up a little from the futon, because the Doctor put his hand on my shoulder and gently pushed me back down.

I'm sure this sort of talk would be enough to quash some men's appetite for what they were about to do; but the Doctor wasn't that sort of man. When he'd finished his explanation, he said to me, 'This is the second time I will have the opportunity of collecting a specimen of your blood. May I show you?'

I'd noticed that he'd arrived with not only his leather overnight bag, but also a small wooden case. The Doctor fetched a key ring from the pocket of his trousers in the closet and unlocked the case. He brought it over and swung it open down the middle to make a kind of freestanding display. On both sides were shelves with tiny glass vials, all plugged with corks and held in place by straps. Along the bottom shelf were a few instruments, such as scissors and tweezers; but the rest of the case was crowded with these glass vials, perhaps as many as forty or fifty of them. Except for a few empty ones on the top shelf, they all held something inside, but I had no idea what. Only when the Doctor brought the lamp from the table was I able to see white labels along the tops of each vial, marked with the names of various geisha. I saw Mameha's name there, as well as the great Mamekichi's. I saw quite a number of other familiar names as well, including Hatsumomo's friend Korin.

'This one,' the Doctor said as he removed one of the vials, 'belongs to you.'

He'd written my name wrong, with a different character for the 'ri' of Sayuri. But inside the vial was a shriveled-looking thing I thought resembled a pickled plum, though it was brownish rather than purple. The Doctor removed the cork and used tweezers to take it out.

'This is a cotton swab that was drenched in your blood,' he said, 'from the time you cut your leg, you'll recall. I don't normally save the blood of my patients, but I was . . . very taken with you. After collecting this sample, I made up my mind that I would be your *mizuage* patron. I think you'll agree it will make an unusual specimen, to possess not just a sample of your blood collected at *mizuage*, but also a sample taken from a laceration on your leg quite a number of months earlier.'

I hid my disgust while the Doctor went on to show me several other vials, including Mameha's. Hers contained not a cotton swab, but a small wadding of white fabric that was stained the color of rust and had grown quite stiff. Dr. Crab seemed to find all these samples fascinating, but for my part . . . well, I pointed my face in their direction in order to be polite, but when the Doctor wasn't watching, I looked elsewhere.

Finally he closed his case and set it aside before taking off his glasses, folding them and putting them on the table nearby. I was afraid the moment had come, and indeed, Dr. Crab moved my legs apart and arranged himself on his knees between them. I think my heart was beating at about the same speed as a mouse's. When the Doctor untied the sash of his sleeping robe, I closed my eyes and brought a hand up to cover my mouth, but I thought better of it at the last moment in case I should make a bad impression, and let my hand settle near my head instead.

The Doctor's hands burrowed around for a while, making me very uncomfortable in much the same way as the young silver-haired doctor had a few weeks earlier. Then he lowered himself until his body was poised just above mine. I put all the force of my mind to work in making a sort of mental barrier between the Doctor and me, but it wasn't enough to keep me from feeling the Doctor's 'eel,' as Mameha might have called it, bump against the inside of my thigh. The lamp was still lit, and I searched the shadows on the ceiling for something to distract me, because now I felt the Doctor pushing so hard that my head shifted on the pillow. I couldn't think what to do with my hands, so I grabbed the pillow with them and squeezed my eyes tighter. Soon there was a great deal of activity going on above me, and I could feel all sorts of movement inside me as well. There must have been a very great deal of blood, because the air had an unpleasant metallic smell. I kept reminding myself how much the Doctor had paid for this privilege; and I remember hoping at one point that he was enjoying himself more than I was. I felt no more pleasure there than if someone had rubbed a file over and over against the inside of my thigh until I bled.

Finally the homeless eel marked its territory, I suppose, and the Doctor lay heavily upon me, moist with sweat. I didn't at all like being so close to him, so I pretended to have trouble breathing in the hopes he would take his weight off me. For a long while he didn't move, but then all at once he got to his knees and was very businesslike again. I didn't watch him, but from the corner of my eye I couldn't help seeing that he wiped himself off using one of the towels beneath me. He tied the sash of his robe, and then put on his glasses, not noticing a little smear of blood at the edge of one lens, and began to wipe between my legs using towels and cotton swabs and the like, just as though we were back in one of the treatment rooms at the hospital. The worst of my discomfort had passed by this time, and I have to admit I was almost fascinated lying there, even with my legs spread apart so revealingly, as I watched him open the wooden case and take out the scissors. He cut away a piece of the bloody towel beneath me and stuffed it, along with a cotton ball he'd used, into the glass vial with my misspelled name on it. Then he gave a formal bow and said, 'Thank you very much.' I couldn't very well bow back while lying down, but it made no difference, because the Doctor stood at once and went off to the bath again.

I hadn't realized it, but I'd been breathing very quickly from nervousness. Now that it was over and I was able to catch my breath, I probably looked as though I were in the middle of being operated upon, but I felt such relief I broke into a smile. Something about the whole experience seemed so utterly ridiculous to me; the more I thought about it, the funnier it seemed, and in a moment I was laughing. I had to keep quiet because the Doctor was in the next room. But to think that the course of my entire future had been altered by this? I imagined the mistress of the Ichiriki making telephone calls to Nobu and the Baron while the bidding was under way, all the money that had been spent, and all the trouble. How strange it would have been with Nobu, since I was beginning to think of him as a friend. I didn't even want to wonder what it might have been like with the Baron.

While the Doctor was still in the bath, I tapped on the door to Mr. Bekku's room. A maid rushed in to change the bedsheets, and Mr. Bekku came to help me put on a sleeping robe. Later, after the Doctor had fallen asleep, I got up again and bathed quietly. Mameha had instructed me to stay awake all night, in case the Doctor should awaken and need something. But even though I tried not to sleep, I couldn't help drifting off. I did manage to awaken in the morning in time to make myself presentable before the Doctor saw me.

After breakfast, I saw Dr. Crab to the front door of the inn and helped him into his shoes. Just before he walked away, he thanked me for the evening and gave me a small package. I couldn't make up my mind whether it might be a jewel like Nobu had given me or a few cuttings from the bloody towel of the night before! But when I worked up my courage to open it back in the room, it turned out to be a package of Chinese herbs. I didn't know what to make of them until I asked Mr. Bekku, who said I should make tea once a day with the herbs to discourage pregnancy. 'Be cautious with them, because they're very costly,' he said. 'But don't be too cautious. They're still cheaper than an abortion.'

It's strange and very hard to explain, but the world looked different to me after *mizuage*. Pumpkin, who hadn't yet had hers, now seemed inexperienced and childlike to me somehow, even though she was older. Mother and Auntie, as well as Hatsumomo and Mameha had all been through it, of course, and I was probably much more aware than they were of having this peculiar thing in common with them. After *mizuage* an apprentice wears her hair in a new style, and with a red silk band at the base of the pincushion bun, rather than a patterned one. For a time I was so aware of which apprentices had red hair bands and which had patterned ones that I scarcely seemed to notice anything else while walking along the street, or in the hallways of the little school. I had a new respect for the ones who had been through *mizuage*, and felt much more worldly than the ones who hadn't.

I'm sure all apprentices feel changed by the experience of *mizuage* in much the same way I did. But for me it wasn't just a matter of seeing the world differently. My day-to-day life changed as well, because of Mother's new view of me. She was the sort of person, I'm sure you realize, who noticed things only if they had price tags on them. When she walked down the street, her mind was probably working like an abacus: 'Oh, there's little Yukiyo, whose stupidity cost her poor older sister nearly a hundred yen last year! And here comes Ichimitsu, who must be very pleased at the payments her new *danna* is making.' If Mother were to walk alongside the Shirakawa Stream on a lovely spring day when you could almost see beauty itself dripping into the water from the tendrils of the cherry trees, she probably wouldn't even notice any of it – unless . . . I don't know . . . she had a plan to make money from selling the trees, or some such thing.

Before my *mizuage*, I don't think it made any difference to Mother that Hatsumomo was causing trouble for me in Gion. But now that I had a high price tag on me, she put a stop to Hatsumomo's troublemaking without my even having to ask it of her. I don't know how she did it. Probably she just said, 'Hatsumomo, if your behavior causes problems for Sayuri and costs this okiya money, you'll be the one to pay it!' Ever since my mother had grown ill, my life had certainly been difficult; but now for a time, things became remarkably uncomplicated. I won't say I never felt tired or disappointed; in fact, I felt tired much of the time. Life in Gion is hardly relaxing for the women who make a living there. But it was certainly a great relief to be freed from the threat of Hatsumomo. Inside the okiya too, life was almost pleasurable. As the adopted daughter, I ate when I wanted. I chose my kimono first instead of waiting for Pumpkin to choose hers – and the moment I'd made my choice, Auntie set to work sewing the seams to the proper width, and basting the collar onto my underrobe, before she'd touched even Hatsumomo's. I didn't mind when Hatsumomo looked at me with resentment and hatred because of the special treatment I now received. But when Pumpkin passed me in the okiya with a worried look, and kept her eyes averted from mine even when we were face-to-face, it caused me terrible pain. I'd always had the feeling our friendship would have grown if only circumstances hadn't come between us. I didn't have that feeling any longer.

With my *mizuage* behind me, Dr. Crab disappeared from my life almost completely. I say 'almost' because even though Mameha and I no longer went to the Shirae Teahouse to entertain him, I did run into him occasionally at parties in Gion. The Baron, on the other hand, I never saw again. I didn't yet know about the role he'd played in driving up the price of my *mizuage*, but as I look back I can understand why Mameha may have wanted to keep us apart. Probably I would have felt every bit as uncomfortable around the Baron as Mameha would have felt having me there. In any case, I can't pretend I missed either of these men.

But there was one man I was very eager to see again, and I'm sure I don't need to tell you I'm talking about the Chairman. He hadn't played any role in Mameha's plan, so I didn't expect my relationship with him to change or come to an end just because my *mizuage* was over. Still, I have to admit I felt very relieved a few weeks afterward to learn that Iwamura Electric had called to request my company once again. When I arrived that evening, both the Chairman and Nobu were present. In the past I would certainly have gone to sit beside Nobu; but now that Mother had adopted me, I wasn't obliged to think of him as my savior any longer. As it happened, a space beside the Chairman was vacant, and so with a feeling of excitement I went to take it. The Chairman was very cordial when I poured him sake, and thanked me by raising his cup in the air before drinking it; but all evening long he never looked at me. Whereas Nobu, whenever I glanced in his direction, glared back at me as though I were the only person in the room he was aware of. I certainly knew what it was like to long for someone, so before the evening was over I made a point of going to spend a bit of time with him. I was careful never to ignore him again after this.

A month or so passed, and then one evening during a party I happened to mention to Nobu that Mameha had arranged for me to appear in a festival in Hiroshima. I wasn't sure he was listening when I told him, but the very next day when I returned to the okiya after my lessons, I found in my room a new wooden travel trunk he'd sent me as a gift. The trunk was much finer even than the one I'd borrowed from Auntie for the Baron's party in Hakone. I felt terribly ashamed of myself for having thought I could simply discard Nobu now that he was no longer central to any plans Mameha might have had. I wrote him a note of thanks, and told him I looked forward to expressing my gratitude in person when I saw him the following week, at a large party Iwamura Electric had planned some months in advance.

But then a peculiar thing happened. Shortly before the party I received a message that my company wouldn't be needed after all. Yoko, who worked at the telephone in our okiya, was under the impression the party had been canceled. As it happened, I had to go to the Ichiriki that night anyway for another party. Just as I was kneeling in the hallway to enter, I saw the door to a large banquet room down at the end slide open, and a young geisha named Katsue came out. Before she closed the door, I heard what I felt certain was the sound of the Chairman's laughter coming from inside the room. I was very puzzled by this, so I rose from my knees and went to catch Katsue before she left the teahouse.

'I'm very sorry to trouble you,' I said, 'but have you just come from the party given by Iwamura Electric?'

'Yes, it's quite lively. There must be twenty-five geisha and nearly fifty men . . .'

'And . . . Chairman Iwamura and Nobu-san are both there?' I asked her.

'Not Nobu. Apparently he went home sick this morning. He'll be very sorry to have missed it. But the Chairman is there; why do you ask?'

I muttered something – I don't remember what it was – and she left.

Up until this moment I'd somehow imagined that the Chairman valued my company as much as Nobu did. Now I had to wonder whether it had all been an illusion, and Nobu was the only one who cared.

25

MAMEHA MAY ALREADY have won her bet with Mother, but she still had quite a stake in my future. So during the next few years she worked to make my face familiar to all her best customers, and to the other geisha in Gion as well. We were still emerging from the Depression at this time; formal banquets weren't as common as Mameha would have liked. But she took me to plenty of informal gatherings, not only parties in the teahouses, but swimming excursions, sightseeing tours, Kabuki plays, and so on. During the heat of summer when everyone felt most relaxed, these casual gatherings were often quite a lot of fun, even for those of us supposedly hard at work entertaining. For example, a group of men sometimes decided to go floating in a canal boat along the Kamo River, to sip sake and dangle their feet in the water. I was too young to join in the carousing, and often ended up with the job of shaving ice to make snow cones, but it was a pleasant change nevertheless.

Some nights, wealthy businessmen or aristocrats threw geisha parties just for themselves. They spent the evening dancing and singing, and drinking with the geisha, often until well after midnight. I remember on one of these occasions, the wife of our host stood at the door to hand out envelopes containing a generous tip as we left. She gave Mameha two of them, and asked her the favor of delivering the second to the geisha Tomizuru, who had 'gone home earlier with a headache,' as she put it. Actually she knew as well as we did that Tomizuru was her husband's mistress, and had gone with him to another wing of the house to keep him company for the night.

Many of the glamorous parties in Gion were attended by famous artists, and writers, and Kabuki actors, and sometimes they were very exciting events. But I'm sorry to tell you that the average geisha party was something much more mundane. The host was likely to be the division head of a small company, and the guest of honor one of his suppliers, or perhaps one of his employees he'd just promoted, or something along those lines. Every so often, some well-meaning geisha admonished me that as an apprentice, my responsibility – besides trying to look pretty – was to sit quietly and listen to conversations in the hopes of one day becoming a clever conversationalist myself. Well, most of the conversations I heard at these parties didn't strike me as very clever at all. A man might turn to the geisha beside him and say, 'The weather certainly is unusually warm, don't you think?' And the geisha would reply with something like, 'Oh, yes, very warm!' Then she'd begin playing a drinking game with him, or try to get all the men singing, and soon the man who'd spoken with her was too drunk to remember he wasn't having as good a time as he'd hoped. For my part, I always considered this a terrible waste. If a man has come to Gion just for the purpose of having a relaxing time, and ends up involved in some childish game such as paper-scissors-stone . . . well, in my view he'd have been better off staying at home and playing with his own children or grandchildren – who, after all, are probably more clever than this poor, dull geisha he was so unfortunate as to sit beside.

Every so often, though, I was privileged to overhear a geisha who really was clever, and Mameha was certainly one of these. I learned a great deal from her conversations. For example, if a man said to her, 'Warm weather, don't you think?' she had a dozen replies ready. If he was old and lecherous, she might say to him, 'Warm? Perhaps it's just the effect on you of being around so many lovely women!' Or if he was an arrogant young businessman who didn't seem to know his place, she might take him off his guard by saying, 'Here you are sitting with a half-dozen of the best geisha in Gion, and all you can think to talk about is the weather.' One time when I happened to be watching her, Mameha knelt beside a very young man who couldn't have been more than nineteen or twenty; he probably wouldn't have been at a geisha party at all if his father hadn't been the host. Of course, he didn't know what to say or how to behave around geisha, and I'm sure he felt nervous; but he turned to Mameha very bravely and said to her, 'Warm, isn't it?' She lowered her voice and answered him like this:

'Why, you're certainly right about it being warm. You should have seen me when I stepped out of the bath this morning! Usually when I'm completely naked, I feel so cool and relaxed. But this morning, there were little beads of sweat covering my skin all the way up my body – along my thighs, and on my stomach, and . . . well, other places too.'

When that poor boy set his sake cup down on the table, his fingers were trembling. I'm sure he never forgot that geisha party for the rest of his life.

If you ask me why most of these parties were so dull, I think probably there are two reasons. First, just because a young girl has been sold by her family and raised from an early age to be a geisha doesn't mean she'll turn out to be clever, or have anything interesting to say. And second, the same thing goes for the men. Just because a man has made enough money to come to Gion and waste it however he chooses doesn't mean he's fun to be around. In fact, many of the men are accustomed to being treated with a great deal of respect. Sitting back with their hands on their knees and big frowns on their faces is about as much work as they plan to do in the way of being entertaining. One time I listened to Mameha spend an entire hour telling stories to a man who never even looked in her direction, but just watched the others in the room while she talked. Oddly enough, this was just what he wanted, and he always asked for Mameha when he came to town.

After two more years of parties and outings – all the while continuing with my studies and participating in dance performances whenever I could – I made the shift from being an apprentice to being a geisha. This was in the summer of 1938, when I was eighteen years old. We call this change 'turning the collar,' because an apprentice wears a red collar while a geisha wears a white one. Though if you were to see an apprentice and a geisha side by side, their collars would be the last thing you'd notice. The apprentice, with her elaborate, long-sleeved kimono and dangling obi, would probably make you think of a Japanese doll, whereas the geisha would look simpler, perhaps, but also more womanly.

The day I turned my collar was one of the happiest days of Mother's life; or at least, she acted more pleased than I'd ever seen her. I didn't understand it at the time, but it's perfectly clear to me now what she was thinking. You see, a geisha, unlike an apprentice, is available to a man for more than just pouring his tea, provided the terms are suitable. Because of my connection with Mameha and my popularity in Gion, my standing was such that Mother had plenty of cause for excitement – excitement being, in Mother's case, just another word for money.

Since moving to New York I've learned what the word 'geisha' really means to most Westerners. From time to time at elegant parties, I've been introduced to some young woman or other in a splendid dress and jewelry. When she learns I was once a geisha in Kyoto, she forms her mouth into a sort of smile, although the corners don't turn up quite as they should. She has no idea what to say! And then the burden of conversation falls to the man or woman who has introduced us – because I've never really learned much English, even after all these years. Of course, by this time there's little point even in trying, because this woman is thinking, 'My goodness . . . I'm talking with a prostitute . . .' A moment later she's rescued by her escort, a wealthy man a good thirty or forty years older than she is. Well, I often find myself wondering why she can't sense how much we really have in common. She is a kept woman, you see, and in my day, so was I.

I'm sure there are a great many things I don't know about these young women in their splendid dresses, but I often have the feeling that without their wealthy husbands or boyfriends, many of them would be struggling to get by and might not have the same proud opinions of themselves. And of course the same thing is true for a first-class geisha. It is all very well for a geisha to go from party to party and be popular with a great many men; but a geisha who wishes to become a star is completely dependent on having a *danna*. Even Mameha, who became famous on her own because of an advertising campaign, would soon have lost her standing and been just another geisha if the Baron hadn't covered the expenses to advance her career.

No more than three weeks after I turned my collar, Mother came to me one day while I was eating a quick lunch in the reception room, and sat across the table a long while puffing on her pipe. I'd been reading a magazine, but I stopped out of politeness – even though Mother didn't seem at first to have much to say to me. After a time she put down her pipe and said, 'You shouldn't eat those yellow pickles. They'll rot your teeth. Look at what they did to mine.'

It had never occurred to me that Mother believed her stained teeth had anything to do with eating pickles. When she'd finished giving me a good view of her mouth, she picked up her pipe again and took in a puff of smoke.

'Auntie loves yellow pickles, ma'am,' I said, 'and her teeth are fine.'

'Who cares if Auntie's teeth are fine? She doesn't make money from having a pretty little mouth. Tell the cook not to give them to you. Anyway, I didn't come here to talk with you about pickles. I came to tell you that this time next month you'll have a *danna*.'

'A *danna*? But, Mother, I'm only eighteen . . .'

'Hatsumomo didn't have a danna until she was twenty. And of course, that didn't last . . . You ought to be very pleased.'

'Oh, I am very pleased. But won't it require a lot of my time to keep a *danna* happy? Mameha thinks I should establish my reputation first, just for a few years.'

'Mameha! What does she know about business? The next time I want to know when to giggle at a party, I'll go and ask her.'

Nowadays young girls, even in Japan, are accustomed to jumping up from the table and shouting at their mothers, but in my day we bowed and said, 'Yes, ma'am,' and apologized

334

for having been troublesome; and that's exactly how I responded.

'Leave the business decisions to me,' Mother went on. 'Only a fool would pass up an offer like the one Nobu Toshikazu has made.'

My heart nearly stopped when I heard this. I suppose it was obvious that Nobu would one day propose himself as my *danna*. After all, he'd made an offer for my *mizuage* several years earlier, and since then had certainly asked for my company more frequently than any other man. I can't pretend I hadn't thought of this possibility; but that isn't to say I'd ever believed it was the course my life would really take. On the day I first met Nobu at the sumo tournament, my almanac reading had been, 'A balance of good and bad can open the door to destiny.' Nearly every day since, I'd thought of it in one way or another. Good and bad . . . well, it was Mameha and Hatsumomo; it was my adoption by Mother and the *mizuage* that had brought it about; and of course it was the Chairman and Nobu. I don't mean to suggest I disliked Nobu. Quite the opposite. But to become his mistress would have closed off my life from the Chairman forever.

Mother must have noticed something of the shock I felt at hearing her words – or in any case, she wasn't pleased at my reaction. But before she could respond we heard a noise in the hallway outside like someone suppressing a cough, and in a moment Hatsumomo stepped into the open doorway. She was holding a bowl of rice, which was very rude of her – she never should have walked away from the table with it. When she'd swallowed, she let out a laugh.

'Mother!' she said. 'Are you trying to make me choke?' Apparently she'd been listening to our conversation while she ate her lunch. 'So the famous Sayuri is going to have Nobu Toshikazu for her *danna*,' she went on. 'Isn't that sweet!'

'If you've come here to say something useful, then say it,' Mother told her.

'Yes, I have,' Hatsumomo said gravely, and she came and knelt at the table. 'Sayuri-san, you may not realize it, but one of the things that goes on between a geisha and her *danna* can cause the geisha to become pregnant, do you understand?

335

And a man will become very upset if his mistress gives birth to another man's child. In your case, you must be especially careful, because Nobu will know at once, if the child should happen to have two arms like the rest of us, that it can't possibly be his!'

Hatsumomo thought her little joke was very funny.

'Perhaps you should cut off one of your arms, Hatsumomo,' said Mother, 'if it will make you as successful as Nobu Toshikazu has been.'

'And probably it would help, too, if my face looked like this!' she said, smiling, and picked up her rice bowl so we could see what was in it. She was eating rice mixed with red adzuki beans and, in a sickening way, it did look like blistered skin.

As the afternoon progressed I began to feel dizzy; with a strange buzzing in my head, and soon made my way to Mameha's apartment to talk with her. I sat at her table sipping at my chilled barley tea – for we were in the heat of summer – and trying not to let her see how I felt. Reaching the Chairman was the one hope that had motivated me all through my training. If my life would be nothing more than Nobu, and dance recitals, and evening after evening in Gion, I couldn't think why I had struggled so.

Already Mameha had waited a long while to hear why I'd come, but when I set my glass of tea down on the table, I was afraid my voice would crack if I tried to speak. I took a few more moments to compose myself, and then finally swallowed and managed to say, 'Mother tells me that within a month it's likely I'll have a *danna*.'

'Yes, I know. And the *danna* will be Nobu Toshikazu.'

By this time I was concentrating so hard on holding myself back from crying, I could no longer speak at all.

'Nobu-san is a good man,' she said, 'and very fond of you.'

'Yes, but, Mameha-san . . . I don't know how to say it . . . this was never what I imagined!'

'What do you mean? Nobu-san has always treated you kindly.'

'But, Mameha-san, I don't want kindness!'

336

'Don't you? I thought we all wanted kindness. Perhaps what you mean is that you want something more than kindness. And that is something you're in no position to ask.'

Of course, Mameha was quite right. When I heard these words, my tears simply broke through the fragile wall that had held them, and with a terrible feeling of shame, I laid my head upon the table and let them drain out of me. Only when I'd composed myself afterward did Mameha speak.

'What did you expect, Sayuri?' she asked

'Something besides this!'

'I understand you may find Nobu difficult to look at, perhaps. But –'

'Mameha-san, it isn't that. Nobu-san is a good man, as you say. It's just that –'

'It's just that you want your destiny to be like Shizue's. Is that it?'

Shizue, though she wasn't an especially popular geisha, was considered by everyone in Gion to be the most fortunate of women. For thirty years she'd been the mistress of a pharmacist. He wasn't a wealthy man, and she wasn't a beauty; but you could have looked all over Kyoto and not found two people who enjoyed each other's company as they did. As usual, Mameha had come closer to the truth than I wanted to admit.

'You're eighteen years old, Sayuri,' she went on. 'Neither you nor I can know your destiny. You may never know it! Destiny isn't always like a party at the end of the evening. Sometimes it's nothing more than struggling through life from day to day.'

'But, Mameha-san, how cruel!'

'Yes, it is cruel,' she said. 'But none of us can escape destiny.'

'Please, it isn't a matter of escaping my destiny, or anything of that sort. Nobu-san is a good man, just as you say. I know I should feel nothing but gratitude for his interest, but . . . there are so many things I've dreamed about.'

'And you're afraid that once Nobu has touched you, after that they can never be? Really, Sayuri, what did you think life as a geisha would be like? We don't become geisha so our lives

337

will be satisfying. We become geisha because we have no other choice.'

'Oh, Mameha-san . . . please . . . have I really been so foolish to keep my hopes alive that perhaps one day –'

'Young girls hope all sorts of foolish things, Sayuri. Hopes are like hair ornaments. Girls want to wear too many of them. When they become old women they look silly wearing even one.'

I was determined not to lose control of my feelings again. I managed to hold in all my tears except the few that squeezed out of me like sap from a tree.

'Mameha-san,' I said, 'do you have. . . strong feelings for the Baron?'

'The Baron has been a good *danna* to me.'

'Yes, of course that's true, but do you have feelings for him as a man? I mean, some geisha do have feelings for their *danna*, don't they?'

'The Baron's relationship with me is convenient for him, and very beneficial to me. If our dealings were tinged with passion . . . well, passion can quickly slip over into jealousy, or even hatred. I certainly can't afford to have a powerful man upset with me. I've struggled for years to carve out a place for myself in Gion, but if a powerful man makes up his mind to destroy me, well, he'll do it! If you want to be successful, Sayuri, you must be sure that men's feelings remain always under your control. The Baron may be hard to take at times, but he has plenty of money, and he's not afraid to spend it. And he doesn't want children, thank heavens. Nobu will certainly be a challenge for you. He knows his own mind much too well. I won't be surprised if he expects more of you than the Baron has expected of me.'

'But, Mameha-san, what about your own feelings? I mean, hasn't there ever been a man . . .'

I wanted to ask if there had ever been a man who brought out feelings of passion in her. But I could see that her irritation with me, if it had been only a bud until then, had burst into full bloom now. She drew herself up with her hands in her lap; I think she was on the point of rebuking me, but I apologized for my rudeness at once, and she settled back again.

'You and Nobu have an *en*, Sayuri, and you can't escape it,' she said.

I knew even then that she was right. An *en* is a karmic bond lasting a lifetime. Nowadays many people seem to believe their lives are entirely a matter of choice; but in my day we viewed ourselves as pieces of clay that forever show the fingerprints of everyone who has touched them. Nobu's touch had made a deeper impression on me than most. No one could tell me whether he would be my ultimate destiny, but I had always sensed the *en* between us. Somewhere in the landscape of my life Nobu would always be present. But could it really be that of all the lessons I'd learned, the hardest one lay just ahead of me? Would I really have to take each of my hopes and put them away where no one would ever see them again, where not even I would ever see them?

'Go back to the okiya, Sayuri,' Mameha told me. 'Prepare for the evening ahead of you. There's nothing like work for getting over a disappointment.'

I looked up at her with the idea of making one last plea, but when I saw the expression on her face, I thought better of it. I can't say what she was thinking; but she seemed to be peering into nothingness with her perfect oval face creased in the corners of her eyes and mouth from strain. And then she let out a heavy breath, and gazed down into her teacup with what I took as a look of bitterness.

A woman living in a grand house may pride herself on all her lovely things; but the moment she hears the crackle of fire she decides very quickly which are the few she values most. In the days after Mameha and I had spoken, I certainly came to feel that my life was burning down around me; and yet when I struggled to find even a single thing that would still matter to me after Nobu had become my *danna*, I'm sorry to say that I failed. One evening while I was kneeling at a table in the Ichiriki Teahouse, trying not to think too much about my feelings of misery, I had a sudden thought of a child lost in the snowy woods; and when I looked up at the white-haired men I was entertaining, they looked so much like snowcapped trees all around me that I felt for one horrifying moment I might be the sole living human in all the world.

The only parties at which I managed to convince myself that my life might still have some purpose, however small, were the ones attended by military men. Already in 1938, we'd all grown accustomed to daily reports about the war in Manchuria; and we were reminded every day of our troops overseas by things like the so-called Rising Sun Lunch Box – which was a pickled plum in the center of a box of rice, looking like the Japanese flag. For several generations, army and navy officers had come to Gion to relax. But now they began to tell us, with watery eyes after their seventh or eighth cup of sake, that nothing kept their spirits up so much as their visits to Gion. Probably this was the sort of thing military officers say to the women they talk with. But the idea that I – who was nothing more than a young girl from the seashore – might truly be contributing something important to the nation . . . I won't pretend these parties did anything to lessen my suffering; but they did help remind me just how selfish my suffering really was.

A few weeks passed, and then one evening in a hallway at the Ichiriki, Mameha suggested the time had come to collect on her bet with Mother. I'm sure you'll recall that the two of them had wagered about whether my debts would be repaid before I was twenty. As it turned out, of course, they'd been repaid already though I was only eighteen. 'Now that you've turned your collar,' Mameha said to me, 'I can't see any reason to wait longer.'

This is what she said, but I think the truth was more complicated. Mameha knew that Mother hated settling debts, and would hate settling them still more when the stakes went higher. My earnings would go up considerably after I took a *danna*; Mother was certain to grow only more protective of the income. I'm sure Mameha thought it best to collect what she was owed as soon as possible, and worry about future earnings in the future.

Several days afterward, I was summoned downstairs to the reception room of our okiya to find Mameha and Mother across the table from each other, chatting about the summer weather. Beside Mameha was a gray-haired woman named Mrs. Okada, whom I'd met a number of times. She was mistress of the okiya where Mameha had once lived, and she still took care of Mameha's accounting in exchange for a portion of the income. I'd never seen her look more serious, peering down at the table with no interest in the conversation at all.

'There you are!' Mother said to me. 'Your older sister has kindly come to visit, and has brought Mrs. Okada with her. You certainly owe them the courtesy of joining us.'

Mrs. Okada spoke up, with her eyes still on the tabletop. 'Mrs. Nitta, as Mameha may have mentioned on the telephone, this is more a business call than a social call. There's no need for Sayuri to join us. I'm sure she has other things to do.'

'I won't have her showing disrespect to the two of you,' Mother replied. 'She'll join us at the table for the few minutes you're here.'

So I arranged myself beside Mother, and the maid came in to serve tea. Afterward Mameha said, 'You must be very proud, Mrs. Nitta, of how well your daughter is doing. Her fortunes have surpassed expectations! Wouldn't you agree?'

'Well now, what do I know about your expectations, Mameha-san?' said Mother. After this she clenched her teeth and gave one of her peculiar laughs, looking from one of us to the other to be sure we appreciated her cleverness. No one laughed with her, and Mrs. Okada just adjusted her glasses and cleared her throat. Finally Mother added, 'As for my own expectations, I certainly wouldn't say Sayuri has surpassed them.'

'When we first discussed her prospects a number of years ago,' Mameha said, 'I had the impression you didn't think much of her. You were reluctant even to have me take on her training.'

'I wasn't sure it was wise to put Sayuri's future in the hands of someone outside the okiya, if you'll forgive me,' said Mother. 'We do have our Hatsumomo, you know.'

'Oh, come now, Mrs. Nitta!' Mameha said with a laugh.

'Hatsumomo would have strangled the poor girl before she'd have trained her!'

'I admit Hatsumomo can be difficult. But when you spot a girl like Sayuri with something a little different, you have to be sure to make the right decisions at the right times – such as the arrangement you and I made, Mameha-san. I expect you've come here today to settle our account?'

'Mrs. Okada has been kind enough to write up the figures,' Mameha replied. 'I'd be grateful if you would have a look at them.'

Mrs. Okada straightened her glasses and took an accounting book from a bag at her knee. Mameha and I sat in silence while she opened it on the table and explained her columns of figures to Mother.

'These figures for Sayuri's earnings over the past year,' Mother interrupted. 'My goodness, I only wish we'd been so fortunate as you seem to think! They're higher even than the total earnings for our okiya.'

'Yes, the numbers are most impressive,' Mrs. Okada said, 'but I do believe they are accurate. I've kept careful track through the records of the Gion Registry Office.'

Mother clenched her teeth and laughed at this, I suppose because she was embarrassed at having been caught in her lie. 'Perhaps I haven't watched the accounts as carefully as I should have,' she said.

After ten or fifteen minutes the two women agreed on a figure representing how much I'd earned since my debut. Mrs. Okada took a small abacus from her bag and made a few calculations, writing down numbers on a blank page of the account book. At last she wrote down a final figure and underscored it. 'Here, then, is the amount Mameha-san is entitled to receive.'

'Considering how helpful she has been to our Sayuri,' Mother said, 'I'm sure Mameha-san deserves even more. Unfortunately, according to our arrangements, Mameha agreed to take half of what a geisha in her position might usually take, until after Sayuri had repaid her debts. Now that the debts are repaid, Mameha is of course entitled to the other half, so that she will have earned the full amount.'

'My understanding is that Mameha did agree to take half wages,' Mrs Okada said, 'but was ultimately to be paid double. This is why she agreed to take a risk. If Sayuri had failed to repay her debts, Mameha would have received nothing more than half wages. But Sayuri has succeeded, and Mameha is entitled to double.'

'Really, Mrs. Okada, can you imagine me agreeing to such terms?' Mother said. 'Everyone in Gion knows how careful I am with money. It's certainly true that Mameha has been helpful to our Sayuri. I can't possibly pay double, but I'd like to propose offering an additional ten percent. If I may say so, it seems generous, considering that our okiya is hardly in a position to throw money around carelessly.'

The word of a woman in Mother's position should have been assurance enough – and with any woman but Mother, it certainly would have been. But now that she'd made up her mind to lie . . . well, we all sat in silence a long moment. Finally Mrs. Okada said, 'Mrs. Nitta, I do find myself in a difficult position. I remember quite clearly what Mameha told me.'

'Of course you do,' Mother said. 'Mameha has her memory of the conversation, and I have mine. What we need is a third party and happily, we have one here with us. Sayuri may only have been a girl at the time, but she has quite a head for numbers.'

'I'm sure her memory is excellent,' Mrs. Okada remarked. 'But one can hardly say she has no personal interest. After all, she is the daughter of the okiya.'

'Yes, she is,' said Mameha; and this was the first time she'd spoken up in quite a while. 'But she's also an honest girl. I'm prepared to accept her answer, provided that Mrs. Nitta will accept it too.'

'Of course I will,' Mother said, and put down her pipe. 'Now then, Sayuri, which is it?'

If I'd been given a choice between sliding off the roof to break my arm again just the way I did as a child, or sitting in that room until I came up with an answer to the question they were asking me, I certainly would have marched right up the stairs and climbed the ladder onto the roof. Of all the women in Gion, Mameha and Mother were the two most influential in my life, and it was clear to me I was going to make one of them angry. I had no doubt in my mind of the truth; but on the other hand, I had to go on living in the okiya with Mother. Of course, Mameha had done more for me than anyone in Gion. I could hardly take Mother's side against her.

'Well?' Mother said to me.

'As I recall, Mameha did accept half wages. But you agreed to pay her double earnings in the end, Mother. I'm sorry, but this is the way I remember it.'

There was a pause, and then Mother said, 'Well, I'm not as young as I used to be. It isn't the first time my memory has misled me.'

'We all have these sorts of problems from time to time,' Mrs. Okada replied. 'Now, Mrs. Nitta, what was this about offering Mameha an additional ten percent? I assume you meant ten percent over the double you originally agreed to pay her.'

'If only I were in a position to do such a thing,' Mother said.

'But you offered it only a moment ago. Surely you haven't changed your mind so quickly?'

Mrs. Okada wasn't gazing at the tabletop any longer, but was staring directly at Mother. After a long moment she said, 'I suppose we'll let it be. In any case, we've done enough for one day. Why don't we meet another time to work out the final figure?'

Mother wore a stern expression on her face, but she gave a little bow of assent and thanked the two of them for coming.

'I'm sure you must be very pleased,' Mrs. Okada said, while putting away her abacus and her accounting book, 'that Sayuri will soon be taking a *danna*. And at only eighteen years of age! How young to take such a big step.'

'Mameha would have done well to take a *danna* at that age herself,' Mother replied.

'Eighteen is a bit young for most girls,' Mameha said, 'but I'm certain Mrs. Nitta has made the right decision in Sayuri's case.'

Mother puffed on her pipe a moment, peering at Mameha across the table. 'My advice to you, Mameha-san,' she said, 'is that you stick to teaching Sayuri about that pretty way of rolling her eyes. When it comes to business decisions, you may leave them to me.'

'I would never presume to discuss business with you, Mrs. Nitta. I'm convinced your decision is for the best . . . But may I ask? Is it true the most generous offer has come from Nobu Toshikazu?'

'His has been the only offer. I suppose that makes it the most generous.'

'The only offer? What a pity . . . The arrangements are so much more favorable when several men compete. Don't you find it so?'

'As I say, Mameha-san, you can leave the business decisions to me. I have in mind a very simple plan for arranging favorable terms with Nobu Toshikazu.'

'If you don't mind,' Mameha said, 'I'd be very eager to hear it.'

Mother put her pipe down on the table. I thought she was going to reprimand Mameha, but in fact she said, 'Yes, I'd like to tell it to you, now that you mention it. You may be able to help me. I've been thinking that Nobu Toshikazu will be more generous if he finds out an Iwamura Electric heater killed our Granny. Don't you think so?'

'Oh, I know very little about business, Mrs. Nitta.'

'Perhaps you or Sayuri should let it slip in conversation the next time you see him. Let him know what a terrible blow it was. I think he'll want to make it up to us.'

'Yes, I'm sure that's a good idea,' Mameha said. 'Still, it's disappointing . . . I had the impression another man had expressed interest in Sayuri.'

'A hundred yen is a hundred yen, whether it comes from this man or that one.'

'That would be true in most cases,' Mameha said. 'But the man I'm thinking of is General Tottori Junnosuke . . .'

At this point in the conversation, I lost track of what the two of them were saying; for I'd begun to realize that Mameha was making an effort to rescue me from Nobu. I certainly hadn't expected such a thing. I had no idea whether she'd changed her mind about helping me, or whether she was thanking me for taking her side against Mother . . . Of course, it was possible she wasn't really trying to help me at all, but had some other purpose. My mind went on racing with these thoughts, until I felt Mother tapping my arm with the stem of her pipe.

'Well?' she said.

'Ma'am?'

'I asked if you know the General.'

'I've met him a few times, Mother,' I said. 'He comes to Gion often.'

I don't know why I gave this response. The truth is, I'd met the General more than a few times. He came to parties in Gion every week, though always as the guest of someone else. He was a bit on the small side – shorter than I was, in fact. But he wasn't the sort of person you could overlook, any more than you could overlook a machine gun. He moved very briskly and was always puffing on one cigarette after another, so that wisps of smoke drifted in the air around him like the clouds around a train idling on the tracks. One evening while slightly drunk, the General had talked to me for the longest time about all the various ranks in the army and found it very funny that I kept mixing them up. General Tottori's own rank was *sho-jo*, which meant 'little general' – that is to say, the lowest of the generals – and foolish girl that I was, I had the impression this wasn't very high. He may have played down the importance of his rank from modesty; and I didn't know any better than to believe him.

By now Mameha was telling Mother that the General had just taken a new position. He'd been put in charge of something called 'military procurement' – though as Mameha went on to explain it, the job sounded like nothing more than a housewife going to the market. If the army had a shortage of ink pads, for example, the General's job was to make sure it got the ink pads it needed, and at a very favorable price.

'With his new job,' said Mameha, 'the General is now in a position to take a mistress for the first time. And I'm quite sure he has expressed an interest in Sayuri.'

'Why should it matter to me if he's expressed an interest in Sayuri?' Mother said. 'These military men never take care of

346

a geisha the way a businessman or an aristocrat does.'

'That may be true, Mrs. Nitta. But I think you'll find that General Tottori's new position could be of great help to the okiya.'

'Nonsense! I don't need help taking care of the okiya. All I need is steady, generous income, and that's the one thing a military man can't give me.'

'Those of us in Gion have been fortunate so far,' Mameha said. 'But shortages will affect us, if the war continues.'

'I'm sure they would, if the war continued,' Mother said. 'This war will be over in six months.'

'And when it is, the military will be in a stronger position than ever before. Mrs. Nitta, please don't forget that General Tottori is the man who oversees all the resources of the military. No one in Japan is in a better position to provide you with everything you could want, whether the war continues or not. He approves every item passing through all the ports in Japan.'

As I later learned, what Mameha had said about General Tottori wasn't quite true. He was in charge of only one of five large administrative areas. But he was senior to the men who oversaw the other districts, so he may as well have been in charge. In any case, you should have seen how Mother behaved after Mameha had said this. You could almost see her mind at work as she thought about having the help of a man in General Tottori's position. She glanced at the teapot, and I could just imagine her thinking, 'Well, I haven't had any trouble getting tea; not yet . . . though the price has gone up . . .' And then probably without even realizing what she was doing, she put one hand inside her obi and squeezed her silk bag of tobacco as if to see how much remained.

Mother spent the next week going around Gion and making one phone call after another to learn as much as she could about General Tottori. She was so immersed in this task that sometimes when I spoke to her; she didn't seem to hear me. I think she was so busy with her thoughts, her mind was like a train pulling too many cars.

During this period I continued seeing Nobu whenever he

347

came to Gion, and did my best to act as though nothing had changed. Probably he'd expected I would be his mistress by the middle of July. Certainly I'd expected it; but even when the month came to a close, his negotiations seemed to have led nowhere. Several times during the following weeks I noticed him looking at me with puzzlement. And then one night he greeted the mistress of the Ichiriki Teahouse in the curtest manner I'd ever seen, by strolling past without so much as a nod. The mistress had always valued Nobu as a customer and gave me a look that seemed surprised and worried all at once. When I joined the party Nobu was giving, I couldn't help noticing signs of anger – a rippling muscle in his jaw, and a certain briskness with which he tossed sake into his mouth. I can't say I blamed him for feeling as he did. I thought he must consider me heartless, to have repaid his many kindnesses with neglect. I fell into a gloomy spell thinking these thoughts, until the sound of a sake cup set down with a *tick* startled me out of it. When I looked up, Nobu was watching me. Guests all around him were laughing and enjoying themselves, and there he sat with his eyes fixed on me, as lost in his thoughts as I had been in mine. We were like two wet spots in the midst of burning charcoal.

26

DURING SEPTEMBER OF that year, while I was still eighteen years old, General Tottori and I drank sake together in a ceremony at the Ichiriki Teahouse. This was the same ceremony I'd first performed with Mameha when she became my older sister; and later with Dr. Crab just before my *miziuage*. In the weeks afterward, everyone congratulated Mother for having made such a favorable alliance.

On that very first night after the ceremony, I went on the General's instructions to a small inn in the northwest of Kyoto called Suruya, with only three rooms. I was so accustomed by this time to lavish surroundings that the shabbiness of the Suruya surprised me. The room smelled of mildew, and the tatami were so bloated and sodden that they seemed to make a sighing noise when I stepped on them. Plaster had crumbled near the floor in one corner. I could hear an old man reading a magazine article aloud in an adjacent room. The longer I knelt there, the more out of sorts I felt, so that I was positively relieved when the General finally arrived – even though he did nothing more, after I had greeted him, than turn on the radio and sit drinking a beer.

After a time he went downstairs to take a bath. When he returned to the room, he took off his robe at once and walked around completely naked toweling his hair; with his little round belly protruding below his chest and a great patch of hair beneath it. I had never seen a man naked before, and I found the General's sagging bottom almost comical. But when he faced me I must admit my eyes went straight to where . . . well, to where his 'eel' ought to have been. Something was flapping around there, but only when the

General lay on his back and told me to take off my clothes did it begin to surface. He was such a strange little nugget of a man, but completely unabashed about telling me what to do. I'd been afraid I'd have to find some way of pleasing him, but as it turned out, all I had to do was follow orders. In the three years since my *mizuage*, I'd forgotten the sheer terror I'd felt when the Doctor finally lowered himself onto me. I remembered it now, but the strange thing was that I didn't feel terror so much as a kind of vague queasiness. The General left the radio on – and the lights as well, as if he wanted to be sure I saw the drabness of the room clearly, right down to the water stain on the ceiling.

As the months passed, this queasiness went away, and my encounters with the General became nothing more than an unpleasant twice-weekly routine. Sometimes I wondered what it might be like with the Chairman; and to tell the truth, I was a bit afraid it might be distasteful, just as with the Doctor and the General. Then something happened to make me see things differently. Around this time a man named Yasuda Akira, who'd been in all the magazines because of the success of a new kind of bicycle light he'd designed, began coming to Gion regularly. He wasn't welcome at the Ichiriki yet and probably couldn't have afforded it in any case, but he spent three or four evenings a week at a little teahouse called Tatematsu, in the Tominagacho section of Gion, not far from our okiya. I first met him at a banquet one night during the spring of 1939, when I was nineteen years old. He was so much younger than the men around him – probably no more than thirty – that I noticed him the moment I came into the room. He had the same sort of dignity as the Chairman. I found him very attractive sitting there with his shirtsleeves rolled up and his jacket behind him on the mats. For a moment I watched an old man nearby, who raised up his chopsticks with a little piece of braised tofu and his mouth already as wide as it would go; this gave me the impression of a door being slid open so that a turtle could march slowly through. By contrast it made me almost weak to see the way Yasuda-san, with his graceful, sculpted arm, put a bite of braised beef into his mouth with his lips parted sensuously.

I made my way around the circle of men, and when I came to him and introduced myself, he said, 'I hope you'll forgive me.'

'Forgive you? Why, what have you done?' I asked him.

'I've been very rude,' he replied. 'I haven't been able to take my eyes off you all evening.'

On impulse I reached into my obi for the brocade card holder I kept there, and discreetly removed one card, which I passed to him. Geisha always carry name cards with them just as businessmen carry business cards. Mine was very small, half the size of an ordinary calling card, printed on heavy rice paper with only the words 'Gion' and 'Sayuri' written on it in calligraphy. It was spring, so I was carrying cards decorated with a colorful spray of plum blossoms in the background. Yasuda admired it for a moment before putting it into his shirt pocket. I had the feeling no words we spoke could be as eloquent as this simple interaction, so I bowed to him and went on to the next man.

From that day, Yasuda-san began asking me to the Tatematsu Teahouse every week to entertain him. I was never able to go as often as he wanted me. But about three months after we first met, he brought me a kimono one afternoon as a gift. I felt very flattered, even though in truth it wasn't a sophisticated robe – woven with a poor quality silk in somewhat garish colors, and with a commonplace design of flowers and butterflies. He wanted me to wear it for him one evening soon, and I promised him I would. But when I returned to the okiya with it that night, Mother saw me carrying the package up the stairs and took it away from me to have a look. She sneered when she saw the robe, and said she wouldn't have me seen in anything so unattractive. The very next day, she sold it.

When I found out what she'd done, I said to her as boldly as I dared that the robe had been given to me as a gift, not to the okiya, and that it wasn't right for her to have sold it.

'Certainly it was your robe,' she said. 'But you are the daughter of the okiya. What belongs to the okiya belongs to you, and the other way around as well.'

I was so angry at Mother after this that I couldn't even

bring myself to look at her. As for Yasuda-san, who'd wanted to see the robe on me, I told him that because of its colors and its butterfly motif, I could wear it only very early in the spring, and since it was now already summer; nearly a year would have to pass before he could see me in it. He didn't seem too upset to hear this.

'What is a year?' he said, looking at me with penetrating eyes. 'I'd wait a good deal longer; depending on what I was waiting for.'

We were alone in the room, and Yasuda-san put his beer glass down on the table in a way that made me blush. He reached out for my hand, and I gave it to him expecting that he wanted to hold it a long moment in both of his before letting it go again. But to my surprise he brought it quickly to his lips and began kissing the inside of my wrist quite passionately, in a way I could feel as far down as my knees. I think of myself as an obedient woman; up until this time I'd generally done the things told to me by Mother; or Mameha, or even Hatsumomo when I'd had no other choice; but I felt such a combination of anger at Mother and longing for Yasuda-san that I made up my mind right then to do the very thing Mother had ordered me most explicitly not to do. I asked him to meet me in that very teahouse at midnight, and I left him there alone.

Just before midnight I came back and spoke to a young maid. I promised her an indecent sum of money if she would see to it that no one disturbed Yasuda-san and me in one of the upstairs rooms for half an hour. I was already there, waiting in the dark, when the maid slid open the door and Yasuda-san stepped inside. He dropped his fedora onto the mats and pulled me to my feet even before the door was closed. To press my body against his felt so satisfying, like a meal after a long spell of hunger. No matter how hard he pressed himself against me, I pressed back harder. Somehow I wasn't shocked to see how expertly his hands slipped through the seams in my clothing to find my skin. I won't pretend I experienced none of the clumsy moments I was accustomed to with the General, but I certainly didn't notice them in the same way. My encounters with the General reminded me of a time as a child when I'd struggled to climb a tree and pluck away a certain leaf at the top. It was all a matter of careful movements, bearing the discomfort until I finally reached my goal. But with Yasuda-san I felt like a child running freely down a hill. Sometime later when we lay exhausted upon the mats together, I moved his shirttail aside and put my hand on his stomach to feel his breathing. I had never in my life been so close to another human being before, though we hadn't spoken a word.

It was only then that I understood: it was one thing to lie still on the futon for the Doctor or the General. It would be something quite different with the Chairman.

Many a geisha's day-to-day life has changed dramatically after taking a *danna*; but in my case, I could hardly see any change at all. I still made the rounds of Gion at night just as I had over the past few years. From time to time during the afternoons I went on excursions, including some very peculiar ones, such as accompanying a man on a visit to his brother in the hospital. But as for the changes I'd expected – the prominent dance recitals paid for by my *danna*, lavish gifts provided by him, even a day or two of paid leisure time – well, none of these things happened. It was just as Mother had said. Military men didn't take care of a geisha the way a business-man or an aristocrat did.

The General may have brought about very little change in my life, but it was certainly true that his alliance with the okiya was invaluable, at least from Mother's point of view. He covered many of my expenses just as a *danna* usually does – including the cost of my lessons, my annual registration fee, my medical expenses, and . . . oh, I don't even know what else – my socks, probably. But more important, his new position as director of military procurement was everything Mameha had suggested, so that he was able to do things for us no other *danna* could have done. For example, Auntie grew ill during March of 1939. We were terribly worried about her; and the doctors were of no help; but after a telephone call to the General, an important doctor from the military hospital in the Kamigyo Ward called on us and provided Auntie with a packet of medicine that cured her. So although the General may not have sent me to Tokyo for dance recitals, or presented me with precious gems, no one could suggest our okiya didn't do well by him. He sent regular deliveries of tea and sugar; as well as chocolates, which were becoming scarce even in Gion. And of course, Mother had been quite wrong about the war ending within six months. We couldn't have believed it at the time, but we'd scarcely seen the beginning of the dark years just yet.

During that fall when the General became my *danna*, Nobu ceased inviting me to parties where I'd so often entertained him. Soon I realized he'd stopped coming to the Ichiriki altogether. I couldn't think of any reason he should do this, unless it was to avoid me. With a sigh, the mistress of the Ichiriki agreed that I was probably right. At the New Year I wrote Nobu a card, as I did with all of my patrons, but he didn't respond. It's easy for me to look back now and tell you casually how many months passed; but at the time I lived in anguish. I felt I'd wronged a man who had treated me kindly – a man I'd come to think of as a friend. What was more, without Nobu's patronage, I was no longer invited to Iwamura Electric's parties, which meant I hardly stood any chance at all of seeing the Chairman.

Of course, the Chairman still came regularly to the Ichiriki even though Nobu didn't. I saw him quietly upbraiding a junior associate in the hallway one evening, gesturing with a fountain pen for emphasis, and I didn't dare disturb him to say hello. Another night, a worried-looking young apprentice named Naotsu, with a terrible underbite, was walking him to the toilet when he caught sight of me. He left Naotsu standing there to come and speak with me. We exchanged the usual pleasantries. I thought I saw in his faint smile, the kind of subdued pride men often seem to feel when gazing on their own children. Before he continued on his way, I said to him, 'Chairman, if there's ever an evening when the presence of another geisha or two might be helpful . . .'

This was very forward of me, but to my relief the Chairman didn't take offense.

'That's a fine idea, Sayuri,' he said. 'I'll ask for you.'

But the weeks passed, and he didn't.

One evening late in March I dropped in on a very lively party given by the Governor of Kyoto Prefecture at a teahouse called Shunju. The Chairman was there, on the losing end of a drinking game, looking exhausted in shirtsleeves and with his tie loosened. Actually the Governor had lost most of the rounds, as I learned, but held his sake better than the Chairman.

'I'm so glad you're here, Sayuri,' he said to me. 'You've got to help me. I'm in trouble.'

To see the smooth skin of his face splotched red, and his arms protruding from rolled-up shirtsleeves, I thought at once of Yasuda-san on that night at the Tatematsu Teahouse. For the briefest moment I had a feeling that everything in the room had vanished but the Chairman and me, and that in his slightly drunken state I might lean in toward him until his arms went around me, and put my lips on his. I even had a flicker of embarrassment that I'd been so obvious in my thoughts that the Chairman must have understood them . . . but if so, he seemed to regard me just the same. To help him, all I could do was conspire with another geisha to slow the pace of the game. The Chairman seemed grateful for this, and when it was all over, he sat and talked with me a long while, drinking glasses of water to sober up. Finally he took a handkerchief from his pocket, identical to the one tucked inside my obi, and wiped his forehead with it, and then smoothed his coarse hair back along his head before saying to me:

'When was the last time you spoke with your old friend Nobu?'

'Not in quite some time, Chairman,' I said. 'To tell the truth, I have the impression Nobu-san may be angry with me.'

The Chairman was looking down into his handkerchief as he refolded it. 'Friendship is a precious thing, Sayuri,' he said. 'One mustn't throw it away.'

I thought about this conversation often over the weeks that followed. Then one day late in April, I was putting on my makeup for a performance of *Dances of the Old Capital*, when a young apprentice I hardly knew came to speak with me. I put down my makeup brush, expecting her to ask a favor – because our okiya was still well supplied with things others in Gion had learned to do without. But instead she said:

'I'm terribly sorry to trouble you, Sayuri-san, but my name is Takazuru. I wondered if you would mind helping me. I know you were once very good friends with Nobu-san . . .'

After months and months of wondering about him, and feeling terribly ashamed for what I'd done, just to hear Nobu's name when I didn't expect it was like opening storm shutters and feeling the first draft of air.

'We must all help each other whenever we can, Takazuru,' I said. 'And if it's a problem with Nobu-san, I'm especially interested. I hope he's well.'

'Yes, he is well, ma'am, or at least I think so. He comes to the Awazumi Teahouse, in East Gion. Do you know it?'

'Oh, yes, I know it,' I said. 'But I had no idea Nobu-san visited there.'

'Yes, ma'am, quite often,' Takazuru told me. 'But . . . may I ask, Sayuri-san? You've known him a long while, and . . . well, Nobu-san is a kind man, isn't he?'

'Takazuru-san, why do you ask me? If you've been spending time with him, surely you know whether or not he is kind!'

'I'm sure I must sound foolish. But I'm so confused! He asks for me every time he comes to Gion, and my older sister tells me he's as good a patron as any girl could hope for. But now she's angry with me because I've cried in front of him several times. I know I shouldn't do it, but I can't even promise I won't do it again!'

'He is being cruel to you, is he?'

By way of answering, poor Takazuru clenched her trembling lips together, and in a moment tears began to pool at the edges of her lids, so much that her little round eyes seemed to gaze up at me from two puddles.

'Sometimes Nobu-san doesn't know how harsh he sounds,' I told her. 'But he must like you, Takazuru-san. Otherwise, why would he ask for you?'

'I think he asks for me only because I'm someone to be mean to,' she said. 'One time he did say my hair smelled clean, but then he told me what a nice change that was.'

'It's strange that you see him so often,' I said. 'I've been hoping for months to run into him.'

'Oh, please don't, Sayuri-san! He already says how nothing about me is as good as you. If he sees you again, he'll only think the worse of me. I know I shouldn't bother you with my problems, ma'am, but . . . I thought you might know something I could do to please him. He likes stimulating conversation, but I never know what to say. Everyone tells me I'm not a very bright girl.'

People in Kyoto are trained to say things like this; but it struck me that this poor girl might be telling the truth. It wouldn't have surprised me if Nobu regarded her as nothing more than the tree where the tiger might sharpen its claws. I couldn't think of anything helpful, so in the end I suggested she read a book about some historical event Nobu might find interesting, and tell the story to him bit by bit when they met. I myself had done this sort of thing from time to time – for there were men who liked nothing more than to sit back with their eyes watery and half-closed, and listen to the sound of a woman's voice. I wasn't sure it would work with Nobu, but Takazuru seemed very grateful for the idea.

Now that I knew where to find Nobu, I was determined to go and see him. I felt terribly sorry I'd made him angry with me; and of course, I might never see the Chairman again without him. I certainly didn't want to cause Nobu pain, but I thought perhaps by meeting with him I could find some way of resuming our friendship. The trouble was, I couldn't drop in uninvited at the Awazumi, for I had no formal relationship with the teahouse. So in the end I made up my mind to stroll past during the evening whenever I could, in the hopes of bumping into Nobu on his way there. I knew his habits well enough to make a fair guess about the time he might arrive.

For eight or nine weeks I kept up this plan. Then at last one evening I spotted him emerging from the back of a limousine in the dark alleyway ahead of me. I knew it was him, because the empty sleeve of his jacket, pinned at the shoulder, gave him an unmistakable silhouette. The driver was handing him his briefcase as I neared. I stopped in the light of a lantern there in the alley, and let out a little gasp that would sound like delight. Nobu looked in my direction just as I'd hoped.

'Well, well,' he said. 'One forgets how lovely a geisha can look.' He spoke in such a casual tone, I had to wonder whether he knew it was me.

'Why, sir, you sound like my old friend Nobu-san,' I said. 'But you can't be him, for I have the impression he has disappeared completely from Gion!'

The driver closed the door, and we stood in silence until the car pulled away.

'I'm so relieved,' I said, 'to see Nobu-san again at last! And what luck for me that he should be standing in the shadows rather than in the light.'

'Sometimes I don't have the least idea what you're talking about, Sayuri. You must have learned this from Mameha. Or maybe they teach it to all geisha.'

'With Nobu-san standing in the shadows, I'm unable to see the angry expression on his face.'

'I see,' he said. 'So you think I'm angry with you?'

'What else am I to think, when an old friend disappears for so many months? I suppose you're going to tell me that you've been too busy to come to the Ichiriki.'

'Why do you say it as if it couldn't possibly be true?'

'Because I happen to know that you've been coming to Gion often. But don't bother to ask me how I know. I won't tell you unless you agree to come on a stroll with me.'

'All right,' said Nobu. 'Since it's a pleasant evening –'

'Oh, Nobu-san, don't say that. I'd much rather you said, "Since I've bumped into an old friend I haven't seen in so long, I can't think of anything I'd rather do than go on a stroll with her."'

'I'll take a walk with you,' he said. 'You may think whatever you like about my reasons for doing it.'

I gave a little bow of assent to this, and we set off together down the alley in the direction of Maruyama Park. 'If Nobu-san wants me to believe he isn't angry,' I said, 'he should act friendlier, instead of like a panther who hasn't been fed for months. No wonder poor Takazuru is so terrified of you . . .'

'So she's spoken to you, has she?' said Nobu. 'Well, if she weren't such an infuriating girl –'

'If you don't like her, why do you ask for her every time you come to Gion?'

'I've never asked for her, not even once! It's her older sister who keeps pushing her at me. It's bad enough you've reminded me of her. Now you're going to take advantage of bumping into me tonight to try to shame me into liking her!'

'Actually, Nobu-san, I didn't "bump" into you at all. I've been strolling down that alley for weeks just for the purpose of finding you.'

This seemed to give Nobu something to think about, for we walked along in silence a few moments. Finally he said, 'I shouldn't be surprised. You're as conniving a person as I know.'

'Nobu-san! What else was I to do?' I said. 'I thought you had disappeared completely. I might never have known where to find you, if Takazuru hadn't come to me in tears to say how badly you've been treating her.'

'Well, I have been hard on her, I suppose. But she isn't as clever as you – or as pretty, for that matter. If you've been thinking I'm angry with you, you're quite right.'

'May I ask what I have done to make an old friend so angry?'

Here Nobu stopped and turned to me with a terribly sad look in his eyes. I felt a fondness welling up in me that I've known for very few men in my life. I was thinking how much I had missed him, and how deeply I had wronged him. But though I'm ashamed to admit it, my feelings of fondness were tinged with pity.

'After a considerable amount of effort,' he said, 'I have discovered the identity of your *danna*.'

'If Nobu-san had asked me, I would have been glad to tell him.'

'I don't believe you. You geisha are the most close-mouthed group of people. I asked around Gion about your *danna*, and one after another they all pretended not to know. I never would have found out, if I hadn't asked Michizono to come entertain me one night, just the two of us.'

Michizono, who was about fifty at the time, was a sort of legend in Gion. She wasn't a beautiful woman, but she could sometimes put even Nobu in a good mood just from the way she crinkled her nose at him when she bowed hello.

'I made her play drinking games with me,' he went on, 'and I won and won until poor Michizono was quite drunk. I could have asked her anything at all and she would have told me.'

'What a lot of work!' I said.

'Nonsense. She was very enjoyable company. There was nothing like work about it. But shall I tell you something? I have lost respect for you, now that I know your *danna* is a little man in uniform whom no one admires.'

'Nobu-san speaks as if I have any choice over who my *danna* is. The only choice I can ever make is what kimono I'll wear. And even then –'

'Do you know why that man has a desk job? It's because no one trusts him with anything that matters. I understand the army very well, Sayuri. Even his own superiors have no use for him. You may as well have made an alliance with a beggar! Really, I was once very fond of you, but –'

'Once? Is Nobu-san not fond of me any longer?'

'I have no fondness for fools.'

'What a cold thing to say! Are you only trying to make me cry? Oh, Nobu-san! Am I a fool because my *danna* is a man you can't admire?'

'You geisha! There was never a more irritating group of people. You go around consulting your almanacs, saying, "Oh, I can't walk toward the east today, because my horo-scope says it's unlucky!" But then when it's a matter of something affecting your entire lives, you simply look the other way.'

'It's less a matter of looking the other way than of closing our eyes to what we can't stop from happening.'

'Is that so? Well, I learned a few things from my talk with Michizono that night when I got her drunk. You are the daughter of the okiya, Sayuri. You can't pretend you have no

360

influence at all. It's your duty to use what influence you have, unless you want to drift through life like a fish belly-up on the stream.'

'I wish I could believe life really is something more than a stream that carries us along, belly-up.'

'All right, if it's a stream, you're still free to be in this part of it or that part, aren't you? The water will divide again and again. If you bump, and tussle, and fight, and make use of whatever advantages you might have –'

'Oh, that's fine, I'm sure, when we have advantages.'

'You'd find them everywhere, if you ever bothered to look! In my case, even when I have nothing more than – I don't know – a chewed-up peach pit, or something of the sort, I won't let it go to waste. When it's time to throw it out, I'll make good and certain to throw it at somebody I don't like!'

'Nobu-san, are you counseling me to throw peach pits?'

'Don't joke about it; you know perfectly well what I'm saying. We're very much alike, Sayuri. I know they call me "Mr. Lizard" and all of that, and here you are, the loveliest creature in Gion. But that very first time I saw you at the sumo tournament years ago – what were you, fourteen? – I could see what a resourceful girl you were even then.'

'I've always believed that Nobu-san thinks me more worthy than I really am.'

'Perhaps you're right. I thought you had something more to you, Sayuri. But it turns out you don't even understand where your destiny lies. To tie your fortunes to a man like the General! I would have taken proper care of you, you know. It makes me so furious to think about it! When this General is gone from your life, he'll leave nothing for you to remember him by. Is this how you intend to waste your youth? A woman who acts like a fool is a fool, wouldn't you say?'

If we rub a fabric too often, it will quickly grow threadbare; and Nobu's words had rasped against me so much, I could no longer maintain that finely lacquered surface Mameha had always counseled me to hide behind. I felt lucky to be standing in shadow, for I was certain Nobu would think still less of me if he saw the pain I was feeling. But I suppose my silence must have betrayed me; for with his one hand he took my shoulder and turned me just a fraction, until the light fell on my face. And when he looked me in the eyes, he let out a long sigh that sounded at first like disappointment.

'Why do you seem so much older to me, Sayuri?' he said after a moment. 'Sometimes I forget you're still a girl. Now you're going to tell me I've been too harsh with you.'

'I cannot expect that Nobu-san should act like anyone but Nobu-san,' I said.

'I react very badly to disappointment, Sayuri. You ought to know that. Whether you failed me because you're too young or because you aren't the woman I thought . . . either way you failed me, didn't you?'

'Please, Nobu-san, it frightens me to hear you say these things. I don't know if I can ever live my life by the standards you use for judging me . . .'

'What standards are those, really? I expect you to go through life with your eyes open! If you keep your destiny in mind, every moment in life becomes an opportunity for moving closer to it. I wouldn't expect this sort of awareness from a foolish girl like Takazuru, but –'

'Hasn't Nobu-san been calling me foolish all evening?'

'You know better than to listen to me when I'm angry.'

'So Nobu-san isn't angry any longer. Then will he come to see me at the Ichiriki Teahouse? Or invite me to come and see him? In fact, I'm in no particular hurry this evening. I could come in even now, if Nobu-san asked me to.'

By now we had walked around the block, and were standing at the entrance to the teahouse. 'I won't ask you,' he said, and rolled open the door.

I couldn't help but let out a great sigh when I heard this; and I call it a great sigh because it contained many smaller sighs within it – one sigh of disappointment, one of frustration, one of sadness . . . and I don't know what else.

'Oh, Nobu-san,' I said, 'sometimes you're so difficult for me to understand.'

'I'm a very easy man to understand, Sayuri,' he said. 'I don't like things held up before me that I cannot have.'

Before I had a chance to reply, he stepped into the teahouse and rolled the door shut behind him.

27

DURING THE SUMMER of that year, 1939, I was so busy with engagements, occasional meetings with the General, dance performances, and the like, that in the morning when I tried to get up from my futon, I often felt like a bucket filled with nails. Usually by midafternoon I managed to forget my fatigue, but I often wondered how much I was earning through all my efforts. I never really expected to find out, however, so I was quite taken aback when Mother called me into her room one afternoon and told me I'd earned more in the past six months than both Hatsumomo and Pumpkin combined.

'Which means,' she said, 'that it's time for you to exchange rooms with them.'

I wasn't as pleased to hear this as you might imagine. Hatsumomo and I had managed to live side by side these past few years by keeping away from each other. But I regarded her as a sleeping tiger, not a defeated one. Hatsumomo certainly wasn't going to think of Mother's plan as 'exchanging rooms'; she was going to feel that her room had been taken away from her.

When I saw Mameha that evening, I told her what Mother had said to me, and mentioned my fears that the fire inside Hatsumomo might flare up again.

'Oh, well, that's fine,' said Mameha. 'That woman won't be beaten once and for all until we see blood. And we haven't seen it yet. Let's give her a bit of a chance and see what sort of a mess she makes for herself this time.'

Early the next morning, Auntie came upstairs in the okiya to lay down the rules for moving our belongings. She began by taking me into Hatsumomo's room and announcing that a certain corner now belonged to me; I could put anything I wanted there, and no one else could touch it. Then she brought Hatsumomo and Pumpkin into my smaller room and set up a similar space for the two of them. After we'd swapped all our belongings, the move would be complete.

I set to work that very afternoon carrying my things through the hall. I wish I could say I'd accumulated a collection of beautiful objects as Mameha probably had by my age; but the mood of the nation had changed greatly. Cosmetics and permanents had recently been banned as luxuries by the military government – though of course those of us in Gion, as playthings of the men in power, still did more or less as we pleased. Lavish gifts, however, were almost unheard of, so I'd accumulated nothing more over the years than a few scrolls, inkstones, and bowls, as well as a collection of stereoscopic photos of famous views, with a lovely viewer made of sterling silver, which the Kabuki actor Onoe Yoegoro XVII had given to me. In any case, I carried these things across the hall – along with my makeup, undergarments, books, and magazines – and piled them in the corner of the room. But as late as the following evening, Hatsumomo and Pumpkin still hadn't begun moving their things out. On the way back from my lessons at noon on the third day, I made up my mind that if Hatsumomo's bottles and ointments were still crowded together on the makeup stand, I would go ask Auntie to help me.

When I reached the top of the stairs, I was surprised to see both Hatsumomo's door and mine standing open. A jar of white ointment lay broken on the hallway floor. Something seemed to be amiss, and when I stepped into my room, I saw what it was. Hatsumomo was sitting at my little table, sipping at what looked like a small glass of water – and reading a notebook that belonged to me!

Geisha are expected to be discreet about the men they know; so you may be puzzled to hear that several years earlier while still an apprentice, I'd gone into a paper store one afternoon and bought a beautiful book of blank pages to begin keeping a diary about my life. I wasn't foolish enough to write down the sorts of things a geisha is never expected to reveal. I wrote only about my thoughts and feelings. When I had something to say about a particular man, I gave him a code name. So for example, I referred to Nobu as 'Mr. Tsu,' because he sometimes made a little scornful noise with his mouth that sounded like 'Tsu!' And I referred to the Chairman as 'Mr. Haa,' because on one occasion he'd taken in a deep breath and let it out slowly in a way that sounded like 'Haa,' and I'd imagined him waking up beside me as he said it – so of course, it made a strong impression on me. But I'd never thought for a moment that anyone would see the things I'd written.

'Why, Sayuri, I'm so pleased to see you!' Hatsumomo said 'I've been waiting to tell you how much I'm enjoying your diary. Some of the entries are *most* interesting . . . and really, your writing style is charming! I'm not much impressed with your calligraphy, but –'

'Did you happen to notice the interesting thing I wrote on the front page?'

'I don't think I did. Let's see . . . "Private." Well, now here's an example of what I'm talking about with your calligraphy.'

'Hatsumomo, please put the book down on the table and leave my room.'

'Really! I'm shocked at you, Sayuri. I'm only trying to be helpful! Just listen for a moment, and you'll see. For example: Why did you choose to give Nobu Toshikazu the name "Mr. Tsu"? It doesn't suit him at all. I think you should have called him "Mr. Blister" or maybe "Mr. One-Arm." Don't you agree? You can change it if you want and you don't even have to give me any credit.'

'I don't know what you're talking about, Hatsumomo. I haven't written anything about Nobu at all.'

Hatsumomo sighed, as if to tell me what an inept liar I was, and then began paging through my journal. 'If it isn't Nobu you were writing about, I want you to tell me the name of the man you're referring to here. Let's see . . . ah, here it is: "Sometimes I see Mr. Tsu's face blooming with anger when a geisha has been staring at him. But for my part, I can look at him as long as I want, and he seems to be pleased by it. I think his fondness for me grows from his feeling that I don't find the look of his skin and his missing arm as strange and frightening as so many girls do." I guess what you're telling me is that you know someone else who looks *just like* Nobu. I think you should introduce them! Think how much they'll have in common.'

By this time I was feeling sick at heart – I can't think of any better way of describing it. For it's one thing to find your secrets suddenly exposed, but when your own foolishness has exposed them . . . well, if I was prepared to curse anyone, it was myself for keeping the journal in the first place and stowing it where Hatsumomo could find it. A shopkeeper who leaves his window open can hardly be angry at the rainstorm for ruining his wares.

I went to the table to take the journal from Hatsumomo, but she clutched it to her chest and stood. In her other hand she picked up the glass of what I'd thought was water. Now that I stood close to her I could smell the odor of sake. It wasn't water at all. She was drunk.

'Sayuri, *of course* you want your journal back, and *of course* I'm going to give it to you,' she said. But she was walking toward the door as she said it. 'The trouble is, I haven't finished reading it. So I'll take it back to my room . . . unless you'd rather I took it to Mother. I'm sure she'll be pleased to see the passages you've written about her.'

I mentioned earlier that a broken bottle of ointment lay on the floor of the hallway. This was how Hatsumomo did things, making a mess and not even bothering to tell the maids. But now as she left my room, she got what she deserved. Probably she'd forgotten about the bottle because she was drunk; in any case she stepped right into the broken glass and let out a little shriek. I saw her look at her foot a moment and make a gasping noise, but then she kept on going.

I felt myself panicking as she stepped into her room. I thought of trying to wrestle the book from her hands . . . but then I remembered Mameha's realization at the sumo tournament. To rush after Hatsumomo was the obvious thing. I'd be better off to wait until she began to relax, thinking she'd won, and then take the journal from her when she wasn't expecting it. This seemed to me a fine idea . . . until a moment later when I had an image of her hiding it in a place I might never find.

By now she'd closed the door. I went to stand outside it and called out quietly, 'Hatsumomo-san, I'm sorry if I seemed angry. May I come in?'

'No, you may not,' she said.

I slid the door open anyway. The room was in terrible disarray, because Hatsumomo had put things everywhere in her efforts at moving. The journal was sitting on the table while Hatsumomo held a towel against her foot. I had no idea how I would distract her, but I certainly didn't intend to leave the room without the journal.

She may have had the personality of a water rat, but Hatsumomo was no fool. If she'd been sober, I wouldn't even have tried to outsmart her right then. But considering her state at the moment . . . I looked around the floor at the piles of underclothing, bottles of perfume, and all the other things she'd scattered in disarray. The closet door was open, and the tiny safe where she kept her jewelry stood ajar; pieces were spilling out onto the mats as though she'd sat there earlier in the morning drinking and trying them on. And then one object caught my eye as clearly as a single star burning in a black sky.

It was an emerald obi brooch, the very one Hatsumomo had accused me of stealing years earlier; on the night I'd found her and her boyfriend in the maids' room. I'd never expected to see it again. I walked directly to the closet and reached down to pluck it from among the jewelry lying there.

'What a wonderful idea!' Hatsumomo said. 'Go ahead and steal a piece of my jewelry. Truthfully, I'd rather have the cash you'll have to pay me.'

'I'm so pleased you don't mind!' I told her. 'But how much cash will I have to pay for this?'

As I said these words, I walked over and held the brooch up before her. The radiant smile she'd worn now faded, just as the darkness fades from a valley when the sun rises on it. In that moment, while Hatsumomo sat stunned, I simply reached down to the table with my other hand and took the journal away.

I had no notion how Hatsumomo would react, but I walked out the door and closed it behind me. I thought of going straight to Mother to show her what I'd found, but of course, I couldn't very well go there with the journal in my hand. As quickly as I could, I slid open the door to the closet where in-season kimono were kept and stashed the journal on a shelf between two robes wrapped in tissue paper. It took no more than a few seconds; but all the while my back tingled from the sensation that at any moment Hatsumomo might open her door and spot me. After I'd shut the closet door again, I rushed into my room and began opening and closing the drawers to my makeup stand to give Hatsumomo the impression I'd hid the journal there.

When I came out into the hallway, she was watching me from the doorway of her room, wearing a little smile as though she found the whole situation amusing. I tried to look worried – which wasn't too difficult – and carried the brooch with me into Mother's room to lay it on the table before her. She put aside the magazine she was reading and held it up to admire it.

'This is a lovely piece,' she said, 'but it won't go far on the black market these days. No one pays much for jewels like this one.'

'I'm sure Hatsumomo will pay very dearly for it, Mother,' I said. 'Do you remember the brooch I'm supposed to have stolen from her years ago, the one that was added to my debts? This is it. I've just found it on the floor near her jewelry box.'

'Do you know,' said Hatsumomo, who had come into the room and now stood behind me. 'I believe Sayuri is right. That is the brooch I lost! Or at least, it looks like it. I never thought I'd see it again!'

'Yes, it's very difficult to find things when you're drunk all the time,' I said. 'If only you'd looked in your jewelry box more closely.'

Mother put the brooch down on the table and went on glowering at Hatsumomo.

'I found it in her room,' Hatsumomo said. 'She'd hidden it in her makeup stand.'

'Why were you looking through her makeup stand?' Mother said.

'I didn't want to have to tell you this, Mother, but Sayuri left something on her table and I was trying to hide it for her. I know I should have brought it to you at once, but . . . she's been keeping a journal, you see. She showed it to me last year. She's written some very incriminating things about certain men, and . . . truthfully, there are some passages about you too, Mother.'

I thought of insisting it wasn't true; but none of it mattered in any case. Hatsumomo was in trouble, and nothing she was going to say would change the situation. Ten years earlier when she had been the okiya's principal earner, she probably could have accused me of anything she'd wanted. She could have claimed I'd eaten the tatami mats in her room, and Mother would have charged me the cost of new ones. But now at last the season had changed; Hatsumomo's brilliant career was dying on the branch, while mine had begun to blossom. I was the daughter of the okiya and its prime geisha. I don't think Mother even cared where the truth lay.

'There is no journal, Mother,' I said. 'Hatsumomo is making it up.'

'Am I?' said Hatsumomo. 'I'll just go find it, then, and while Mother reads through it, you can tell her how I made it up.'

Hatsumomo went to my room, with Mother following. The hallway floor was a terrible mess. Not only had Hatsumomo broken a bottle and then stepped on it, she'd tracked ointment and blood all around the upstairs hall – and much worse, onto the tatami mats in her own room, Mother's room, and now mine as well. She was kneeling at my dressing table when I looked in, closing the drawers very slowly and looking a bit defeated.

'What journal is Hatsumomo talking about?' Mother asked me.

'If there's a journal, I'm certain Hatsumomo will find it,' I said.

At this, Hatsumomo put her hands into her lap and gave a

little laugh as though the whole thing had been some sort of game, and she'd been cleverly outwitted.

'Hatsumomo,' Mother said to her, 'you'll repay Sayuri for the brooch you accused her of stealing. What's more, I won't have the tatami in this okiya defiled with blood. They'll be replaced, and at your expense. This has been a very costly day for you, and it's hardly past noon. Shall I hold off calculating the total, just in case you're not quite finished?'

I don't know if Hatsumomo heard what Mother said. She was too busy glaring at me, and with a look on her face I wasn't accustomed to seeing.

If you'd asked me, while I was still a young woman, to tell you the turning point in my relationship with Hatsumomo, I would have said it was my *mizuage*. But even though it's quite true that my *mizuage* lifted me onto a high shelf where Hatsumomo could no longer reach me, she and I might well have gone on living side by side until we were old women, if nothing else had happened between us. This is why the real turning point, as I've since come to see it, occurred the day when Hatsumomo read my journal, and I discovered the obi brooch she'd accused me of stealing.

By way of explaining why this is so, let me tell you something Admiral Yamamoto Isoroku once said during an evening at the Ichiriki Teahouse. I can't pretend I was well acquainted with Admiral Yamamoto – who's usually described as the father of the Japanese Imperial Navy – but I was privileged to attend parties with him on a number of occasions. He was a small man; but keep in mind that a stick of dynamite is small too. Parties always grew noisier after the Admiral arrived. That night, he and another man were in the final round of a drinking game, and had agreed that the loser would go buy a condom at the nearest pharmacy – just for the embarrassment of it, you understand; not for any other purpose. Of course, the Admiral ended up winning, and the whole crowd broke into cheers and applause.

'It's a good thing you didn't lose, Admiral,' said one of his aides. 'Think of the poor pharmacist looking up to find Admiral Yamamoto Isoroku on the other side of the counter!'

Everyone thought this was very funny, but the Admiral replied that he'd never had any doubt about winning.

'Oh, come now!' said one of the geisha. 'Everyone loses from time to time! Even you, Admiral!'

'I suppose it's true that everyone loses at some time,' he said. 'But never me.'

Some in the room may have considered this an arrogant thing to say, but I wasn't one of them. The Admiral seemed to me the sort of man who really was accustomed to winning. Finally someone asked him the secret of his success.

'I never seek to defeat the man I am fighting,' he explained. 'I seek to defeat his confidence. A mind troubled by doubt cannot focus on the course to victory. Two men are equals – *true* equals – only when they both have equal confidence.'

I don't think I realized it at the time, but after Hatsumomo and I quarreled over my journal, her mind – as the Admiral would have put it – began to be troubled by doubt. She knew that under no circumstances would Mother take her side against me any longer; and because of that, she was like a fabric taken from its warm closet and hung out of doors where the harsh weather will gradually consume it.

If Mameha were to hear me explaining things in this way, she would certainly speak up and say how much she disagreed. Her view of Hatsumomo was quite different from mine. She believed Hatsumomo was a woman bent on self-destruction, and that all we needed to do was to coax her along a path she was certain to follow in any case. Perhaps Mameha was right; I don't know. It's true that in the years since my *mizuage*, Hatsumomo had gradually been afflicted by some sort of disease of the character – if such a thing exists. She'd lost all control over her drinking, for example, and of her bouts of cruelty too. Until her life began to fray, she'd always used her cruelty for a purpose, just as a samurai draws his sword – not for slashing at random, but for slashing at enemies. But by this time in her life, Hatsumomo seemed to have lost sight of who her enemies were, and sometimes struck out even at Pumpkin. From time to time during parties, she even made insulting comments to the men she was entertaining. And another thing: she was no longer as beautiful as she'd once been. Her skin was waxy-looking, and her features puffy. Or perhaps I was only seeing her that way. A tree may look as beautiful as ever; but when you notice the insects infesting it, and the tips of the branches that are brown from disease, even the trunk seems to lose some of its magnificence.

Everyone knows that a wounded tiger is a dangerous beast; and for this reason, Mameha insisted that we follow Hatsumomo around Gion during the evenings over the next few weeks. Partly, Mameha wanted to keep an eye on her, because neither of us would have been surprised if she'd sought out Nobu to tell him about the contents of my journal, and about all my secret feelings for 'Mr. Haa,' whom Nobu might have recognized as the Chairman. But more important, Mameha wanted to make Hatsumomo's life difficult for her to bear.

'When you want to break a board,' Mameha said, 'cracking it in the middle is only the first step. Success comes when you bounce up and down with all your weight until the board snaps in half.'

So every evening, except when she had an engagement she couldn't miss, Mameha came to our okiya around dusk and waited to walk out the door behind Hatsumomo. Mameha and I weren't always able to stay together, but usually at least one of us managed to follow her from engagement to engagement for a portion of the evening. On the first night we did this, Hatsumomo pretended to find it amusing. But by the end of the fourth night she was looking at us through squinted, angry eyes, and had difficulty acting cheerful around the men she tried to entertain. Then early the following week, she suddenly wheeled around in an alleyway and came toward us.

'Let me see now,' she said. 'Dogs follow their owners. And the two of you are following me around, sniffing and sniffing. So I guess you want to be treated like dogs! Shall I show you what I do with dogs I don't like?'

And with this, she drew back her hand to strike Mameha on the side of the head. I screamed, which must have made Hatsumomo stop to think about what she was doing. She stared at me a moment with eyes burning before the fire went out of them and she walked away. Everyone in the alley had noticed what was happening, and a few came over to see if Mameha was all right. She assured them she was fine and then said sadly:

'Poor Hatsumomo! It must be just as the doctor said. She really does seem to be losing her mind.'

There was no doctor, of course, but Mameha's words had the effect she'd hoped for. Soon a rumor had spread all over Gion that a doctor had declared Hatsumomo mentally unstable.

For years Hatsumomo had been very close to the famous Kabuki actor Bando Shojiro VI. Shojiro was what we call an *onna-gata*, which means that he always played women's roles. Once, in a magazine interview, he said that Hatsumomo was the most beautiful woman he'd ever seen, and that on the stage he often imitated her gestures to make himself seem more alluring. So you can well imagine that whenever Shojiro was in town, Hatsumomo visited him.

One afternoon I learned that Shojiro would attend a party later that evening at a teahouse in the geisha district of Pontocho, on the other side of the river from Gion. I heard this bit of news while preparing a tea ceremony for a group of naval officers on leave. Afterward I rushed back to the okiya, but Hatsumomo had already dressed and snuck out. She was doing what I'd once done, leaving early so that no one would follow her. I was very eager to explain to Mameha what I'd learned, so I went straight to her apartment. Unfortunately, her maid told me she'd left a half hour earlier 'to worship.' I knew exactly what this meant: Mameha had gone to a little temple just at the eastern edge of Gion to pray before the three tiny *jizo* statues she'd paid to have erected there. A *jizo*, you see, honors the soul of a departed child; in Mameha's case, they were for the three children she'd aborted at the Baron's request. Under other circumstances I might have gone searching for her, but I couldn't possibly disturb her in such a private moment; and besides, she might not have wanted me to know even that she'd gone there. Instead I sat in her apartment and permitted Tatsumi to serve me tea while I waited. At last, with something of a weary look about her; Mameha came home. I didn't want to raise the subject at first, and so for a time we chatted about the upcoming Festival of the Ages, in which Mameha was scheduled to portray Lady Murasaki Shikibu, author of *The Tale of Genji*. Finally Mameha looked up with a smile from her cup of brown tea – Tatsumi had been roasting the leaves when I arrived – and I told her what I'd discovered during the course of the afternoon.

'How perfect!' she said. 'Hatsumomo's going to relax and think she's free of us. With all the attention Shojiro is certain to give her at the party, she may feel renewed. Then you and I will come drifting in like some sort of horrid smell from the alleyway, and ruin her evening completely.'

Considering how cruelly Hatsumomo had treated me over the years, and how very much I hated her, I'm sure I ought to have been elated at this plan. But somehow conspiring to make Hatsumomo suffer wasn't the pleasure I might have imagined. I couldn't help remembering one morning as a child, when I was swimming in the pond near our tipsy house and suddenly felt a terrible burning in my shoulder. A wasp had stung me and was struggling to free itself from my skin. I was too busy screaming to think of what to do, but one of the boys pulled the wasp off and held it by the wings upon a rock, where we all gathered to decide exactly how to murder it. I was in great pain because of the wasp, and certainly felt no kindness toward it. But it gave me a terrible sensation of weakness in my chest to know that this tiny struggling creature could do nothing to save itself from the death that was only moments away. I felt the same sort of pity toward Hatsumomo.

During evenings when we trailed her around Gion until she returned to the okiya just to get away from us, I felt almost as though we were torturing her.

In any case, around nine o'clock that night, we crossed the river to the Pontocho district. Unlike Gion, which sprawls over many blocks, Pontocho is just a single long alleyway stretched out along one bank of the river. People call it an 'eel's bed' because of its shape. The autumn air was a bit chilly that night, but Shojiro's party was outdoors anyway, on a wooden verandah standing on stilts above the water. No one paid us much attention when we stepped out through the glass doors. The verandah was beautifully lit with paper lanterns, and the river shimmered gold from the lights of a restaurant on the opposite bank. Everyone was listening to Shojiro, who was in the middle of telling a story in his singsong voice; but you should have seen the way Hatsumomo's expression soured when she caught sight of us. I couldn't help remembering a damaged pear I'd held in my hand the day before, because amid the cheerful faces, Hatsumomo's expression was like a terrible bruise.

Mameha went to kneel on a mat right beside Hatsumomo, which I considered very bold of her. I knelt toward the other end of the verandah, beside a gentle-looking old man who turned out to be the koto player Tachibana Zensaku, whose scratchy old records I still own. Tachibana was blind, I discovered that night. Regardless of my purpose in coming, I would have been content to spend the evening just chatting with him, for he was such a fascinating, endearing man. But we'd hardly begun to talk when suddenly everyone burst out laughing.

Shojiro was quite a remarkable mimic. He was slender like the branch of a willow, with elegant, slow-moving fingers, and a very long face he could move about in extraordinary ways; he could have fooled a group of monkeys into thinking he was one of them. At that moment he was imitating the geisha beside him, a woman in her fifties. With his effeminate gestures – his pursed lips, his rolls of the eyes – he managed to look so much like her that I didn't know whether to laugh or just sit with my hand over my mouth in astonishment. I'd seen Shojiro on the stage, but this was something much better.

Tachibana leaned in toward me and whispered, 'What's he doing?'

'He's imitating an older geisha beside him.'

'Ah,' said Tachibana. 'That would be Ichiwari.' And then he tapped me with the back of his hand to make sure he had my attention. 'The director of the Minamiza Theater,' he said, and held out his little finger below the table where no one else could see it. In Japan, you see, holding up the little finger means 'boyfriend' or 'girlfriend.' Tachibana was telling me that the older geisha, the one named Ichiwari, was the theater director's mistress. And in fact the director was there too, laughing louder than anyone.

A moment later, still in the midst of his mimicry, Shojiro stuck one of his fingers up his nose. At this, everyone let out a laugh so loud you could feel the verandah trembling. I didn't know it at the time, but picking her nose was one of Ichiwari's well-known habits. She turned bright red when she saw this, and held a sleeve of her kimono over her face, and Shojiro, who had drunk a good bit of sake, imitated her even then. People laughed politely, but only Hatsumomo seemed to find it really funny; for at this point Shojiro was beginning to cross the line into cruelty. Finally the theater director said, 'Now, now, Shojiro-san, save some energy for your show tomorrow! Anyway, don't you know you're sitting near one of Gion's greatest dancers? I propose that we ask for a performance.'

Of course, the director was talking about Mameha.

'Heavens, no. I don't want to see any dancing just now,' Shojiro said. As I came to understand over the years, he preferred to be the center of attention himself. 'Besides, I'm having fun.'

'Shojiro-san, we mustn't pass up an opportunity to see the famous Mameha,' the director said, speaking this time without a trace of humor. A few geisha spoke up as well, and finally Shojiro was persuaded to ask her if she would perform, which he did as sulkily as a little boy. Already I could see Hatsumomo looking displeased. She poured more sake for Shojiro, and he poured more for her. They exchanged a long look as if to say their party had been spoiled.

A few minutes passed while a maid was sent to fetch a shamisen and one of the geisha tuned it and prepared to play. Then Mameha took her place against the backdrop of the teahouse and performed a few very short pieces. Nearly anyone would have agreed that Mameha was a lovely woman, but very few people would have found her more beautiful than Hatsumomo; so I can't say exactly what caught Shojiro's eye. It may have been the sake he'd drunk, and it may have been Mameha's extraordinary dancing – for Shojiro was a dancer himself. Whatever it was, by the time Mameha came back to join us at the table, Shojiro seemed quite taken with her and asked that she sit beside him. When she did, he poured her a cup of sake, and turned his back on Hatsumomo as if she were just another adoring apprentice.

Well, Hatsumomo's mouth hardened, and her eyes shrank to about half their size. As for Mameha, I never saw her flirt with anyone more deliberately than she did with Shojiro. Her voice grew high and soft, and her eyes swished from his chest to his face and back again. From time to time she drew the fingertips of her hand across the base of her throat as though she felt self-conscious about the splotchy blush that had appeared there. There wasn't really any blush, but she acted it so convincingly, you wouldn't have known it without looking closely. Then one of the geisha asked Shojiro if he'd heard from Bajiru-san.

'Bajiru-san,' said Shojiro, in his most dramatic manner, 'has abandoned me!'

I had no idea who Shojiro was talking about, but Tachibana, the old koto player, was kind enough to explain in a whisper that 'Bajiru-san' was the English actor Basil Rathbone – though I'd never heard of him at the time. Shojiro had taken a trip to London a few years earlier and staged a Kabuki performance there. The actor Basil Rathbone had admired it so much that with the help of an interpreter the two of them had developed something of a friendship. Shojiro may have lavished attention on women like Hatsumomo or Mameha, but the fact remained that he was homosexual; and since his trip to England, he'd made it a running joke that his heart was destined to be broken because Bajiru-san had no interest in men.

'It makes me sad,' said one of the geisha quietly, 'to witness the death of a romance.'

Everyone laughed except for Hatsumomo, who went on glowering at Shojiro.

'The difference between me and Bajiru-san is this. I'll show you,' Shojiro said; and with this he stood and asked Mameha to join him. He led her off to one side of the room, where they had a bit of space.

'When I do my work, I look like this,' he said. And he sashayed from one side of the room to the other, waving his folding fan with a most fluid wrist, and letting his head roll back and forth like a ball on a seesaw. 'Whereas when Bajiru-san does his work, he looks like this.' Here he grabbed Mameha, and you should have seen the astonished expression on her face when he dipped her toward the floor in what looked like a passionate embrace, and planted kisses all over her face. Everyone in the room cheered and clapped. Everyone except Hatsumomo, that is.

'What is he doing?' Tachibana asked me quietly. I didn't think anyone else had heard, but before I could reply, Hatsumomo cried out:

'He's making a fool of himself! That's what he's doing.'

'Oh, Hatsumomo-san,' said Shojiro, 'you're jealous, aren't you!'

'Of course she is!' said Mameha. 'Now you must show us how the two of you make up. Go on, Shojiro-san. Don't be shy! You must give her the very same kisses you gave to me! It's only fair. And in the same way.'

Shojiro didn't have an easy time of it, but soon he succeeded in getting Hatsumomo to her feet. Then with the crowd behind him, he took her in his arms and bent her back. But after only an instant, he jerked upright again with a shout, and grabbed his lip. Hatsumomo had bitten him; not enough to make him bleed, but certainly enough to give him a shock. She was standing with her eyes squinted in anger and her teeth exposed; and then she drew back her hand and slapped him. I think her aim must have been bad from all the sake she'd drunk, because she hit the side of his head rather than his face.

'What happened?' Tachibana asked me. His words were as clear in the quiet of the room as if someone had rung a bell. I didn't answer, but when he heard Shojiro's whimper and the heavy breathing of Hatsumomo, I'm sure he understood.

'Hatsumomo-san, please,' said Mameha, speaking in a voice so calm it sounded completely out of place, 'as a favor to me . . . *do* try to calm down.'

I don't know if Mameha's words had the precise effect she was hoping for, or whether Hatsumomo's mind had already shattered. But Hatsumomo threw herself at Shojiro and began hitting him everywhere. I do think that in a way she went crazy. It wasn't just that her mind seemed to have fractured; the moment itself seemed disconnected from everything else. The theater director got up from the table and rushed over to restrain her. Somehow in the middle of all this, Mameha slipped out and returned a moment later with the mistress of the teahouse. By that time the theater director was holding Hatsumomo from behind. I thought the crisis was over, but then Shojiro shouted at Hatsumomo so loudly, we heard it echo off the buildings across the river in Gion.

'You monster!' he screamed. 'You've bitten me!'

I don't know what any of us would have done without the calm thinking of the mistress. She spoke to Shojiro in a soothing voice, while at the same time giving the theater director a signal to take Hatsumomo away. As I later learned, he didn't just take her inside the teahouse; he took her downstairs to the front and shoved her out onto the street.

Hatsumomo didn't return to the okiya at all that night. When she did come back the following day, she smelled as if she had been sick to her stomach, and her hair was in disarray. She was summoned at once to Mother's room and spent a long while there.

A few days afterward, Hatsumomo left the okiya, wearing a simple cotton robe Mother had given her, and with her hair as I'd never seen it, hanging in a mass around her shoulders. She carried a bag containing her belongings and jewelry, and didn't say good-bye to any of us, but just walked out to the street. She didn't leave voluntarily; Mother had thrown her out. And in fact, Mameha believed Mother had probably been trying to get rid of Hatsumomo for years. Whether or not this is true, I'm sure Mother was pleased at having fewer mouths to feed, since Hatsumomo was no longer earning what she once had, and food had never been more difficult to come by.

If Hatsumomo hadn't been renowned for her wickedness, some other okiya might have wanted her even after what she'd done to Shojiro. But she was like a teakettle that even on a good day might still scald the hand of anyone who used it.

Everyone in Gion understood this about her.

I don't know for sure what ever became of Hatsumomo. A few years after the war, I heard she was making a living as a prostitute in the Miyagawa-cho district. She couldn't have been there long, because on the night I heard it, a man at the same party swore that if Hatsumomo was a prostitute, he would find her and give her some business of his own. He did go looking for her, but she was nowhere to be found. Over the years, she probably succeeded in drinking herself to death. She certainly wouldn't have been the first geisha to do it.

In just the way that a man can grow accustomed to a bad leg, we'd all grown accustomed to having Hatsumomo in our okiya. I don't think we quite understood all the ways her presence had afflicted us until long after she'd left, when things that we hadn't realized were ailing slowly began to heal. Even when Hatsumomo had been doing nothing more than sleeping in her room, the maids had known she was there, and that during the course of the day she would abuse them. They'd lived with the kind of tension you feel if you walk across a frozen pond whose ice might break at any moment. And as for Pumpkin, I think she'd grown to be dependent on her older sister and felt strangely lost without her.

I'd already become the okiya's principal asset, but even I took some time to weed out all the peculiar habits that had taken root because of Hatsumomo. Every time a man looked at me strangely, I found myself wondering if he'd heard something unkind about me from her; even long after she was gone. Whenever I climbed the stairs to the second floor of the okiya, I still kept my eyes lowered for fear that Hatsumomo would be waiting there on the landing, eager for someone to abuse. I can't tell you how many times I reached that last step and looked up suddenly with the realization that there was no Hatsumomo, and there never would be again. I knew she was gone, and yet the very emptiness of the hall seemed to suggest something of her presence. Even now, as an older woman, I sometimes lift the brocade cover on the mirror of my makeup stand, and have the briefest flicker of a thought that I may find her there in the glass, smirking at me.

28

IN JAPAN WE refer to the years from the Depression through World War II as *kuraitani* – the valley of darkness, when so many people lived like children whose heads had slipped beneath the waves. As is often the case, those of us in Gion didn't suffer quite as badly as others. While most Japanese lived in the dark valley all through the 1930s, for example, in Gion we were still warmed by a bit of sun. And I'm sure I don't need to tell you why; women who are mistresses of cabinet ministers and naval commanders are the recipients of enormous good fortune, and they pass that good fortune along to others. You might say Gion was like a pond high up on a mountaintop, fed by streams of rich springwater. More water poured in at some spots than others, but it raised the pond as a whole.

Because of General Tottori, our okiya was one of the spots where the rich springwater came pouring in. Things grew worse and worse around us during the course of several years; and yet long after the rationing of goods had begun, we continued to receive regular supplies of foodstuffs, tea, linens, and even some luxuries like cosmetics and chocolate. We might have kept these things to ourselves and lived behind closed doors, but Gion isn't that sort of place. Mother passed much of it along and considered it well spent, not because she was a generous woman, of course, but because we were all like spiders crowded together on the same web. From time to time people came asking for help, and we were pleased to give it when we could. At some point in the fall of 1941 for example, the military police found a maid with a box containing probably ten times more ration coupons than her okiya was supposed to have. Her mistress sent her to us for safekeeping until arrangements could be made to take her to the countryside, because of course, every okiya in Gion hoarded coupons; the better the okiya, the more it usually had. The maid was sent to us rather than to someone else because General Tottori had instructed the military police to leave us alone. So you see, even within that mountaintop pond that was Gion, we were the fish swimming in the very warmest water of all.

As the darkness continued to settle over Japan, there did finally come a time when even the pinpoint of light in which we'd managed to keep ourselves suddenly went out. It happened at a single moment, early one afternoon just a few weeks before New Year's Day, in December 1942. I was eating my breakfast – or at least, my first meal of the day, for I'd been busy helping to clean the okiya in preparation for the New Year – when a man's voice called out at our entrance. I thought he was probably just making a delivery, so I went on with my meal, but a moment later the maid interrupted me to say a military policeman had come looking for Mother.

'A military policeman?' I said. 'Tell him Mother is out.'

'Yes, I did, ma'am. He'd like to speak with you instead.'

When I reached the front hall, I found the policeman removing his boots in the entryway. Probably most people would have felt relieved just to note that his pistol was still snapped inside its leather case, but as I say, our okiya had lived differently right up until that moment. Ordinarily a policeman would have been more apologetic even than most visitors, since his presence would alarm us. But to see him tugging at his boots . . . well, this was his way of saying he planned to come in whether we invited him or not.

I bowed and greeted him, but he did nothing more than glance at me as though he would deal with me later. Finally he pulled up his socks and pulled down his cap, and then stepped up into the front entrance hall and said he wanted to see our vegetable garden. Just like that, with no word of apology for troubling us. You see, by this time nearly everyone in Kyoto, and probably the rest of the country, had converted their decorative gardens into vegetable gardens – everyone but people like us, that is. General Tottori provided us with enough food that we didn't need to plow up our garden, and were instead able to go on enjoying the hair moss and spearflowers, and the tiny maple in the corner. Since it was winter, I hoped the policeman would look only at the spots of frozen ground where the vegetation had died back, and imagine that we'd planted squash and sweet potatoes amid the decorative plants. So after I'd led him down to the courtyard, I didn't say a word; I just watched as he knelt down and touched the dirt with his fingers. I suppose he wanted to feel whether or not the ground had been dug up for planting.

I was so desperate for something to say that I blurted out the first thing that came to mind. 'Doesn't the dusting of snow on the ground make you think of foam on the ocean?' He didn't answer me, but just stood up to his full height and asked what vegetables we had planted.

'Officer,' I said, 'I'm terribly sorry, but the truth is, we haven't had an opportunity to plant any vegetables at all. And now that the ground is so hard and cold . . .'

'Your neighborhood association was quite right about you!' he said, taking off his cap. He brought out from his pocket a slip of paper and began to read a long list of misdeeds our okiya had committed. I don't even remember them all – hoarding cotton materials, failing to turn in metal and rubber goods needed for the war effort, improper use of ration tickets, all sorts of things like that. It's true we had done these things, just as every other okiya in Gion had. Our crime, I suppose, was that we'd enjoyed more good fortune than most, and had survived longer and in better shape than all but a very few.

Luckily for me, Mother returned just then. She didn't seem at all surprised to find a military policeman there; and in fact, she behaved more politely toward him than I'd ever seen her behave toward anyone. She led him into our reception room and served him some of our ill-gotten tea. The door was closed, but I could hear them talking for a long while. At one point when she came out to fetch something, she pulled me aside and told me this:

'General Tottori was taken into custody this morning. You'd better hurry and hide our best things, or they'll be gone tomorrow.'

Back in Yoroido I used to swim on chilly spring days, and afterward lie on the rocks beside the pond to soak up the heat of the sun. If the sunlight vanished suddenly behind a cloud, as it often did, the cold air seemed to close about my skin like a sheet of metal. The moment I heard of the General's misfortune, standing there in the front entrance hall, I had that same feeling. It was as though the sun had vanished, possibly for good, and I was now condemned to stand wet and naked in the icy air. Within a week of the policeman's visit, our okiya had been stripped of the things other families had lost long ago, such as stores of food, undergarments, and so forth. We'd always been Mameha's source for packets of tea; I think she'd been using them to purchase favors. But now her supplies were better than ours, and she became our source instead. Toward the end of the month, the neighborhood association began confiscating many of our ceramics and scrolls to sell them on what we called the 'gray market,' which was different from the black market. The black market was for things like fuel oil, foods, metals, and so on – mostly items that were rationed or illegal to trade. The gray market was more innocent; it was mainly housewives selling off their precious things to raise cash. In our case, though, our things were sold to punish us as much as for any other reason, and so the cash went to benefit others. The head of the neighborhood association, who was mistress of a nearby okiya, felt deeply sorry whenever she came to take our things away But the military police had given orders; no one could do anything but obey.

If the early years of the war had been like an exciting voyage out to sea, you might say that by about the middle of 1943 we all realized the waves were simply too big for our craft. We thought we would drown, all of us; and many did. It wasn't just that day-to-day life had grown increasingly miserable; no one dared admit it, but I think we'd all begun worrying about the outcome of the war. No one had fun any longer; many people seemed to feel it was unpatriotic even to have a good time. The closest thing to a joke I heard during this period was something the geisha Raiha said one night. For months we'd heard rumors that the military government planned to shut down all the geisha districts in Japan; lately we'd begun to realize that it really was going to happen. We were all wondering what would become of us, when suddenly Raiha spoke up.

'We can't waste our time thinking about such things,' she said. 'Nothing is bleaker than the future, except perhaps the past.'

It may not sound funny to you; but that night we laughed until tears beaded in the corners of our eyes. One day soon the geisha districts would indeed close. When they did, we were certain to end up working in the factories. To give you some idea of what life in the factories was like, let me tell you about Hatsumomo's friend Korin.

During the previous winter, the catastrophe that every geisha in Gion feared most had actually happened to Korin. A maid tending the bath in her okiya had tried to burn newspapers to heat the water, but had lost control of the flames. The entire okiya was destroyed, along with its collection of kimono. Korin ended up working in a factory south of the city fitting lenses into the equipment used for dropping bombs from airplanes. She came back to visit Gion from time to time as the months passed, and we were horrified at how much she'd changed. It wasn't just that she seemed more and more unhappy; we'd all experienced unhappiness, and were prepared for it in any case. But she had a cough that was as much a part of her as a song is part of a bird; and her skin was stained as though she'd soaked it in ink – since the coal the factories used was of a very low grade and covered everything in soot as it burned. Poor Korin was forced to work double shifts while being fed no more than a bowl of weak broth with a few noodles once a day, or watery rice gruel flavored with potato skin.

So you can imagine how terrified we were of the factories. Every day that we awakened to find Gion still open, we felt grateful.

Then one morning in January of the following year, I was standing in line at the rice store in the falling snow, holding my ration coupons, when the shopkeeper next door put out his head and called into the cold:

'It's happened!'

We all of us looked at one another. I was too numbed with cold to care what he was talking about, for I wore only a heavy shawl around my peasant's clothing; no one wore kimono during the day any longer. Finally the geisha in front of me brushed the snow from her eyebrows and asked him what he was talking about. 'The war hasn't come to an end, has it?' she asked.

'The government has announced the closing of the geisha districts,' he said. 'All of you are to report to the registry office tomorrow morning.'

For a long moment we listened to the sound of a radio inside his shop. Then the door rumbled closed again, and there was nothing but the soft hiss of the falling snow. I looked at the despair on the faces of the other geisha around me and knew in an instant that we were all thinking the same thing: Which of the men we knew would save us from life in the factories?

Even though General Tottori had been my *danna* until the previous year, I certainly wasn't the only geisha acquainted with him. I had to reach him before anyone else did. I wasn't properly dressed for the weather, but I put my ration coupons back into the pocket of my peasant pants and set out at once for the northwest of the city. The General was rumored to be living in the Suruya Inn, the same one where we'd met during the evenings twice a week for so many years.

I arrived there an hour or so later, burning with the cold and dusted all over with snow. But when I greeted the mistress, she took a long look at me before bowing in apology and saying she had no idea who I was.

'It's me, mistress . . . Sayuri! I've come to speak with the General.'

'Sayuri-san . . . my heavens! I never thought to see you looking like the wife of a peasant.'

She led me inside at once, but wouldn't present me to the

General until she'd first taken me upstairs and dressed me in one of her kimono. She even put on me a bit of makeup she'd stashed away, so the General would know me when he saw me.

When I entered his room, General Tottori was sitting at the table listening to a drama on the radio. His cotton robe hung open, exposing his bony chest and the thin gray hairs. I could see that his hardships of the past year had been far worse than mine. After all, he'd been accused of awful crimes – negligence, incompetence, abuse of power, and so forth; some people considered him lucky to have escaped prison. An article in a magazine had even blamed him for the Imperial Navy's defeats in the South Pacific, saying that he'd failed to oversee the shipment of supplies. Still, some men bear hardships better than others; and with one look at the General I could see that the weight of this past year had pressed down upon him until his bones had grown brittle, and even his face had come to look a bit misshapen. In the past he'd smelled of sour pickles all the time. Now as I bowed low on the mats near him, he had a different sort of sour smell.

'You're looking very well, General,' I said, though of course this was a lie. 'What a pleasure it is to see you again!'

The General switched off the radio. 'You're not the first to come to me,' he said. 'There's nothing I can do to help you, Sayuri.'

'But I rushed here so quickly! I can't imagine how anyone reached you before I did!'

'Since last week nearly every geisha I know has been to see me, but I don't have friends in power any longer. I don't know why a geisha of your standing should come to me anyway. You're liked by so many men with influence.'

'To be liked and to have true friends willing to help are two very different things,' I said.

'Yes, so they are. What sort of help have you come to me for anyway?'

'Any help at all, General. We talk about nothing these days in Gion but how miserable life in a factory will be.'

'Life will be miserable for the lucky ones. The rest won't even live to see the end of the war.'

'I don't understand.'

'The bombs will fall soon,' the General said. 'You can be certain the factories will take more than their share. If you want to be alive when this war is over, you'd better find someone who can tuck you away in a safe place. I'm sorry I'm not that man. I've already exhausted what influence I had.'

The General asked after Mother's health, and Auntie's, and soon bid me good-bye. I learned only much later what he meant about exhausting his influence. The proprietress of the Suruya had a young daughter; the General had arranged to send her to a town in northern Japan.

On the way back to the okiya, I knew the time had come for me to act; but I couldn't think what to do. Even the simple task of holding my panic at arm's length seemed more than I could manage. I went by the apartment where Mameha was now living – for her relationship with the Baron had ended several months earlier and she'd moved into a much smaller space. I thought she might know what course I should take, but in fact, she was in nearly as much of a panic as I was.

'The Baron will do nothing to help me,' she said, her face pale with worry. 'I've been unable to reach the other men I have in mind. You had better think of someone, Sayuri, and go to him as quickly as you can.'

I'd been out of touch with Nobu for more than four years by that time; I knew at once I couldn't approach him. As for the Chairman . . . well, I would have grabbed at any excuse just to speak with him, but I could never have asked him for a favor. However warmly he may have treated me in the hallways, I wasn't invited to his parties, even when lesser geisha were. I felt hurt by this, but what could I do? In any case, even if the Chairman had wanted to help me, his quarrels with the military government had been in the news-papers lately. He had too many troubles of his own.

So I spent the rest of that afternoon going from teahouse to teahouse in the biting cold, asking about a number of men I hadn't seen in weeks or even months. None of the mistresses knew where to find them.

That evening, the Ichiriki was busy with farewell parties. It was fascinating to see how differently all the geisha reacted to the news. Some looked as though their spirits had been murdered within them; others were like statues of the Buddha – calm and lovely, but painted over with a layer of sadness. I can't say how I myself looked, but my mind was like an abacus. I was so busy with scheming and plotting – thinking which man I would approach, and how I would do it – that I scarcely heard the maid who told me I was wanted in another room. I imagined a group of men had requested my company; but she led me up the stairs to the second floor and along a corridor to the very back of the teahouse. She opened the door of a small tatami room I'd never entered before. And there at the table, alone with a glass of beer, sat Nobu.

Before I could even bow to him or speak a word, he said, 'Sayuri-san, you've disappointed me!'

'My goodness! I haven't had the honor of your company for four years, Nobu-san, and already in an instant I've disappointed you. What could I have done wrong so quickly?'

'I had a little bet with myself that your mouth would fall open at the sight of me.'

'The truth is, I'm too startled even to move!'

'Come inside and let the maid close the door. But first, tell her to bring another glass and another beer. There's something you and I must drink to.'

I did as Nobu told me, and then knelt at the end of the table with a corner between us. I could feel Nobu's eyes upon my face almost as though he were touching me. I blushed as one might blush under the warmth of the sun, for I'd forgotten how flattering it felt to be admired.

'I see angles in your face I've never seen before,' he said to me. 'Don't tell me you're going hungry like everyone else. I'd never expected such a thing of you.'

'Nobu-san looks a bit thin himself.'

'I have food enough to eat, just no time for eating it.'

'I'm glad at least that you are keeping busy.'

'That's the most peculiar thing I've ever heard. When you see a man who has kept himself alive by dodging bullets, do you feel glad for him that he has something to occupy his time?'

'I hope Nobu-san doesn't mean to say that he is truly in fear for his life . . .'

'There's no one out to murder me, if that's what you mean. But if Iwamura Electric is my life, then yes, I'm certainly in fear for it. Now tell me this: What has become of that *danna* of yours?'

'The General is doing as well as any of us, I suppose. How kind of you to ask.'

'Oh, I don't mean it kindly at all.'

'Very few people wish him well these days. But to change the subject, Nobu-san, am I to suppose that you have been coming here to the Ichiriki night after night, but keeping yourself hidden from me by using this peculiar upstairs room?'

'It is a peculiar room, isn't it? I think it's the only one in the teahouse without a garden view. It looks out on the street, if you open those paper screens.'

'Nobu-san knows the room well.'

'Not really. It's the first time I've used it.'

I made a face at him when he said this, to show I didn't believe him.

'You may think what you want, Sayuri, but it's true I've never been in this room before. I think it's a bedroom for overnight guests, when the mistress has any. She was kind enough to let me use it tonight when I explained to her why I'd come.'

'How mysterious . . . So you had a purpose in coming. Will I find out what it is?'

'I hear the maid returning with our beer,' Nobu said. 'You'll find out when she's gone.'

The door slid open, and the maid placed the beer on the table. Beer was a rare commodity during this period, so it was quite something to watch the gold liquid rising in the glass. When the maid had left, we raised our glasses, and Nobu said:

'I have come here to toast your *danna*!'

I put down my beer when I heard this. 'I must say, Nobu-san, there are few things any of us can find to be cheerful about. But it would take me weeks even to begin imagining why you should wish to drink in honor of my *danna*.'

'I should have been more specific. Here's to the foolishness of your *danna*! Four years ago I told you he was an unworthy

390

man, and he has proved me right. Wouldn't you say?'

'The truth is . . . he isn't my *danna* any longer.'

'Just my point! And even if he were, he couldn't do a thing for you, could he? I know Gion is going to close, and everyone's in a panic about it. I received a telephone call at my office today from a certain geisha . . . I won't name her . . . but can you imagine? She asked if I could find her a job at Iwamura Electric.'

'If you don't mind my asking, what did you tell her?'

'I don't have a job for anyone, hardly even myself. Even the Chairman may be out of a job soon, and end up in prison if he doesn't start doing as the government orders. He's persuaded them we don't have the means to manufacture bayonets and bullet casings, but now they want us to design and build fighter airplanes! I mean, honestly, fighter airplanes? We manufacture appliances! Sometimes I wonder what these people are thinking.'

'Nobo-san should speak more quietly.'

'Who's going to hear me? That General of yours?'

'Speaking of the General,' I said, 'I did go to see him today, to ask for his help.'

'You're lucky he was still alive to see you.'

'Has he been ill?'

'Not ill. But he'll get around to killing himself one of these days, if he has the courage.'

'Please, Nobu-san.'

'He didn't help you, did he?'

'No, he said he'd already used up whatever influence he had.'

'That wouldn't have taken him long. Why didn't he save what little influence he had for you?'

'I haven't seen him in more than a year.'

'You haven't seen me in more than four years. And I have saved my best influence for you. Why didn't you come to me before now?'

'But I've imagined you angry with me all this time. Just look at you, Nobu-san! How could I have come to you?'

'How could you not? I can save you from the factories. I have access to the perfect haven. And believe me, it is perfect,

391

just like a nest for a bird. You're the only one I'll give it to, Sayuri. And I won't give it even to you, until you've bowed on the floor right here in front of me and admitted how wrong you were for what happened four years ago. You're certainly right I'm angry with you! We may both be dead before we see each other again. I may have lost the one chance I had. And it isn't enough that you brushed me aside: you wasted the very ripest years of your life on a fool, a man who won't pay even the debt he owes to his country, much less to you. He goes on living as if he's done nothing wrong!'

You can imagine how I was feeling by this time; for Nobu was a man who could hurl his words like stones. It wasn't just the words themselves or their meaning, but the way he said them. At first I'd been determined not to cry, regardless of what he said; but soon it occurred to me that crying might be the very thing Nobu wanted of me. And it felt so easy, like letting a piece of paper slip from my fingers. Every tear that slid down my cheeks I cried for a different reason. There seemed so much to mourn! I cried for Nobu, and for myself; I cried at wondering what would become of us all. I even cried for General Tottori, and for Korin, who had grown so gray and hollow from life in the factory. And then I did what Nobu demanded of me. I moved away from the table to make room, and I bowed low to the floor.

'Forgive me for my foolishness,' I said.

'Oh, get up off the mats. I'm satisfied if you tell me you won't make the same mistake again.'

'I will not.'

'Every moment you spent with that man was wasted! That's just what I told you would happen, isn't it? Perhaps you've learned enough by now to follow your destiny in the future.'

'I will follow my destiny, Nobu-san. There's nothing more I want from life.'

'I'm pleased to hear that. And where does your destiny lead you?'

'To the man who runs Iwamura Electric,' I said. Of course, I was thinking of the Chairman.

'So it does,' Nobu said. 'Now let us drink our beers together.'

392

I wet my lips – for I was far too confused and upset to be thirsty. Afterward Nobu told me about the nest he'd set aside. It was the home of his good friend Arashino Isamu, the kimono maker. I don't know if you remember him, but he was the guest of honor at the party on the Baron's estate years earlier at which Nobu and Dr. Crab were present. Mr. Arashino's home, which was also his workshop, was on the banks of the Kamo River shallows, about five kilometers upstream from Gion. Until a few years earlier, he and his wife and daughter had made kimono in the lovely Yuzen style for which he was famous. Lately, however, all the kimono makers had been put to work sewing parachutes – for they were accustomed to working with silk, after all. It was a job I could learn quickly, said Nobu, and the Arashino family was very willing to have me. Nobu himself would make the necessary arrangements with the authorities. He wrote the address of Mr. Arashino's home on a piece of paper and gave it to me.

I told Nobu a number of times how grateful I was. Each time I told him, he looked more pleased with himself. Just as I was about to suggest that we take a walk together in the newly fallen snow, he glanced at his watch and drained the last sip of his beer.

'Sayuri,' he said to me, 'I don't know when we will see each other again or what the world will be like when we do. We may both have seen many horrible things. But I will think of you every time I need to be reminded that there is beauty and goodness in the world.'

'Nobu-san! Perhaps you ought to have been a poet!'

'You know perfectly well there's nothing poetic about me.'

'Do your enchanting words mean you're about to leave? I was hoping we might take a stroll together.'

'It's much too cold. But you may see me to the door, and we'll say good-bye there.'

I followed Nobu down the stairs and crouched in the entry-way of the teahouse to help him into his shoes. Afterward I slipped my feet into the tall wooden *geta* I was wearing because of the snow, and walked Nobu out to the street. Years earlier a car would have been waiting for him, but only government officials had cars these days, for almost no one could find the gasoline to run them. I suggested walking him to the trolley.

'I don't want your company just now,' Nobu said. 'I'm on my way to a meeting with our Kyoto distributor. I have too many things on my mind as it is.'

'I must say, Nobu-san, I much preferred your parting words in the room upstairs.'

'In that case, stay there next time.'

I bowed and told Nobu good-bye. Most men would probably have turned to look over their shoulders at some point; but Nobu just plodded through the snow as far as the corner, and then turned up Shijo Avenue and was gone. In my hand I held the piece of paper he'd given me, with Mr. Arashino's address written on it. I realized I was squeezing it so hard in my fingers that if it were possible to crush it, I'm sure I would have. I couldn't think why I felt so nervous and afraid. But after gazing a moment at the snow still falling all around me, I looked at Nobu's deep footprints leading to the corner and had the feeling I knew just what was troubling me. When would I ever see Nobu again? Or the Chairman? Or for that matter, Gion itself? Once before, as a child, I'd been torn from my home. I suppose it was the memory of those horrible years that made me feel so alone.

29

YOU MAY THINK that because I was a successful young geisha with a great many admirers, someone else might have stepped forward to rescue me even if Nobu hadn't. But a geisha in need is hardly like a jewel dropped on the street, which anyone might be happy to pick up. Every one of the hundreds of geisha in Gion was struggling to find a nest from the war in those final weeks, and only a few were lucky enough to find one. So you see, every day I lived with the Arashino family, I felt myself more and more in Nobu's debt.

I discovered how fortunate I really was during the spring of the following year, when I learned that the geisha Raiha had been killed in the firebombing of Tokyo. It was Raiha who'd made us laugh by saying that nothing was as bleak as the future except the past. She and her mother had been prominent geisha, and her father was a member of a famous merchant family; to those of us in Gion, no one had seemed more likely to survive the war than Raiha. At the time of her death she was apparently reading a book to one of her young nephews on her father's estate in the Denenchofu section of Tokyo, and I'm sure she probably felt as safe there as she had in Kyoto. Strangely, the same air raid that killed Raiha also killed the great sumo wrestler Miyagiyama. Both had been living in relative comfort. And yet Pumpkin, who had seemed so lost to me, managed to survive the war, though the lens factory where she was working on the outskirts of Osaka was bombed five or six times. I learned that year that nothing is so unpredictable as who will survive a war and who won't. Mameha survived, working in a small hospital in Fukui Prefecture as a nurse's assistant; but her maid Tatsumi was killed by the terrible bomb that fell on Nagasaki, and her dresser, Mr. Itchoda, died of a heart attack during an air raid drill. Mr. Bekku, on the other hand, worked on a naval base in Osaka and yet survived somehow. So did General Tottori, who lived in the Suruya Inn until his death in the mid-1950s, and the Baron too – though I'm sorry to say that in the early years of the Allied Occupation, the Baron drowned himself in his splendid pond after his title and many of his holdings were taken away. I don't think he could face a world in which he was no longer free to act on his every whim.

As for Mother, there was never a moment's doubt in my mind that she would survive. With her highly developed ability to benefit from other people's suffering, she fell so naturally into work in the gray market that it was as if she'd done it all along; she spent the war growing richer instead of poorer by buying and selling other people's heirlooms. Whenever Mr. Arashino sold a kimono from his collection in order to raise cash, he asked me to contact Mother so she could recover it for him. Many of the kimono sold in Kyoto passed through her hands, you see. Mr. Arashino probably hoped Mother would forgo her profit and hold his kimono a few years until he could buy them back again; but she never seemed able to find them – or at least, that was what she said.

The Arashinos treated me with great kindness during the years I lived in their home. In the daytime, I worked with them sewing parachutes. At night I slept alongside their daughter and grandson on futons spread out on the floor of the work-shop. We had so little charcoal, we burned compressed leaves for warmth – or newspapers and magazines; anything we could find. Of course food had grown still more scarce; you can't imagine some of the things we learned to eat, such as soybean dregs, usually given to livestock, and a hideous thing called *nukapan*, made by frying rice bran in wheat flour. It looked like old, dried leather though I'm sure leather would probably have tasted better. Very occasionally we had small quantities of potatoes, or sweet potatoes; dried whale meat; sausage made from seals; and sometimes sardines, which we Japanese had never regarded as anything more than fertilizer.

I grew so thin during these years that no one would have recognized me on the streets of Gion. Some days the Arashinos' little grandson, Juntaro, cried from hunger – which is when Mr. Arashino usually decided to sell a kimono from his collection. This was what we Japanese called the 'onion life' – peeling away a layer at a time and crying all the while.

One night in the spring of 1944, after I'd been living with the Arashino family no more than three or four months, we witnessed our first air raid. The stars were so clear, we could see the silhouettes of the bombers as they droned overhead, and also the shooting stars – as they seemed to us – that flew up from the earth and exploded near them. We were afraid we would hear the horrible whistling noise and watch Kyoto burst into flames all around us; and if it had, our lives would have ended right then, whether we had died or not – because Kyoto is as delicate as a moth's wing; if it had been crushed, it could never have recovered as Osaka and Tokyo, and so many other cities, were able to do. But the bombers passed us over, not only that night but every night. Many evenings we watched the moon turn red from the fires in Osaka, and sometimes we saw ashes floating through the air like falling leaves – even there in Kyoto, fifty kilometers away. You can well imagine that I worried desperately about the Chairman and Nobu, whose company was based in Osaka, and who both had homes there as well as in Kyoto. I wondered too what would become of my sister, Satsu, wherever she was. I don't think I'd ever been consciously aware of it, but since the very week she'd run away, I'd carried a belief shrouded somewhere in the back of my mind that the courses of our lives would one day bring us together again. I thought perhaps she might send a letter to me in care of the Nitta okiya, or else come back to Kyoto looking for me. Then one afternoon while I was taking little Juntaro for a walk along the river, picking out stones from the edge of the water and throwing them back in, it occurred to me that Satsu never would come back to Kyoto to find me. Now that I was living an impoverished life myself, I could see that traveling to some far-off city for any reason at all was out of the question. And in any case, Satsu and I probably wouldn't recognize each other on the street even if she did come. As for my fantasy that she might write me a letter . . . well, I felt like a foolish girl again; had it really taken me all these years to understand that Satsu had no way of knowing the name of the Nitta okiya? She couldn't write me if she wanted to – unless she contacted Mr. Tanaka, and she would never do such a thing. While little Juntaro went on throwing stones into the river, I squatted beside him and trickled water onto my face with one hand, smiling at him all the while and pretending I'd done it to cool myself. My little ruse must have worked, because Juntaro seemed to have no idea that anything was the matter.

Adversity is like a strong wind. I don't mean just that it holds us back from places we might otherwise go. It also tears away from us all but the things that cannot be torn, so that afterward we see ourselves as we really are, and not merely as we might like to be. Mr. Arashino's daughter, for example, suffered the death of her husband during the war, and afterward poured herself into two things: caring for her little boy and sewing parachutes for the soldiers. She seemed to live for nothing else. When she grew thinner and thinner, you knew where every gram of her was going. By the war's end, she clutched at that child as though he were the cliff's edge that kept her from falling to the rocks below.

Because I'd lived through adversity once before, what I learned about myself was like a reminder of something I'd once known but had nearly forgotten – namely, that beneath the elegant clothing, and the accomplished dancing, and the clever conversation, my life had no complexity at all, but was as simple as a stone falling toward the ground. My whole purpose in everything during the past ten years had been to win the affections of the Chairman. Day after day I watched the swift water of the Kamo River shallows rushing below the workshop; sometimes I threw a petal into it, or a piece of straw, knowing that it would be carried all the way to Osaka before washing out into the sea. I wondered if perhaps the Chairman, sitting at his desk, might look out his window one afternoon and see that petal or that straw and perhaps think of me. But soon I began to have a troubling thought. The

Chairman might see it, perhaps, though I doubted he would; but even if he did, and he leaned back in his chair to think of the hundred things the petal might bring to mind, I might not be one of them. He had often been kind to me, it was true; but he was a kind man. He'd never shown the least sign of recognizing that I had once been the girl he'd comforted, or that I cared for him, or thought of him.

One day I came to a realization, more painful in some ways even than my sudden understanding that Satsu and I were unlikely to be reunited. I'd spent the previous night nursing a troubling thought, wondering for the first time what might happen if I reached the end of my life and still the Chairman had never taken any special notice of me. That next morning I looked carefully at my almanac in the hopes of finding some sign that my life wouldn't be lived without purpose. I was feeling so dejected that even Mr. Arashino seemed to recognize it, and sent me on an errand to purchase sewing needles at the dry goods store thirty minutes away. On my walk back, strolling along the roadside as the sun was setting, I was nearly run down by an army truck. It's the closest I've ever come to being killed. Only the next morning did I notice that my almanac had warned against travel in the direction of the Rat, precisely the direction in which the dry goods store lay; I'd been looking only for a sign about the Chairman, and hadn't noticed. From this experience I understood the danger of focusing only on what isn't there. What if I came to the end of my life and realized that I'd spent every day watching for a man who would never come to me? What an unbearable sorrow it would be, to realize I'd never really tasted the things I'd eaten, or seen the places I'd been, because I'd thought of nothing but the Chairman even while my life was drifting away from me. And yet if I drew my thoughts back from him, what life would I have? I would be like a dancer who had practiced since childhood for a performance she would never give.

The war ended for us in August of 1945. Most anyone who lived in Japan during this time will tell you that it was the very bleakest moment in a long night of darkness. Our country wasn't simply defeated, it was destroyed – and I don't mean by all the bombs, as horrible as those were. When your country has lost a war and an invading army pours in, you feel as though you yourself have been led to the execution ground to kneel, hands bound, and wait for the sword to fall. During a period of a year or more, I never once heard the sound of laughter – unless it was little Juntaro, who didn't know any better. And when Juntaro laughed, his grandfather waved a hand to shush him. I've often observed that men and women who were young children during these years have a certain seriousness about them; there was too little laughter in their childhoods.

By the spring of 1946, we'd all come to recognize that we would live through the ordeal of defeat. There were even those who believed Japan would one day be renewed. All the stories about invading American soldiers raping and killing us had turned out to be wrong; and in fact, we gradually came to realize that the Americans on the whole were remarkably kind. One day an entourage of them came riding through the area in their trucks. I stood watching them with the other women from the neighborhood. I'd learned during my years in Gion to regard myself as the inhabitant of a special world that separated me from other women; and in fact, I'd felt so separated all these years that I'd only rarely wondered how other women lived – even the wives of the men I'd entertained. Yet there I stood in a pair of torn work pants, with my stringy hair hanging along my back. I hadn't bathed in several days, for we had no fuel to heat the water more than a few times each week. To the eyes of the American soldiers who drove past, I looked no different from the women around me; and as I thought of it, who could say I was any different? If you no longer have leaves, or bark, or roots, can you go on calling yourself a tree? 'I am a peasant,' I said to myself, 'and not a geisha at all any longer.' It was a frightening feeling to look at my hands and see their roughness. To draw my mind away from my fears, I turned my attention again to the truckloads of soldiers driving past. Weren't these the very American soldiers we'd been taught to hate, who had bombed our cities with such horrifying weapons? Now they rode through our neighborhood, throwing pieces of candy to the children.

Within a year after the surrender, Mr. Arashino had been encouraged to begin making kimono once again. I knew nothing about kimono except how to wear them, so I was given the task of spending my days in the basement of the workshop annex, tending to the vats of dye as they boiled. This was a horrid job, partly because we couldn't afford any fuel but *tadon*, which is a kind of coal dust held together by tar; you cannot imagine the stench when it burns. Over time Mr. Arashino's wife taught me how to gather the proper leaves, stems, and bark to make the dyes myself, which may sound like something of a promotion. And it might have been, except that one of the materials – I never found out which – had the strange effect of pickling my skin. My delicate dancer's hands, which I'd once nurtured with the finest creams, now began to peel like the papery outside of an onion, and were stained all over the color of a bruise. During this time – impelled probably by my own loneliness – I became involved in a brief romance with a young tatami maker named Inoue. I thought he looked quite handsome, with his soft eyebrows like smudges on his delicate skin and a perfect smoothness to his lips. Every few nights during the course of several weeks, I sneaked into the annex to let him in. I didn't realize quite how gruesome my hands looked until one night when the fire under the vats was burning so brightly we could see each other. After Inoue caught a glimpse of my hands, he wouldn't let me touch him with them!

To allow my skin some relief, Mr. Arashino gave me the task of gathering spiderworts during the summertime. The spiderwort is a flower whose juice is used for painting the silks before they're masked with starch and then dyed. They tend to grow around the edges of ponds and lakes during the rainy season. I thought gathering them sounded like a pleasant job, so one morning in July, I set out with my rucksack, ready to enjoy the cool, dry day; but soon I discovered that spiderworts are devilishly clever flowers. As far as I could tell, they'd enlisted every insect in western Japan as an ally. Whenever I tore off a handful of flowers, I was attacked by divisions of ticks and mosquitoes; and to make matters worse, one time I stepped on a hideous little frog. Then after I'd spent a miserable week gathering the flowers, I took on what I thought would be a much easier task, of squeezing them in a press to extract their juices. But if you've never smelled the juice of a spiderwort . . . well, I was very glad at the end of the week to go back to boiling dyes once again.

I worked very hard during those years. But every night when I went to bed, I thought of Gion. All the geisha districts in Japan had reopened within a few months of the surrender; but I wasn't free to go back until Mother summoned me. She was making quite a good living selling kimono, artwork, and Japanese swords to American soldiers. So for the time being, she and Auntie remained on the little farm west of Kyoto where they had set up shop, while I continued to live and work with the Arashino family.

Considering that Gion was only a few kilometers away, you may think I visited there often. And yet in the nearly five years I lived away, I went only once. It was one afternoon during the spring, about a year after the end of the war, while I was on my way back from picking up medicine for little Juntaro at the Kamigyo Prefectural Hospital. I took a walk along Kawaramachi Avenue as far as Shijo and crossed the bridge from there into Gion. I was shocked to see whole families crowded together in poverty along the river's edge.

In Gion I recognized a number of geisha, though of course they didn't recognize me; and I didn't speak a word to them, hoping for once to view the place as an outsider might. In truth, though, I could scarcely see Gion at all as I strolled through it; I saw instead only my ghostly memories. When I walked along the banks of the Shirakawa Stream, I thought of the many afternoons Mameha and I had spent walking there. Nearby was the bench where Pumpkin and I had sat with two bowls of noodles on the night I asked for her help. Not far away was the alleyway where Nobu had chastened me for taking the General as my *danna*. From there I walked half a block to the corner of Shijo Avenue where I'd made the young delivery man drop the lunch boxes he was carrying. In all of these spots, I felt I was standing on a stage many hours after the dance had ended, when the silence lay as heavily upon the empty theater as a blanket of snow. I went to our okiya and stared with longing at the heavy iron padlock on the door. When I was locked in, I wanted to be out. Now life had changed so much that, finding myself locked out, I wanted to be inside again. And yet I was a grown woman – free, if I wished, to stroll out of Gion at that very moment and never come back.

One bitter cold afternoon in November, three years after the end of the war, I was warming my hands over the dye vats in the annex when Mrs. Arashino came down to say that some-one wished to see me. I could tell from her expression that the visitor wasn't just another of the women from the neighbor-hood. But you can imagine my surprise when I reached the top of the stairs and saw Nobu. He was sitting in the work-shop with Mr. Arashino, holding an empty teacup as though he'd been there chatting for some time already. Mr. Arashino stood when he saw me.

'I have some work in the next room, Nobu-san,' he said. 'You two can stay here and talk. I'm delighted you've come to see us.'

'Don't fool yourself, Arashino,' Nobu replied. 'Sayuri is the person I've come to see.'

I thought this an unkind thing for Nobu to have said, and not at all funny; but Mr. Arashino laughed when he heard it and rolled the door of the workshop closed behind him.

'I thought the whole world had changed,' I said. 'But it can't be so, for Nobu-san has stayed exactly the same.'

'I never change,' he said. 'But I haven't come here to chat. I want to know what's the matter with you.'

'Nothing is the matter. Hasn't Nobu-san been receiving my letters?'

'Your letters all read like poems! You never talk about anything but "the beautiful, trickling water" or some such nonsense.'

'Why, Nobu-san, I'll never waste another letter on you!'

'I'd rather you didn't, if that's how they sound. Why can't you just tell me the things I want to know, such as when you're coming back to Gion? Every month I telephone the Ichiriki to ask about you, and the mistress gives some excuse or other. I thought I might find you ill with some horrible disease. You're skinnier than you were, I suppose, but you look healthy enough to me. What's keeping you?'

'I certainly think of Gion every day.'

'Your friend Mameha came back a year or more ago. Even Michizono, as old as she is, showed up the day it reopened. But no one has been able to tell me why Sayuri won't come back.'

'To tell the truth, the decision isn't mine. I've been waiting for Mother to reopen the okiya. I'm as eager to get back to Gion as Nobu-san is to have me there.'

'Then call that mother of yours and tell her the time has come. I've been patient the past six months. Didn't you understand what I was telling you in my letters?'

'When you said you wanted me back in Gion, I thought you meant that you hoped to see me there soon.'

'If I say I want to see you back in Gion, what I mean is, I want you to pack your bags and go back to Gion. I don't see why you need to wait for that mother of yours anyway! If she hasn't had the sense to go back by now, she's a fool.'

'Few people have anything good to say about her, but I can assure you she's no fool. Nobu-san might even admire her, if he came to know her. She's making a fine living selling souvenirs to American soldiers.'

'The soldiers won't be here forever. You tell her your good friend Nobu wants you back in Gion.' At this, he took a little package with his one hand and tossed it onto the mats next to me. He didn't say a word afterward, but only sipped at his tea and looked at me.

'What is Nobu-san throwing at me?' I said.

'It's a gift I've brought. Open it.'

'If Nobu-san is giving me a gift, first I must bring my gift for him.'

I went to the corner of the room, where I kept my trunk of belongings, and found a folding fan I'd long ago decided to give to Nobu. A fan may seem a simple gift for the man who'd saved me from life in the factories. But to a geisha, the fans we use in dance are like sacred objects – and this wasn't just an ordinary dancer's fan, but the very one my teacher had given me when I reached the level of *shisho* in the Inoue School of dance. I'd never before heard of a geisha parting with such a thing – which was the very reason I'd decided to give it to him.

I wrapped the fan in a square of cotton and went back to present it to him. He was puzzled when he opened it, as I knew he would be. I did my best to explain why I wanted him to have it.

'It's kind of you,' he said, 'but I'm unworthy of this gift. Offer it to someone who appreciates dance more than I do.'

'There's no one else I would give it to. It's a part of me, and I have given it to Nobu-san.'

'In that case, I'm very grateful and I'll cherish it. Now open the package I've brought you.'

Wrapped inside paper and string, and padded with layers of newspaper, was a rock about the size of a fist. I'm sure I was at least as puzzled to receive a rock as Nobu must have been by the fan I'd given him. When I looked at it more closely, I saw it wasn't a rock at all, but a piece of concrete.

'You have in your hand some rubble from our factory in Osaka,' Nobu told me. 'Two of our four factories were destroyed. There's a danger our whole company may not survive the next few years. So you see, if you've given me a piece of yourself with that fan, I suppose I've just given you a piece of myself as well.'

'If it's a piece of Nobu-san, then I will cherish it.'

'I didn't give it to you to cherish. It's a piece of concrete! I want you to help me turn it into a lovely jewel for you to keep.'

'If Nobu-san knows how to do such a thing, please tell me, and we'll all be rich!'

'I have a task for you to do in Gion. If it works out as I hope, our company will be back on its feet in a year or so. When I ask you for that piece of concrete back and replace it with a jewel instead, the time will have come at last for me to become your *danna*.'

My skin felt as cold as glass when I heard this; but I showed no sign of it. 'How mysterious, Nobu-san. A task *I* could undertake, which would be helpful to Iwamura Electric?'

'It's an awful task. I won't lie to you. During the final two years before Gion closed, there was a man named Sato who used to go to parties as a guest of the Prefectural Governor. I want you to come back so you can entertain him.'

I had to laugh when I heard this. 'How horrible a task can that be? However much Nobu-san dislikes him, I'm sure I've entertained worse.'

'If you remember him, you'll know exactly how horrible it is. He's irritating, and he acts like a pig. He tells me he always sat across the table so he could stare at you. You're the only thing he ever talks about – when he talks, that is; because mostly he just sits. Maybe you saw him mentioned in the news magazines last month; he was just appointed to be a Deputy Minister of Finance.'

'My goodness!' I said. 'He must be very capable.'

'Oh, there are fifteen or more men who hold that title. I know he's capable of pouring sake into his mouth; that's the only thing I've ever seen him do. It's a tragedy that the future of a great company like ours should be affected by a man like him! It's a terrible time to be alive, Sayuri.'

'Nobu-san! You mustn't say a thing like that.'

'Why on earth not? No one's going to hear me.'

'It isn't a matter of who hears you. It's your attitude! You shouldn't think that way.'

'Why shouldn't I? The company has never been in worse condition. All through the war, the Chairman resisted what the government told him to do. By the time he finally agreed to cooperate, the war was almost over, and nothing we ever made for them – not one thing – was taken into battle. But has that stopped the Americans from classifying Iwamura Electric as a *zaibatsu* just like Mitsubishi? It's ridiculous. Compared to Mitsubishi, we were like a sparrow watching a lion. And there's something worse: if we can't convince them of our case, Iwamura Electric will be seized, and its assets sold to pay war reparations! Two weeks ago I'd have said that was bad enough, but now they've appointed this fellow Sato to make a recommendation about our case. Those Americans think they were clever to appoint a Japanese. Well, I'd rather have seen a dog take the job than this man.' Suddenly Nobu interrupted himself. 'What on earth is the matter with your hands?'

Since coming up from the annex, I'd kept my hands hidden as best I could. Obviously Nobu had caught sight of them somehow. 'Mr. Arashino was kind enough to give me the job of making dyes.'

'Let's hope he knows how to remove those stains,' said Nobu. 'You can't go back to Gion looking like that.'

'Nobu-san, my hands are the least of my problems. I'm not sure I can go back to Gion at all. I'll do my best to persuade Mother, but truthfully, it isn't my decision. Anyway, I'm sure there are other geisha who'll be helpful –'

'There aren't other geisha! Listen to me, I took Deputy Minister Sato to a teahouse the other day with half a dozen people. He didn't speak a word for an hour, and then finally he cleared his throat and said, "This isn't the Ichiriki." So I told him, "No, it's not. You certainly got that right!" He grunted like a pig, and then said, "Sayuri entertains at the Ichiriki." So I told him, "No, Minister, if she were in Gion at all, she would come right here and entertain us. But I told you – she isn't in Gion!" So then he took his sake cup –'

'I hope you were more polite with him than that,' I said.

'I certainly wasn't! I can tolerate his company for about half an hour. After that I'm not responsible for the things I say. That's exactly the reason I want you there! And don't tell me again it isn't your decision. You owe this to me, and you know it perfectly well. Anyway, the truth is . . . I'd like the chance to spend some time with you myself . . .'

'And I would like to spend time with Nobu-san.'

'Just don't bring any illusions with you when you come.'

'After the past few years, I'm sure I don't have any left. But is Nobu-san thinking of something in particular?'

'Don't expect me to become your *danna* in a month, that's what I'm saying. Until Iwamura Electric has recovered, I'm in no position to make such an offer. I've been very worried about the company's prospects. But to tell the truth, Sayuri, I feel better about the future after seeing you again.'

'Nobu-san! How kind!'

'Don't be ridiculous, I'm not trying to flatter you. Your destiny and mine are intertwined. But I'll never be your *danna* if Iwamura Electric doesn't recover. Perhaps the recovery, just like my meeting you in the first place, is simply meant to be.'

During the final years of the war, I'd learned to stop wondering what was meant to be and what wasn't. I'd often said to the women in the neighborhood that I wasn't sure if I'd ever go back to Gion – but the truth is, I'd always known I would. My destiny, whatever it was, awaited me there. In these years away, I'd learned to suspend all the water in my personality by turning it to ice, you might say. Only by stopping the natural flow of my thoughts in this way could I bear the waiting. Now to hear Nobu refer to my destiny . . . well, I felt he'd shattered the ice inside me and awakened my desires once again.

'Nobu-san,' I said, 'if it's important to make a good impression on Deputy Minister Sato, perhaps you should ask the Chairman to be there when you entertain him.'

'The Chairman is a busy man.'

'But surely if the Minister is important to the future of the company –'

'You worry about getting yourself there. I'll worry about what's best for the company. I'll be very disappointed if you're not back in Gion by the end of the month.'

Nobu rose to leave, for he had to be back in Osaka before nightfall. I walked him to the entryway to help him into his coat and shoes, and put his fedora on his head for him. When I was done, he stood looking at me a long while. I thought he was about to say he found me beautiful – for this was the sort of comment he sometimes made after gazing at me for no reason.

'My goodness, Sayuri, you do look like a peasant!' he said. He had a scowl on his face as he turned away.

30

THAT VERY NIGHT while the Arashinos slept, I wrote to Mother by the light of the *tadon* burning under the dye vats in the annex. Whether my letter had the proper effect or whether Mother was already prepared to reopen the okiya, I don't know; but a week later an old woman's voice called out at the Arashinos' door, and I rolled it open to find Auntie there. Her cheeks had sunken where she'd lost teeth, and the sickly gray of her skin made me think of a piece of sashimi left on the plate overnight. But I could see that she was still a strong woman; she was carrying a bag of coal in one hand and foodstuffs in the other, to thank the Arashinos for their kindness toward me.

The next day I said a tearful farewell and went back to Gion, where Mother, Auntie, and I set about the task of putting things back in order. When I'd had a look around the okiya, the thought crossed my mind that the house itself was punishing us for our years of neglect. We had to spend four or five days on only the worst of the problems: wiping down the dust that lay as heavily as gauze over the woodwork; fishing the remains of dead rodents from the well; cleaning Mother's room upstairs, where birds had torn up the tatami mats and used the straw to make nests in the alcove. To my surprise, Mother worked as hard as any of us, partly because we could afford only a cook and one adult maid, though we did also have a young girl named Etsuko. She was the daughter of the man on whose farm Mother and Auntie had been living. As if to remind me of how many years had passed since I first came to Kyoto as a nine-year-old girl, Etsuko herself was nine. She seemed to regard me with the same fear I'd once felt toward

Hatsumomo, even though I smiled at her whenever I could. She stood as tall and thin as a broom, with long hair that trailed behind her as she scurried about. And her face was narrow like a grain of rice, so that I couldn't help thinking that one day she too would be thrown into the pot just as I had been, and would fluff up white and delicious, to be consumed.

When the okiya was livable again, I set out to pay my respects around Gion. I began by calling on Mameha, who was now in a one-room apartment above a pharmacy near the Gion Shrine; since her return a year earlier, she'd had no *danna* to pay for anything more spacious. She was startled when she first saw me – because of the way my cheekbones protruded, she said. The truth was, I felt just as startled to see her. The beautiful oval of her face was unchanged, but her neck looked sinewy and much too old for her. The strangest thing was that she sometimes held her mouth puckered like an old woman's, because her teeth, though I could see no difference in them, had been quite loose at one time during the war and still caused her pain.

We talked for a long while, and then I asked if she thought *Dances of the Old Capital* would resume the following spring. The performances hadn't been seen in a number of years.

'Oh, why not?' she said. 'The theme can be the "Dance in the Stream"!'

If you've ever visited a hot springs resort or some such place, and been entertained by women masquerading as geisha who are really prostitutes, you'll understand Mameha's little joke. A woman who performs the 'Dance in the Stream' is really doing a kind of striptease. She pretends to wade into deeper and deeper water, all the while raising her kimono to keep the hem dry, until the men finally see what they've been waiting for, and begin to cheer and toast one another with sake.

'With all the American soldiers in Gion these days,' she went on, 'English will get you further than dance. Anyway, the Kaburenjo Theater has been turned into a *kyabarei*.'

I'd never heard this word before, which came from the

410

English 'cabaret,' but I learned soon enough what it meant. Even while living with the Arashino family, I'd heard stories about American soldiers and their noisy parties. Still I was shocked when I stepped into the entryway of a teahouse later that afternoon and found – instead of the usual row of men's shoes at the base of the step – a confusion of army boots, each of which looked as big to me as Mother's little dog Taku had been. Inside the front entrance hall, the first thing I saw was an American man in his underwear squeezing himself beneath the shelf of an alcove while two geisha, both laughing, tried to pull him out. When I looked at the dark hair on his arms and chest, and even on his back, I had the feeling I'd never seen anything quite so beastly. He'd apparently lost his clothing in a drinking game and was trying to hide, but soon he let the women draw him out by the arms and lead him back down the hall and through a door. I heard whistling and cheering when he entered.

About a week after my return, I was finally ready to make my first appearance as a geisha again. I spent a day rushing from the hairdresser's to the fortune-teller's; soaking my hands to remove the last of the stains; and searching all over Gion to find the makeup I needed. Now that I was nearing thirty, I would no longer be expected to wear white makeup except on special occasions. But I did spend a half hour at my makeup stand that day, trying to use different shades of Western-style face powder to hide how thin I'd grown. When Mr. Bekku came to dress me, young Etsuko stood and watched just as I had once watched Hatsumomo; and it was the astonishment in her eyes, more than anything I saw while looking in the mirror, that convinced me I truly looked like a geisha once again.

When at last I set out that evening, all of Gion was blanketed in a beautiful snow so powdery the slightest wind blew the roofs clean. I wore a kimono shawl and carried a lacquered umbrella, so I'm sure I was as unrecognizable as the day I'd visited Gion looking like a peasant. I recognized only about half the geisha I passed. It was easy to tell those who'd lived in Gion before the war, because they gave a little bow of courtesy as they passed, even when they didn't seem to recognize me. The others didn't bother with more than a nod.

Seeing soldiers here and there on the streets, I dreaded what I might find when I reached the Ichiriki. But in fact, the entry-way was lined with the shiny black shoes worn by officers; and strangely enough, the teahouse seemed quieter than in my days as an apprentice. Nobu hadn't yet arrived – or at least, I didn't see any sign of him – but I was shown directly into one of the large rooms on the ground floor and told he would join me there shortly Ordinarily I would have waited in the maids' quarters up the hallway, where I could warm my hands and sip a cup of tea; no geisha likes a man to find her idle. But I didn't mind waiting for Nobu – and besides, I considered it a privilege to spend a few minutes by myself in such a room. I'd been starved for beauty over the past five years, and this was a room that would have astonished you with its loveliness. The walls were covered with a pale yellow silk whose texture gave a kind of presence, and made me feel held by them just as an egg is held by its shell.

I'd expected Nobu to arrive by himself, but when I finally heard him in the hallway, it was clear he'd brought Deputy Minister Sato with him. I didn't mind if Nobu found me waiting, as I've mentioned; but I thought it would be disastrous to give the Minister reason to think I might be unpopular. So I slipped quickly through the adjoining doors into an unused room. As it turned out, this gave me a chance to listen to Nobu struggle to be pleasant.

'Isn't this quite a room, Minister?' he said. I heard a little grunt in reply. 'I requested it especially for you. That painting in the Zen style is really something, don't you think?' Then after a long silence, Nobu added, 'Yes, it's a beautiful night. Oh, did I already ask if you've tasted the Ichiriki Teahouse's own special brand of sake?'

Things continued in this way, with Nobu probably feeling about as comfortable as an elephant trying to act like a butterfly. When at length I went into the hallway and slid open the door, Nobu seemed very relieved to see me.

I got my first good look at the Minister only after intro-ducing myself and going to kneel at the table. He didn't look at all familiar, though he'd claimed to have spent hours staring at me. I don't know how I managed to forget him, because he had a very distinctive appearance; I've never seen anyone who had more trouble just lugging his face around. He kept his chin tucked against his breastbone as though he couldn't quite hold up his head, and he had a peculiar lower jaw that protruded so that his breath seemed to blow right up his nose. After he gave me a little nod and said his name, it was a long while before I heard any sound from him other than grunts, for a grunt seemed to be his way of responding to almost anything.

I did my best to make conversation until the maid rescued us by arriving with a tray of sake. I filled the Minister's cup and was astonished to watch him pour the sake directly into his lower jaw in the same way he might have poured it into a drain. He shut his mouth for a moment and then opened it again, and the sake was gone, without any of the usual signs people make when they swallow. I wasn't really sure he'd swallowed at all until he held out his empty cup.

Things went on like this for fifteen minutes or more while I tried to put the Minister at his ease by telling him stories and jokes, and asking him a few questions. But soon I began to think perhaps there was no such thing as 'the Minister at his ease.' He never gave me an answer of more than a single word. I suggested we play a drinking game; I even asked if he liked to sing. The longest exchange we had in our first half hour was when the Minister asked if I was a dancer.

'Why yes, I am. Would the Minister like me to perform a short piece?'

'No,' he said. And that was the end of it.

The Minister may not have liked making eye contact with people, but he certainly liked to study his food, as I discovered after a maid arrived with dinner for the two men. Before putting anything in his mouth, he held it up with his chopsticks and peered at it, turning it this way and that. And if he didn't recognize it, he asked me what it was. 'It's a piece of yam boiled in soy sauce and sugar,' I told him when he held up something orange. Actually I didn't have the least idea whether it was yam, or a slice of whale liver; or anything else, but I didn't think the Minister wanted to hear that. Later, when he held up a piece of marinated beef and asked me about it, I decided to tease him a bit.

'Oh, that's a strip of marinated leather,' I said. 'It's a specialty of the house here! It's made from the skin of elephants. So I guess I should have said "elephant leather."'

'Elephant leather?'

'Now Minister, you know I'm teasing you! It's a piece of beef. Why do you look at your food so closely? Did you think you would come here and eat dog or something?'

'I've eaten dog, you know,' he said to me.

'That's very interesting. But we don't have any dog here tonight. So don't look at your chopsticks anymore.'

Very soon we began playing a drinking game. Nobu hated drinking games, but he kept quiet after I made a face at him. We may have let the Minister lose a bit more often than we should have, because later, as we were trying to explain the rules to a drinking game he'd never played, his eyes became as unsteady as corks floating in the surf. All at once he stood up and headed off toward one corner of the room.

'Now, Minister,' Nobu said to him, 'exactly where are you planning on going?'

The Minister's answer was to let out a burp, which I considered a very well-spoken reply because it was apparent he was about to throw up. Nobu and I rushed over to help him, but he'd already clamped his hand over his mouth. If he'd been a volcano, he would have been smoking by this time, so we had no choice but to roll open the glass doors to the garden to let him vomit onto the snow there. You may be appalled at the thought of a man throwing up into one of these exquisite decorative gardens, but the Minister certainly wasn't the first. We geisha try to help a man down the hallway to the toilet, but sometimes we can't manage it. If we say to one of the maids that a man has just visited the garden, they all know exactly what we mean and come at once with their cleaning supplies.

Nobu and I did our best to keep the Minister kneeling in the doorway with his head suspended over the snow. But despite our efforts he soon tumbled out headfirst. I did my best to shove him to one side, so he would at least end up in snow that hadn't yet been vomited upon. But the Minister was as bulky as a thick piece of meat. All I really did was turn him onto his side as he fell.

Nobu and I could do nothing but look at each other in dismay at the sight of the Minister lying perfectly still in the deep snow, like a branch that had fallen from a tree.

'Why, Nobu-san,' I said, 'I didn't know how much fun your guest was going to be.'

'I believe we've killed him. And if you ask me, he deserved it. What an irritating man!'

'Is this how you act toward your honored guests? You must take him out onto the street and walk him around a bit to wake him up. The cold will do him good.'

'He's lying in the snow. Isn't that cold enough?'

'Nobu-san!' I said. And I suppose this was enough of a reprimand, for Nobu let out a sigh and stepped down into the garden in his stocking feet to begin the task of bringing the Minister back to consciousness. While he was busy with this, I went to find a maid who could help, because I couldn't see how Nobu would get the Minister back up into the teahouse with only one arm. Afterward I fetched some dry socks for the two men and alerted a maid to tidy the garden after we'd left.

When I returned to the room, Nobu and the Minister were at the table again. You can imagine how the Minister looked – and smelled. I had to peel his wet socks off his feet with my own hands, but I kept my distance from him while doing it. As soon as I was done, he slumped back onto the mats and was unconscious again a moment later.

'Do you think he can hear us?' I whispered to Nobu.

'I don't think he hears us even when he's conscious,' Nobu said. 'Did you ever meet a bigger fool in your life?'

'Nobu-san, quietly!' I whispered. 'Do you think he actually enjoyed himself tonight? I mean, is this the sort of evening you had in mind?'

'It isn't a matter of what I had in mind. It's what he had in mind.'

'I hope that docsn't mean we'll be doing the same thing again next week.'

415

'If the Minister is pleased with the evening, I'm pleased with the evening.'

'Nobu-san, really! You certainly weren't pleased. You looked as miserable as I've ever seen you. Considering the Minister's condition, I think we can assume he isn't having the best night of his life either . . .'

'You can't assume anything, when it comes to the Minister.'

'I'm sure he'll have a better time if we can make the atmosphere more . . . festive somehow. Wouldn't you agree?'

'Bring a few more geisha next time, if you think it will help,' Nobu said. 'We'll come back next weekend. Invite that older sister of yours.'

'Mameha's certainly clever, but the Minister is so exhausting to entertain. We need a geisha who's going to, I don't know, make a lot of noise! Distract everyone. You know, now that I think of it . . . it seems to me we need another guest as well, not just another geisha.'

'I can't see any reason for that.'

'If the Minister is busy drinking and sneaking looks at me, and you're busy growing increasingly fed up with him, we're not going to have a very festive evening,' I said. 'To tell the truth, Nobu-san, perhaps you should bring the Chairman with you next time.'

You may wonder if I'd been plotting all along to bring the evening to this moment. It's certainly true that in coming back to Gion, I'd hoped more than anything else to find a way of spending time with the Chairman. It wasn't so much that I craved the chance to sit in the same room with him again, to lean in and whisper some comment and take in the scent of his skin. If those sorts of moments would be the only pleasure life offered me, I'd be better off shutting out that one brilliant source of light to let my eyes begin to adjust to the darkness. Perhaps it was true, as it now seemed, that my life was falling toward Nobu. I wasn't so foolish as to imagine I could change the course of my destiny. But neither could I give up the last traces of hope.

'I've considered bringing the Chairman,' Nobu replied. 'The Minister is very impressed with him. But I don't know,

Sayuri. I told you once already. He's a busy man.'

The Minister jerked on the mats as if someone had poked him, and then managed to pull himself up until he was sitting at the table. Nobu was so disgusted at the sight of his clothing that he sent me out to bring back a maid with a damp towel. After the maid had cleaned the Minister's jacket and left us alone again, Nobu said:

'Well, Minister, this certainly has been a wonderful evening! Next time we'll have even more fun, because instead of throwing up on just me, you might be able to throw up on the Chairman, and perhaps another geisha or two as well!'

I was very pleased to hear Nobu mention the Chairman, but I didn't dare react.

'I like this geisha,' said the Minister. 'I don't want another one.'

'Her name is Sayuri, and you'd better call her that, or she won't agree to come. Now stand up, Minister. It's time for us to get you home.'

I walked them as far as the entryway, where I helped them into their coats and shoes and watched the two of them set out in the snow. The Minister was having such a hard time, he would have trudged right into the gate if Nobu hadn't taken him by the elbow to steer him.

Later the same night, I dropped in with Mameha on a party full of American officers. By the time we arrived, their translator was of no use to anyone because they'd made him drink so much; but the officers all recognized Mameha. I was a bit surprised when they began humming and waving their arms, signaling to her that they wanted her to put on a dance. I expected we would sit quietly and watch her, but the moment she began, several of the officers went up and started prancing around alongside. If you'd told me it would happen, I might have felt a little uncertain beforehand; but to see it . . . well, I burst out laughing and enjoyed myself more than I had in a long while. We ended up playing a game in which Mameha and I took turns on the shamisen while the American officers danced around the table. Whenever we stopped the music,

417

they had to rush back to their places. The last to sit drank a penalty glass of sake.

In the middle of the party I commented to Mameha how peculiar it was to see everyone having so much fun without speaking the same language – considering that I'd been at a party with Nobu and another Japanese man earlier that evening, and we'd had an awful time. She asked me a bit about the party.

'Three people can certainly be too few,' she said after I'd told her about it, 'particularly if one of them is Nobu in a foul mood.'

'I suggested he bring the Chairman next time. And we need another geisha as well, don't you think? Someone loud and funny'

'Yes,' said Mameha, 'perhaps I'll stop by . . .'

I was puzzled at first to hear her say this. Because really, no one on earth would have described Mameha as 'loud and funny.' I was about to tell her again what I meant, when all at once she seemed to recognize our misunderstanding and said, 'Yes, I'm interested to stop by . . . but I suppose if you want someone loud and funny, you ought to speak to your old friend Pumpkin.'

Since returning to Gion, I'd encountered memories of Pumpkin everywhere. In fact, the very moment I'd stepped into the okiya for the first time, I'd remembered her there in the formal entrance hall on the day Gion had closed, when she'd given me a stiff farewell bow of the sort she was obliged to offer the adopted daughter. I'd gone on thinking of her again and again all during that week as we cleaned. At one point, while helping the maid wipe the dust from the woodwork, I pictured Pumpkin on the walkway right before me, practicing her shamisen. The empty space there seemed to hold a terrible sadness within it. Had it really been so many years since we were girls together? I suppose I might easily have put it all out of my mind, but I'd never quite learned to accept the disappointment of our friendship running dry. I blamed the terrible rivalry that Hatsumomo had forced upon us. My adoption was the final blow of course, but still I couldn't help holding myself partly accountable. Pumpkin had shown me only kindness. I might have found some way to thank her for that.

Strangely, I hadn't thought of approaching Pumpkin until Mameha suggested it. I had no doubt our first encounter would be awkward, but I mulled it over the rest of that night and decided that maybe Pumpkin would appreciate being introduced into a more elegant circle, as a change from the soldiers' parties. Of course, I had another motive as well. Now that so many years had passed, perhaps we might begin to mend our friendship.

I knew almost nothing about Pumpkin's circumstances, except that she was back in Gion, so I went to speak with Auntie, who had received a letter from her several years earlier. It turned out that in the letter, Pumpkin had pleaded to be taken back into the okiya when it reopened, saying she would never find a place for herself otherwise. Auntie might have been willing to do it, but Mother had refused on the grounds that Pumpkin was a poor investment.

'She's living in a sad little okiya over in the Hanami-cho section,' Auntie told me. 'But don't take pity on her and bring her back here for a visit. Mother won't want to see her. I think it's foolish for you to speak with her anyway.'

'I have to admit,' I said, 'I've never felt right about what happened between Pumpkin and me . . .'

'Nothing happened between you. Pumpkin fell short and you succeeded. Anyway, she's doing very well these days. I hear the Americans can't get enough of her. She's crude, you know, in just the right sort of way for them.'

That very afternoon I crossed Shijo Avenue to the Hanami-cho section of Gion, and found the sad little okiya Auntie had told me about. If you remember Hatsumomo's friend Korin, and how her okiya had burned during the darkest years of the war . . . well, that fire had damaged the okiya next door as well, and this was where Pumpkin was now living. Its exterior walls were charred all along one side, and a part of the tiled roof that had burned away was crudely patched with wooden boards. I suppose in sections of Tokyo or Osaka, it might have been the most intact building in the neighborhood; but it stood out in the middle of Kyoto.

A young maid showed me into a reception room that smelled of wet ash, and came back later to serve me a cup of weak tea. I waited a long while before Pumpkin at last came and slid open the door. I could scarcely see her in the dark hallway outside, but just knowing she was there made me feel such warmth, I rose from the table to go and embrace her. She took a few steps into the room and then knelt and gave a bow as formal as if I'd been Mother. I was startled by this, and stopped where I stood.

'Really, Pumpkin . . . it's only me!' I said.

She wouldn't even look at me, but kept her eyes to the mats like a maid awaiting orders. I felt very disappointed and went back to my place at the table.

When we'd last seen each other in the final years of the war, Pumpkin's face had still been round and full just as in childhood, but with a more sorrowful look. She had changed a great deal in the years since. I didn't know it at the time, but after the closing of the lens factory where she'd worked, Pumpkin spent more than two years in Osaka as a prostitute. Her mouth seemed to have shrunken in size – perhaps because she held it taut, I don't know. And though she had the same broad face, her heavy cheeks had thinned, leaving her with a gaunt elegance that was astonishing to me. I don't mean to suggest Pumpkin had become a beauty to rival Hatsumomo or anything of the sort, but her face had a certain woman-liness that had never been there before.

'I'm sure the years have been difficult, Pumpkin,' I said to her, 'but you look quite lovely.'

Pumpkin didn't reply to this. She just inclined her head faintly to indicate she'd heard me. I congratulated her on her popularity and tried asking about her life since the war; but she remained so expressionless that I began to feel sorry I'd come.

Finally after an awkward silence, she spoke.

'Have you come here just to chat, Sayuri? Because I don't have anything to say that will interest you.'

'The truth is,' I said, 'I saw Nobu Toshikazu recently and . . . actually, Pumpkin, he'll be bringing a certain man to Gion from time to time. I thought perhaps you'd be kind enough to help us entertain him.'

'But of course, you've changed your mind now that you've seen me.'

'Why, no,' I said. 'I don't know why you say that. Nobu Toshikazu and the Chairman – Iwamura Ken, I mean . . . Chairman Iwamura – would appreciate your company greatly. It's as simple as that.'

For a moment Pumpkin just knelt in silence, peering down at the mats. 'I've stopped believing that anything in life is "as simple as that," she said at last. 'I know you think I'm stupid –'

'Pumpkin!'

'– but I think you probably have some other reason you're not going to tell me about.'

Pumpkin gave a little bow, which I thought very enigmatic. Either it was an apology for what she'd just said, or perhaps she was about to excuse herself.

'I suppose I do have another reason,' I said. 'To tell the truth, I'd hoped that after all these years, perhaps you and I might be friends, as we once were. We've survived so many things together . . . including Hatsumomo! It seems only natural to me that we should see each other again.'

Pumpkin said nothing.

'Chairman Iwamura and Nobu will be entertaining the Minister again next Saturday at the Ichiriki Teahouse,' I told her. 'If you'll join us, I'd be very pleased to see you there.'

I'd brought her a packet of tea as a gift, and now I untied it from its silk cloth and placed it on the table. As I rose to my feet, I tried to think of something kind to tell her before leaving, but she looked so puzzled, I thought it best just to go.

31

IN THE FIVE or so years since I'd last seen the Chairman, I'd read from time to time in the newspapers about the difficulties he'd suffered – not only his disagreements with the military government in the final years of the war, but his struggle since then to keep the Occupation authorities from seizing his company. It wouldn't have surprised me if all these hardships had aged him a good deal. One photograph of him in the Yomiuri newspaper showed a strained look around his eyes from worry, like the neighbor of Mr. Arashino's who used to squint up at the sky so often, watching for bombers. In any case, as the weekend neared I had to remind myself that Nobu hadn't quite made up his mind that he would bring the Chairman. I could do nothing but hope.

On Saturday morning I awakened early and slid back the paper screen over my window to find a cold rain falling against the glass. In the little alleyway below, a young maid was just climbing to her feet again after slipping on the icy cobblestones. It was a drab, miserable day, and I was afraid even to read my almanac. By noon the temperature had dropped still further; and I could see my breath as I ate lunch in the reception room, with the sound of icy rain tapping against the window. Any number of parties that evening were canceled because the streets were too hazardous, and at nightfall Auntie telephoned the Ichiriki to be sure Iwamura Electric's party was still on. The mistress told us the telephone lines to Osaka were down, and she couldn't be sure. So I bathed and dressed, and walked over to the Ichiriki on the arm of Mr. Bekku, who wore a pair of rubber overshoes he'd borrowed from his younger brother, a dresser in the Pontocho district.

The Ichiriki was in chaos when I arrived. A water pipe had burst in the servants' quarters, and the maids were so busy, I couldn't get the attention of a single one. I showed myself down the hallway to the room where I'd entertained Nobu and the Minister the week before. I didn't really expect anyone to be there, considering that both Nobu and the Chairman would probably be traveling all the way from Osaka – and even Mameha had been out of town and might very well have had trouble returning. Before sliding open the door, I knelt a moment with my eyes closed and one hand on my stomach to calm my nerves. All at once it occurred to me that the hallway was much too quiet. I couldn't hear even a murmur from within the room. With a terrible feeling of disappointment I realized the room must be empty. I was about to stand and leave when I decided to slide open the door just in case; and when I did, there at the table, holding a magazine with both hands, sat the Chairman, looking at me over the top of his reading glasses. I was so startled to see him, I couldn't even speak. Finally I managed to say:

'My goodness, Chairman! Who has left you here all by yourself? The mistress will be very upset.'

'She's the one who left me,' he said, and slapped the magazine shut. 'I've been wondering what happened to her.'

'You don't even have a thing to drink. Let me bring you some sake.'

'That's just what the mistress said. At this rate you'll never come back, and I'll have to go on reading this magazine all night. I'd much rather have your company.' And here he removed his reading glasses, and while stowing them in his pocket, took a long look at me through narrowed eyes.

The spacious room with its pale yellow walls of silk began to seem very small to me as I rose to join the Chairman, for I don't think any room would have been enough to contain all that I was feeling. To see him again after so long awakened something desperate inside me. I was surprised to find myself feeling sad, rather than joyful, as I would have imagined. At times I'd worried that the Chairman might have fallen headlong into old age during the war just as Auntie had done. Even from across the room, I'd noticed that the corners of his eyes were creased more sharply than I remembered them. The skin around his mouth, too, had begun to sag, though it seemed to me to give his strong jaw a kind of dignity. I stole a glimpse of him as I knelt at the table, and found that he was still watching me without expression. I was about to start a conversation, but the Chairman spoke first.

'You are still a lovely woman, Sayuri.'

'Why, Chairman,' I said, 'I'll never believe another word you say. I had to spend a half hour at my makeup stand this evening to hide the sunken look of my cheeks.'

'I'm sure you've suffered worse hardships during the past several years than losing a bit of weight. I know I certainly have.'

'Chairman, if you don't mind my saying it . . . I've heard a little bit from Nobu-san about the difficulties your company is facing –'

'Yes, well, we needn't talk about that. Sometimes we get through adversity only by imagining what the world might be like if our dreams should ever come true.'

He gave me a sad smile that I found so beautiful, I lost myself staring at the perfect crescent of his lips.

'Here's a chance for you to use your charm and change the subject,' he said.

I hadn't even begun to reply before the door slid open and Mameha entered, with Pumpkin right behind her. I was surprised to see Pumpkin; I hadn't expected she would come. As for Mameha, she'd evidently just returned from Nagoya and had rushed to the Ichiriki thinking she was terribly late. The first thing she asked – after greeting the Chairman and thanking him for something he'd done for her the week before – was why Nobu and the Minister weren't present. The Chairman admitted he'd been wondering the same thing.

'What a peculiar day this has been,' Mameha said, talking almost to herself, it seemed. 'The train sat just outside Kyoto Station for an hour, and we couldn't get off. Two young men finally jumped out through the window. I think one of them may have hurt himself. And then when I finally reached the Ichiriki a moment ago, there didn't seem to be anyone here. Poor Pumpkin was wandering the hallways lost! You've met

Pumpkin, haven't you, Chairman?'

I hadn't really looked closely at Pumpkin until now, but she was wearing an extraordinary ash-gray kimono, which was spotted below the waist with brilliant gold dots that turned out to be embroidered fireflies, set against an image of mountains and water in the light of the moon. Neither mine nor Mameha's could compare with it. The Chairman seemed to find the robe as startling as I did, because he asked her to stand and model it for him. She stood very modestly and turned around once.

'I figured I couldn't set foot in a place like the Ichiriki in the sort of kimono I usually wear,' she said. 'Most of the ones at my okiya aren't very glamorous, though the Americans can't seem to tell the difference.'

'If you hadn't been so frank with us, Pumpkin,' Mameha said, 'we might have thought this was your usual attire.'

'Are you kidding me? I've never worn a robe this beautiful in my life. I borrowed it from an okiya down the street. You won't believe what they expect me to pay them, but I'll never have the money, so it doesn't make any difference, now does it?'

I could see that the Chairman was amused – because a geisha never spoke in front of a man about anything as crass as the cost of a kimono. Mameha turned to say something to him, but Pumpkin interrupted.

'I thought some big shot was going to be here tonight.'

'Maybe you were thinking of the Chairman,' Mameha said. 'Don't you think he's a "big shot"?'

'He knows whether he's a big shot. He doesn't need me to tell him.'

The Chairman looked at Mameha and raised his eyebrows in mock surprise. 'Anyway, Sayuri told me about some other guy,' Pumpkin went on.

'Sato Noritaka, Pumpkin,' the Chairman said. 'He's a new Deputy Minister of Finance.'

'Oh, I know that Sato guy. He looks just like a big pig.'

We all laughed at this. 'Really, Pumpkin,' Mameha said, 'the things that come out of your mouth!'

Just then the door slid open and Nobu and the Minister

entered, both glowing red from the cold. Behind them was a maid carrying a tray with sake and snacks. Nobu stood hugging himself with his one arm and stamping his feet, but the Minister just clumped right past him to the table. He grunted at Pumpkin and jerked his head to one side, telling her to move so he could squeeze in beside me. Introductions were made, and then Pumpkin said: 'Hey, Minister, I'll bet you don't remember me, but I know a lot about you.'

The Minister tossed into his mouth the cupful of sake I'd just poured for him, and looked at Pumpkin with what I took to be a scowl.

'What do you know?' said Mameha. 'Tell us something.'

'I know the Minister has a younger sister who's married to the mayor of Tokyo,' Pumpkin said. 'And I know he used to study karate, and broke his hand once.'

The Minister looked a bit surprised, which told me that these things must be true.

'Also, Minister, I know a girl you used to know,' Pumpkin went on. 'Nao Itsuko. We worked in a factory outside Osaka together. You know what she told me? She said the two of you did "you-know-what" together a couple of times.'

I was afraid the Minister would be angry, but instead his expression softened until I began to see what I felt certain was a glimmer of pride.

'She was a pretty girl, she was, that Itsuko,' he said, looking at Nobu with a subdued smile.

'Why, Minister,' Nobu replied, 'I'd never have guessed you had such a way with the ladies.' His words sounded very sincere, but I could see the barely concealed look of disgust on his face. The Chairman's eyes passed over mine; he seemed to find the whole encounter amusing.

A moment later the door slid open and three maids came into the room carrying dinner for the men. I was a bit hungry and had to avert my eyes from the sight of the yellow custard with gingko nuts, served in beautiful celadon cups. Later the maids came back with dishes of grilled tropical fish laid out on beds of pine needles. Nobu must have noticed how hungry I looked, for he insisted I taste it. Afterward the Chairman offered a bite to Mameha, and also to Pumpkin, who refused.

'I wouldn't touch that fish for anything,' Pumpkin said. 'I don't even want to look at it.'

'What's wrong with it?' Mameha asked.

'If I tell you, you'll only laugh at me.'

'Tell us, Pumpkin,' Nobu said.

'Why should I tell you? It's a big, long story, and anyway nobody's going to believe it.'

'Big liar!' I said.

I wasn't actually calling Pumpkin a liar. Back before the closing of Gion, we used to play a game we called 'big liar,' in which everyone had to tell two stories, only one of which was true. Afterward the other players tried to guess which was which; the ones who guessed wrong drank a penalty glass of sake.

'I'm not playing,' said Pumpkin.

'Just tell the fish story then,' said Mameha, 'and you don't have to tell another.'

Pumpkin didn't look pleased at this; but after Mameha and I had glowered at her for a while, she began.

'Oh, all right. It's like this. I was born in Sapporo, and there was an old fisherman there who caught a weird-looking fish one day that was able to speak.'

Mameha and I looked at each other and burst out laughing.

'Laugh if you want to,' Pumpkin said, 'but it's perfectly true.'

'Now, go on, Pumpkin. We're listening,' said the Chairman.

'Well, what happened was, this fisherman laid the fish out to clean it, and it began making noises that sounded just like a person talking, except the fisherman couldn't understand it. He called a bunch of other fishermen over, and they all listened for a while. Pretty soon the fish was nearly dead from being out of the water too long, so they decided to go ahead and kill it. But just then an old man made his way through the crowd and said he could understand every single word the fish was saying, because it was speaking in Russian.'

We all burst out laughing, and even the Minister made a few grunting noises. When we'd calmed down Pumpkin said, 'I knew you wouldn't believe it, but it's perfectly true!'

'I want to know what the fish was saying,' said the Chairman.

'It was nearly dead, so it was kind of . . . whispering. And when the old man leaned down and put his ear to the fish's lips –'

'Fish don't have lips!' I said.

'All right, to the fish's . . . whatever you call those things,' Pumpkin went on. 'To the edges of its mouth. And the fish said, "Tell them to go ahead and clean me. I have nothing to live for any longer. The fish over there who died a moment ago was my wife."'

'So fish get married!' said Mameha. 'They have husbands and wives!'

'That was before the war,' I said. 'Since the war, they can't afford to marry. They just swim around looking for work.'

'This happened way before the war,' said Pumpkin. 'Way, way before the war. Even before my mother was born.'

'Then how do you know it's true?' said Nobu. 'The fish certainly didn't tell it to you.'

'The fish died then and there! How could it tell me if I wasn't born yet? Besides, I don't speak Russian.'

'All right, Pumpkin,' I said, 'so you believe the Chairman's fish is a talking fish too.'

'I didn't say that. But it looks *exactly* like that talking fish did. I wouldn't eat it if I was starving to death.'

'If you hadn't been born yet,' said the Chairman, 'and even your mother hadn't been born, how do you know what the fish looked like?'

'You know what the Prime Minister looks like, don't you?' she said. 'But have you ever met him? Actually, you probably have. Let me pick a better example. You know what the Emperor looks like, but you've never had the honor of meeting him!'

'The Chairman has had the honor, Pumpkin,' Nobu said.

'You know what I mean. Everybody knows what the Emperor looks like. That's what I'm trying to say.'

'There are pictures of the Emperor,' said Nobu. 'You can't have seen a picture of the fish.'

'The fish is famous where I grew up. My mother told me all

428

about it, and I'm telling you, it looks like that thing right there on the table!'

'Thank heavens for people like you, Pumpkin,' said the Chairman. 'You make the rest of us seem positively dull.'

'Well, that's my story. I'm not telling another one. If the rest of you want to play "big liar," somebody else can start.'

'I'll start,' said Mameha. 'Here's my first story. When I was about six years old I went out one morning to draw water from the well in our okiya, and I heard the sound of a man clearing his throat and coughing. It was coming from inside the well. I woke up the mistress, and she came out to listen to it. When we held a lantern over the well, we couldn't find anyone there at all, but we continued to hear him until after the sun had come up. Then the sounds stopped and we never heard them again.'

'The other story is the true one,' said Nobu, 'and I haven't even heard it.'

'You have to listen to them both,' Mameha went on. 'Here's my second. One time I went with several geisha to Osaka to entertain at the home of Akita Masaichi.' He was a famous businessman who'd made a fortune before the war. 'After we sang and drank for hours, Akita-san fell asleep on the mats, and one of the other geisha snuck us into the next room and opened a big chest full of all kinds of pornography. There were pornographic woodblock prints, including some by Hiroshige –'

'Hiroshige never made pornographic prints,' said Pumpkin.

'Yes, he did, Pumpkin,' the Chairman said. 'I've seen some of them.'

'And also,' Mameha went on, 'he had pictures of all sorts of fat European women and men, and some reels of movies.'

'I knew Akita Masaichi well,' said the Chairman. 'He wouldn't have had a collection of pornography. The other one is true.'

'Now, really, Chairman,' Nobu said. 'You believe a story about a man's voice coming out of a well?'

'I don't have to believe it. All that matters is whether Mameha thinks it's true.'

Pumpkin and the Chairman voted for the man in the well.

The Minister and Nobu voted for the pornography. As for me, I'd heard both of these before and knew that the man in the well was the true one. The Minister drank his penalty glass without complaining; but Nobu grumbled all the while, so we made him go next.

'I'm not going to play this game,' he said.

'You're going to play it, or you're going to drink a penalty glass of sake every round,' Mameha told him.

'All right, you want two stories, I'll tell you two stories,' he said. 'Here's the first one. I've got a little white dog, named Kubo. One night I came home, and Kubo's fur was completely blue.'

'I believe it,' said Pumpkin. 'It had probably been kidnapped by some sort of demon.'

Nobu looked as if he couldn't quite imagine that Pumpkin was serious. 'The next day it happened again,' he went on tentatively, 'only this time Kubo's fur was bright red.'

'Definitely demons,' said Pumpkin. 'Demons love red. It's the color of blood.'

Nobu began to look positively angry when he heard this. 'Here's my second story. Last week I went to the office so early in the morning that my secretary hadn't yet arrived. All right, which is the true one?'

Of course, we all chose the secretary except for Pumpkin, who was made to drink a penalty glass of sake. And I don't mean a cup; I mean a glass. The Minister poured it for her, adding drop by drop after the glass was full, until it was bulging over the rim. Pumpkin had to sip it before she could pick the glass up. I felt worried just watching her, for she had a very low tolerance for alcohol.

'I can't believe the story about the dog isn't true,' she said after she'd finished the glass. Already I thought I could hear her words slurring a bit. 'How could you make something like that up?'

'How could I make it up? The question is, how could you believe it? Dogs don't turn blue. Or red. And there aren't demons.'

It was my turn to go next. 'My first story is this. One night some years ago, the Kabuki actor Yoegoro got very drunk and

430

told me he'd always found me beautiful.'

'This one isn't true,' Pumpkin said. 'I know Yoegoro.'

'I'm sure you do. But nevertheless, he told me he found me beautiful, and ever since that night, he's sent me letters from time to time. In the corner of every letter, he glues one little curly black hair.'

The Chairman laughed at this, but Nobu sat up, looking angry; and said, 'Really, these Kabuki actors. What irritating people!'

'I don't get it. What do you mean a *curly* black hair?' Pumpkin said; but you could see from her expression that she figured out the answer right away.

Everyone fell silent, waiting for my second story. It had been on my mind since we'd started playing the game, though I was nervous about telling it, and not at all certain it was the right thing to do.

'Once when I was a child,' I began, 'I was very upset one day, and I went to the banks of the Shirakawa Stream and began to cry . . .'

As I began this story, I felt almost as though I were reaching across the table to touch the Chairman on the hand. Because it seemed to me that no one else in the room would see anything unusual in what I was saying, whereas the Chairman would understand this very private story – or at least, I hoped he would. I felt I was having a conversation with him more intimate than any we'd ever had; and I could feel myself growing warm as I spoke. Just before continuing, I glanced up, expecting to find the Chairman looking at me quizzically. Instead, he didn't seem even to be paying attention. All at once I felt so vain, like a girl posturing for the crowds as she walks along, only to discover the street is empty.

I'm sure everyone in the room had grown tired of waiting for me by this time, because Mameha said, 'Well? Go on.' Pumpkin mumbled something too, but I couldn't understand her.

'I'm going to tell another story,' I said. 'Do you remember the geisha Okaichi? She died in an accident during the war. Many years before, she and I were talking one day, and she told me she'd always been afraid a heavy wooden box would

431

fall right onto her head and kill her. And that's exactly how she died. A crate full of scrap metal fell from a shelf.'

I'd been so preoccupied, I didn't realize until this moment that neither of my stories was true. Both were partially true; but it didn't concern me very much in any case, because most people cheated while playing this game. So I waited until the Chairman had chosen a story – which was the one about Yoegoro and the curly hair – and declared him right. Pumpkin and the Minister had to drink penalty glasses of sake.

After this it was the Chairman's turn.

'I'm not very good at this sort of game,' he said. 'Not like you geisha, who are so adept at lying.'

'Chairman!' said Mameha, but of course she was only teasing.

'I'm concerned about Pumpkin, so I'm going to make this simple. If she has to drink another glass of sake, I don't think she'll make it.'

It was true that Pumpkin was having trouble focusing her eyes. I don't even think she was listening to the Chairman until he said her name.

'Just listen closely, Pumpkin. Here's my first story. This evening I came to attend a party at the Ichiriki Teahouse. And here's my second. Several days ago, a fish came walking into my office – no, forget that. You might even believe in a walking fish. How about this one. Several days ago, I opened my desk drawer; and a little man jumped out wearing a uniform and began to sing and dance. All right, now which one is true?'

'You don't expect me to believe a man jumped out of your drawer,' Pumpkin said.

'Just pick one of the stories. Which is true?'

'The other one. I don't remember what it was.'

'We ought to make you drink a penalty glass for that, Chairman,' said Mameha.

When Pumpkin heard the words 'penalty glass,' she must have assumed she'd done something wrong, because the next thing we knew, she'd drunk half a glassful of sake, and she wasn't looking well. The Chairman was the first to notice, and took the glass right out of her hand.

'You're not a drain spout, Pumpkin.' the Chairman said. She stared at him so blankly, he asked if she could hear him.

'She might be able to hear you,' Nobu said, 'but she certainly can't see you.'

'Come on, Pumpkin,' the Chairman said. 'I'm going to walk you to your home. Or drag you, if I have to.'

Mameha offered to help, and the two of them led Pumpkin out together, leaving Nobu and the Minister sitting at the table with me.

'Well, Minister,' Nobu said at last, 'how was your evening?'

I think the Minister was every bit as drunk as Pumpkin had been; but he muttered that the evening had been very enjoyable. 'Very enjoyable, indeed,' he added, nodding a couple of times. After this, he held out his sake cup for me to fill, but Nobu plucked it from his hand.

32

ALL THROUGH THAT winter and the following spring, Nobu went on bringing the Minister to Gion once or even twice every week. Considering how much time the two of them spent together during these months, you'd think the Minister would eventually have realized that Nobu felt toward him just as an ice pick feels toward a block of ice; but if he did, he never showed the least sign. To tell the truth, the Minister never seemed to notice much of anything, except whether I was kneeling beside him and whether his cup was full of sake. This devotion made my life difficult at times; when I paid too much attention to the Minister, Nobu grew short-tempered, and the side of his face with less scarring turned a brilliant red from anger. This was why the presence of the Chairman, Mameha, and Pumpkin was so valuable to me. They played the same role straw plays in a packing crate.

Of course I valued the Chairman's presence for another reason as well. I saw more of him during these months than I'd ever seen of him before, and over time I came to realize that the image of him in my mind, whenever I lay on my futon at night, wasn't really how he looked, not exactly. For example, I'd always pictured his eyelids smooth with almost no lashes at all; but in fact they were edged with dense, soft hair like little brushes. And his mouth was far more expressive than I'd ever realized – so expressive, in fact, that he often hid his feelings only very poorly. When he was amused by something but didn't want to show it, I could nevertheless spot his mouth quivering in the corners. Or when he was lost in thought – mulling over some problem he'd encountered during the day, perhaps – he sometimes turned a sake cup around and around in his hand and put his mouth into a deep frown that made creases all the way down the sides of his chin. Whenever he was carried away in this state I considered myself free to stare at him unabashedly. Something about his frown, and its deep furrows, I came to find inexpressibly handsome. It seemed to show how thoroughly he thought about things, and how seriously he was taken in the world. One evening while Mameha was telling a long story, I gave myself over so completely to staring at the Chairman that when I finally came to myself again, I realized that anyone watching me would have wondered what I was doing. Luckily the Minister was too dazed with drink to have noticed; as for Nobu, he was chewing a bite of something and poking around on the plate with his chopsticks, paying no attention either to Mameha or to me. Pumpkin, though, seemed to have been watching me all along. When I looked at her, she wore a smile I wasn't sure how to interpret.

One evening toward the end of February, Pumpkin came down with the flu and was unable to join us at the Ichiriki. The Chairman was late that night as well, so Mameha and I spent an hour entertaining Nobu and the Minister by ourselves. We finally decided to put on a dance, more for our own benefit than for theirs. Nobu wasn't much of a devotee, and the Minister had no interest at all. It wasn't our first choice as a way to pass the time, but we couldn't think of anything better.

First Mameha performed a few brief pieces while I accompanied her on the shamisen. Afterward we exchanged places. Just as I was taking up the starting pose for my first dance – my torso bent so that my folding fan reached toward the ground and my other arm stretched out to one side – the door slid open and the Chairman entered. We greeted him and waited while he took a seat at the table. I was delighted he'd arrived, because although I knew he'd seen me on the stage, he'd certainly never watched me dance in a setting as intimate as this one. At first I'd intended to perform a short piece called 'Shimmering Autumn Leaves,' but now I changed my mind and asked Mameha to play 'Cruel Rain' instead. The story behind 'Cruel Rain' is of a young woman who feels deeply moved when her lover takes off his kimono jacket to cover her during a rainstorm, because she knows him to be an enchanted spirit whose body will melt away if he becomes wet. My teachers had often complimented me on the way I expressed the woman's feelings of sorrow; during the section when I had to sink slowly to my knees, I rarely allowed my legs to tremble as most dancers did. Probably I've mentioned this already, but in dances of the Inoue School the facial expression is as important as the movement of the arms or legs. So although I'd like to have stolen glances at the Chairman as I was dancing, I had to keep my eyes positioned properly at all times, and was never able to do it. Instead, to help give feeling to my dance, I focused my mind on the saddest thing I could think of, which was to imagine that my *danna* was there in the room with me – not the Chairman, but rather Nobu. The moment I formulated this thought, everything around me seemed to droop heavily toward the earth. Outside in the garden, the eaves of the roof dripped rain like beads of weighted glass. Even the mats themselves seemed to press down upon the floor. I remember thinking that I was dancing to express not the pain of a young woman who has lost her supernatural lover, but the pain I myself would feel when my life was finally robbed of the one thing I cared most deeply about. I found myself thinking, too, of Satsu; I danced the bitterness of our eternal separation. By the end I felt almost overcome with grief; but I certainly wasn't prepared for what I saw when I turned to look at the Chairman.

He was sitting at the near corner of the table so that, as it happened, no one but me could see him. I thought he wore an expression of astonishment at first, because his eyes were so wide. But just as his mouth sometimes twitched when he tried not to smile, now I could see it twitching under the strain of a different emotion. I couldn't be sure, but I had the impression his eyes were heavy with tears. He looked toward the door, pretending to scratch the side of his nose so he could wipe a finger in the corner of his eye; and he smoothed his eyebrows as though they were the source of his trouble. I was so shocked to see the Chairman in pain that I felt almost disoriented for a moment. I made my way back to the table, and Mameha and Nobu began to talk. After a moment the Chairman interrupted.

'Where is Pumpkin this evening?'

'Oh, she's ill, Chairman,' said Mameha.

'What do you mean? Won't she be here at all?'

'No, not at all,' Mameha said. 'And it's a good thing, considering she has the stomach flu.'

Mameha went back to talking. I saw the Chairman glance at his wristwatch and then, with his voice still unsteady, he said:

'Mameha, you'll have to excuse me. I'm not feeling very well myself this evening.'

Nobu said something funny just as the Chairman was sliding the door shut, and everyone laughed. But I was thinking a thought that frightened me. In my dance, I'd tried to express the pain of absence. Certainly I had upset myself doing it, but I'd upset the Chairman too; and was it possible he'd been thinking of Pumpkin – who, after all, was absent? I couldn't imagine him on the brink of tears over Pumpkin's illness, or any such thing, but perhaps I'd stirred up some darker, more complicated feelings. All I knew was that when my dance ended, the Chairman asked about Pumpkin; and he left when he learned she was ill. I could hardly bring myself to believe it. If I'd made the discovery that the Chairman had developed feelings for Mameha, I wouldn't have been surprised. But Pumpkin? How could the Chairman long for someone so . . . well, so lacking in refinement?

You might think that any woman with common sense ought to have given up her hopes at this point. And I did for a time go to the fortune-teller every day, and read my almanac more carefully even than usual, searching for some sign whether I should submit to what seemed my inevitable destiny. Of course, we Japanese were living in a decade of crushed hopes. I wouldn't have found it surprising if mine had died off just like so many other people's. But on the other hand, many believed the country itself would one day rise again; and we all knew such a thing could never happen if we resigned ourselves to living forever in the rubble. Every time I happened to read an account in the newspaper of some little shop that had made, say, bicycle parts before the war, and was now back in business almost as though the war had never happened, I had to tell myself that if our entire nation could emerge from its own dark valley, there was certainly hope that I could emerge from mine.

Beginning that March and running all through the spring, Mameha and I were busy with *Dances of the Old Capital*, which was being staged again for the first time since Gion had closed in the final years of the war. As it happened, the Chairman and Nobu grew busy as well during these months, and brought the Minister to Gion only twice. Then one day during the first week of June, I heard that my presence at the Ichiriki Teahouse had been requested early that evening by Iwamura Electric. I had an engagement booked weeks before that I couldn't easily miss; so by the time I finally slid open the door to join the party, I was half an hour late. To my surprise, instead of the usual group around the table, I found only Nobu and the Minister.

I could see at once that Nobu was angry. Of course, I imagined he was angry at me for making him spend so much time alone with the Minister – though to tell the truth, the two of them weren't 'spending time together' any more than a squirrel is spending time with the insects that live in the same tree. Nobu was drumming his fingers on the tabletop, wearing a very cross expression, while the Minister stood at the window gazing out at the garden.

'All right, Minister!' Nobu said, when I'd settled myself at the table. 'That's enough of watching the bushes grow. Are we supposed to sit here and wait for you all night?'

The Minister was startled, and gave a little bow of apology before coming to take his place on a cushion I'd set out for him. Usually I had difficulty thinking of anything to say to him, but tonight my task was easier since I hadn't seen him in so long.

'Minister,' I said, 'you don't like me anymore!'

'Eh?' said the Minister, who managed to rearrange his features so they showed a look of surprise.

'You haven't been to see me in more than a month! Is it because Nobu-san has been unkind, and hasn't brought you to Gion as often as he should have?'

'Nobu-san isn't unkind,' said the Minister. He blew several breaths up his nose before adding, 'I've asked too much of him already.'

'Keeping you away for a month? He certainly is unkind. We have so much to catch up on.'

'Yes,' Nobu interrupted, 'mostly a lot of drinking.'

'My goodness, but Nobu-san is grouchy tonight. Has he been this way all evening? And where are the Chairman, and Mameha and Pumpkin? Won't they be joining us?'

'The Chairman isn't available this evening,' Nobu said. 'I don't know where the others are. They're your problem, not mine.'

In a moment, the door slid back, and two maids entered carrying dinner trays for the men. I did my best to keep them company while they ate – which is to say, I tried for a while to get Nobu to talk; but he wasn't in a talking mood; and then I tried to get the Minister to talk, but of course, it would have been easier to get a word or two out of the grilled minnow on his plate. So at length I gave up and just chattered away about whatever I wanted, until I began to feel like an old lady talking to her two dogs. All this while I poured sake as liberally as I could for both men. Nobu didn't drink much, but the Minister held his cup out gratefully every time. Just as the Minister was beginning to take on that glassy-eyed look, Nobu, like a man who has just woken up, suddenly put his own cup firmly on the table, wiped his mouth with his napkin, and said:

'All right, Minister, that's enough for one evening. It's time for you to be heading home.'

'Nobu-san!' I said. 'I have the impression your guest is just beginning to enjoy himself.'

'He's enjoyed himself plenty. We're sending him home early for once, thank heavens. Come on, then, Minister! Your wife will be grateful.'

'I'm not married,' said the Minister. But already he was pulling up his socks and getting ready to stand.

I led Nobu and the Minister up the hallway to the entrance, and helped the Minister into his shoes. Taxis were still uncommon because of gasoline rationing, but the maid summoned a rickshaw and I helped the Minister into it. Already I'd noticed that he was acting a bit strangely, but this evening he pointed his eyes at his knees and wouldn't even say good-bye. Nobu remained in the entryway, glowering out into the night as if he were watching clouds gather, though in fact it was a clear evening. When the Minister had left, I said to him, 'Nobu-san, what in heaven's name is the matter with the two of you?'

He gave me a look of disgust and walked back into the teahouse. I found him in the room, tapping his empty sake cup on the table with his one hand. I thought he wanted sake, but he ignored me when I asked – and the vial turned out to be empty, in any case. I waited a long moment, thinking he had something to say to me, but finally I spoke up.

'Look at you, Nobu-san. You have a wrinkle between your eyes as deep as a rut in the road.'

He let the muscles around his eyes relax a bit, so that the wrinkle seemed to dissolve. 'I'm not as young as I once was, you know,' he told me.

'What is that supposed to mean?'

'It means there are some wrinkles that have become permanent features, and they aren't going to go away just because you say they should.'

'There are good wrinkles and bad wrinkles, Nobu-san. Never forget it.'

'You aren't as young as you once were yourself, you know.'

'Now you've stooped to insulting me! You're in a worse mood even than I'd feared. Why isn't there any alcohol here? You need a drink.'

'I'm not insulting you. I'm stating a fact.'

'There are good wrinkles and bad wrinkles, and there are good facts and bad facts,' I said. 'The bad facts are best avoided.'

I found a maid and asked that she bring a tray with scotch and water, as well as some dried squid as a snack – for it had struck me that Nobu hadn't eaten much of his dinner. When

440

the tray arrived, I poured scotch into a glass, filled it with water; and put it before him.

'There,' I said, 'now pretend that's medicine, and drink it.' He took a sip; but only a very small one. 'All of it,' I said.

'I'll drink it at my own pace.'

'When a doctor orders a patient to take medicine, the patient takes the medicine. Now drink up!'

Nobu drained the glass, but he wouldn't look at me as he did it. Afterward I poured more and ordered him to drink again.

'You're not a doctor!' he said to me. 'I'll drink at my own pace.'

'Now, now, Nobu-san. Every time you open your mouth, you get into worse trouble. The sicker the patient, the more the medication.'

'I won't do it. I hate drinking alone.'

'All right, I'll join you,' I said. I put some ice cubes in a glass and held it up for Nobu to fill. He wore a little smile when he took the glass from me – certainly the first smile I'd seen on him all evening – and very carefully poured twice as much scotch as I'd poured into his, topped by a splash of water. I took his glass from him, dumped its contents into a bowl in the center of the table, and then refilled it with the same amount of scotch he'd put into mine, plus an extra little shot as punishment.

While we drained our glasses, I couldn't help making a face; I find drinking scotch about as pleasurable as slurping up rainwater off the roadside. I suppose making these faces was all for the best, because afterward Nobu looked much less grumpy. When I'd caught my breath again, I said, 'I don't know what has gotten into you this evening. Or the Minister for that matter.'

'Don't mention that man! I was beginning to forget about him, and now you've reminded me. Do you know what he said to me earlier?'

'Nobu-san,' I said, 'it is my responsibility to cheer you up, whether you want more scotch or not. You've watched the Minister get drunk night after night. Now it's time you got drunk yourself.'

Nobu gave me another disagreeable look, but he took up his glass like a man beginning his walk to the execution ground, and looked at it for a long moment before drinking it all down. He put it on the table and afterward rubbed his eyes with the back of his hand as if he were trying to clear them.

'Sayuri,' he said, 'I must tell you something. You're going to hear about it sooner or later. Last week the Minister and I had a talk with the proprietress of the Ichiriki. We made an inquiry about the possibility of the Minister becoming your *danna*.'

'The Minister?' I said. 'Nobu-san, I don't understand. Is that what you wish to see happen?'

'Certainly not. But the Minister has helped us immeasurably, and I had no choice. The Occupation authorities were prepared to make their final judgment *against* Iwamura Electric, you know. The company would have been seized. I suppose the Chairman and I would have learned to pour concrete or something, for we would never have been permitted to work in business again. However, the Minister made them reopen our case, and managed to persuade them we were being dealt with much too harshly. Which is the truth, you know.'

'Yet Nobu-san keeps calling the Minister all sorts of names,' I said. 'It seems to me –'

'He deserves to be called any name I can think of! I don't like the man, Sayuri. It doesn't make me like him any better to know I'm in his debt.'

'I see,' I said. 'So I was to be given to the Minister because –'

'No one was trying to give you to the Minister. He could never have afforded to be your *danna* anyway. I led him to believe Iwamura Electric would be willing to pay – which of course we wouldn't have been. I knew the answer beforehand or I wouldn't have asked the question. The Minister was terribly disappointed, you know. For an instant I felt almost sorry for him.'

There was nothing funny in what Nobu had said. And yet I couldn't help but laugh, because I had a sudden image in my mind of the Minister as my *danna*, leaning in closer and closer to me, with his lower jaw sticking out, until suddenly his breath blew up my nose.

'Oh, so you find it funny, do you?' Nobu said to me.

'Really, Nobu-san . . . I'm sorry but to picture the Minister –'

'I don't want to picture the Minister! It's bad enough to have sat there beside him, talking with the mistress of the Ichiriki.'

I made another scotch and water for Nobu, and he made one for me. It was the last thing I wanted; already the room seemed cloudy. But Nobu raised his glass, and I had no choice but to drink with him. Afterward he wiped his mouth with his napkin and said, 'It's a terrible time to be alive, Sayuri.'

'Nobu-san, I thought we were drinking to cheer ourselves up.'

'We've certainly known each other a long time, Sayuri. Maybe . . . fifteen years! Is that right?' he said. 'No, don't answer. I want to tell you something, and you're going to sit right there and listen to it. I've wanted to tell you this a long while, and now the time has come. I hope you're listening, because I'm only going to say it once. Here's the thing: I don't much like geisha; probably you know that already. But I've always felt that you, Sayuri, aren't exactly like all the others.'

I waited a moment for Nobu to continue, but he didn't.

'Is that what Nobu-san wanted to tell me?' I asked.

'Well, doesn't that suggest that I ought to have done all kinds of things for you? For example . . . ha! For example, I ought to have bought you jewelry.'

'You have bought me jewelry. In fact, you've always been much too kind. To me, that is; you certainly aren't kind to everybody.'

'Well, I ought to have bought you more of it. Anyway, that isn't what I'm talking about. I'm having trouble explaining myself. What I'm trying to say is, I've come to understand what a fool I am. You laughed earlier at the idea of having the Minister for a *danna*. But just look at me: a one-armed man with skin like – what do they call me, the lizard?'

'Oh, Nobu-san, you must never talk about yourself that way . . .'

'The moment has finally come. I've been waiting years. I

443

had to wait all through your nonsense with that General. Every time I imagined him with you . . . well, I don't even want to think about that. And the very idea of this foolish Minister! Did I tell you what he said to me this evening? This is the worst thing of all. After he found out he wasn't going to be your *danna*, he sat there a long while like a pile of dirt, and then finally said, "I thought you told me I could be Sayuri's *danna*." Well, I hadn't said any such thing! "We did the best we could, Minister, and it didn't work out," I told him. So then he said, "Could you arrange it just once?" I said, "Arrange what once? For you to be Sayuri's *danna* just once? You mean, one evening?" And then he nodded! Well, I said, "You listen to me, Minister! It was bad enough going to the mistress of the teahouse to propose a man like you as *danna* to a woman like Sayuri. I only did it because I knew it wouldn't happen. But if you think –" '

'You didn't say that!'

'I certainly did. I said, "But if you think I would arrange for you to have even a quarter of a second alone with her . . . Why should you have her? And anyway, she isn't mine to give, is she? To think that I would go to her and ask such a thing!"'

'Nobu-san, I hope the Minister didn't take this too badly, considering all he's done for Iwamura Electric.'

'Now wait just a moment. I won't have you thinking I'm ungrateful. The Minister helped us because it was his job to help us. I've treated him well these past months, and I won't stop now. But that doesn't mean I have to give up what I've waited more than ten years for, and let him have it instead! What if I'd come to you as he wanted me to? Would you have said, "All right, Nobu-san, I'll do it for you"?'

'Please . . . How can I answer such a question?'

'Easily. Just tell me you would never have done such a thing.'

'But Nobu-san, I owe such a debt to you . . . If you asked a favor of me, I could never turn it down lightly.'

'Well, this is new! Have you changed, Sayuri, or has there always been a part of you I didn't know?'

'I've often thought Nobu-san has much too high an opinion of me . . .'

'I don't misjudge people. If you aren't the woman I think you are, then this isn't the world I thought it was. Do you mean to say you could consider giving yourself to a man like the Minister? Don't you feel there's right and wrong in this world, and good and bad? Or have you spent too much of your life in Gion?'

'My goodness, Nobu-san . . . it's been years since I've seen you so enraged . . .'

This must have been exactly the wrong thing to say because all at once Nobu's face flared in anger. He grabbed his glass in his one hand and slammed it down so hard it cracked, spilling ice cubes onto the tabletop. Nobu turned his hand to see a line of blood across his palm.

'Oh, Nobu-san!'

'Answer me!'

'I can't even think of the question right now . . . please, I have to go fetch something for your hand –'

'Would you give yourself to the Minister, no matter who asked it of you? If you're a woman who would do such a thing, I want you to leave this room right now and never speak to me again!'

I couldn't understand how the evening had taken this dangerous turn; but it was perfectly clear to me I could give only one answer. I was desperate to fetch a cloth for Nobu's hand – his blood had trickled onto the table already – but he was looking at me with such intensity I didn't dare to move.

'I would never do such a thing,' I said.

I thought this would calm him, but for a long, frightening moment he continued to glower at me. Finally he let out his breath.

'Next time, speak up before I have to cut myself for an answer.'

I rushed out of the room to fetch the mistress. She came with several maids and a bowl of water and towels. Nobu wouldn't let her call a doctor; and to tell the truth, the cut wasn't as bad as I'd feared. After the mistress left, Nobu was strangely silent. I tried to begin a conversation, but he showed no interest.

'First I can't calm you down,' I said at last, 'and now I can't get you to speak. I don't know whether to make you drink more, or if the liquor itself is the problem.'

'We've had enough liquor, Sayuri. It's time you went and brought back that rock.'

'What rock?'

'The one I gave you last fall. The piece of concrete from the factory. Go and bring it.'

I felt my skin turn to ice when I heard this – because I knew perfectly well what he was saying. The time had come for Nobu to propose himself as my *danna*.

'Oh, honestly, I've had so much to drink, I don't know whether I can walk at all!' I said. 'Perhaps Nobu-san will let me bring it the next time we see each other?'

'You'll get it tonight. Why do you think I stayed on after the Minister left? Go get it while I wait here for you.'

I thought of sending a maid to retrieve the rock for me; but I knew I could never tell her where to find it. So with some difficulty I made my way down the hall, slid my feet into my shoes, and sloshed my way – as it felt to me, in my drunken state – through the streets of Gion.

When I reached the okiya, I went to my room and found the piece of concrete, wrapped in a square of silk and stowed on a shelf of my closet. I unwrapped it and left the silk on the floor; though I don't know exactly why. As I left, Auntie – who must have heard me stumbling and come up to see what was the matter – met me in the upstairs hallway and asked why I was carrying a rock in my hand.

'I'm taking it to Nobu-san, Auntie,' I said. 'Please, stop me!'

'You're drunk, Sayuri. What's gotten into you this evening?'

'I have to give it back to him. And . . . oh, it will be the end of my life if I do. Please stop me.'

'Drunk, and sobbing. You're worse than Hatsumomo! You can't go back out like this.'

'Then please call the Ichiriki. And have them tell Nobu-san I won't be there. Will you?'

'Why is Nobu-san waiting for you to bring him a rock?'

'I can't explain. I can't . . .'

'It makes no difference. If he's waiting for you, you'll have to go,' she said to me, and led me by the arm back into my room, where she dried my face with a cloth and touched up my makeup by the light of an electric lantern. I was limp while she did it; she had to support my chin in her hand to keep my head from rolling. She grew so impatient that she finally grabbed my head with both hands and made it clear she wanted me to keep it still.

'I hope I never see you acting this way again, Sayuri. Heaven knows what's come over you.'

'I'm a fool, Auntie.'

'You've certainly been a fool this evening,' she said. 'Mother will be very angry if you've done something to spoil Nobu-san's affection for you.'

'I haven't yet,' I said. 'But if you can think of anything that will . . .'

'That's no way to talk,' Auntie said to me. And she didn't speak another word until she was finished with my makeup.

I made my way back to the Ichiriki Teahouse, holding that heavy rock in both my hands. I don't know whether it was really heavy, or whether my arms were simply heavy from too much to drink. But by the time I joined Nobu in the room again, I felt I'd used up all the energy I had. If he spoke to me about becoming his mistress, I wasn't at all sure I would be able to dam up my feelings.

I set the rock on the table. Nobu picked it up with his fingers and held it in the towel wrapped around his hand.

'I hope I didn't promise you a jewel this big,' he said. 'I don't have that much money. But things are possible now that weren't possible before.'

I bowed and tried not to look upset. Nobu didn't need to tell me what he meant.

33

THAT VERY NIGHT while I lay on my futon with the room swaying around I me, I made up my mind to be like the fisherman who hour after hour scoops out fish with his net. Whenever thoughts of the Chairman drifted up from within me, I would scoop them out, and scoop them out again, and again, until none of them were left. It would have been a clever system, I'm sure, if I could have made it work. But when I had even a single thought of him, I could never catch it before it sped away and carried me to the very place from which I'd banished my thoughts. Many times I stopped myself and said: Don't think of the Chairman, think of Nobu instead. And very deliberately, I pictured myself meeting Nobu somewhere in Kyoto. But then something always went wrong. The spot I pictured might be where I'd often imagined myself encountering the Chairman, for example . . . and then in an instant I was lost in thoughts of the Chairman once again.

I went on this way for weeks, trying to remake myself. Sometimes when I was free for a while from thinking about the Chairman, I began to feel as if a pit had opened up within me. I had no appetite even when little Etsuko came late at night carrying me a bowl of clear broth. The few times I did manage to focus my mind clearly on Nobu, I grew so numbed I seemed to feel nothing at all. While putting on my makeup, my face hung like a kimono from a rod. Auntie told me I looked like a ghost. I went to parties and banquets as usual, but I knelt in silence with my hands in my lap.

I knew Nobu was on the point of proposing himself as my *danna*, and so I waited every day for the news to reach me.

But the weeks dragged on without any word. Then one hot afternoon at the end of June, nearly a month after I'd given back the rock, Mother brought in a newspaper while I was eating lunch, and opened it to show me an article entitled 'Iwamura Electric Secures Financing from Mitsubishi Bank.' I expected to find all sorts of references to Nobu and the Minister, and certainly to the Chairman; but mostly the article gave a lot of information I can't even remember. It told that Iwamura Electric's designation had been changed by the Allied Occupation authorities from . . . I don't remember – a Class Something to a Class Something-Else. Which meant, as the article went on to explain, that the company was no longer restricted from entering into contracts, applying for loans, and so forth. Several paragraphs followed, all about rates of interest and lines of credit; and then finally about a very large loan secured the day before from the Mitsubishi Bank. It was a difficult article to read, full of numbers and business terms. When I finished, I looked up at Mother, kneeling on the other side of the table.

'Iwamura Electric's fortunes have turned around completely,' she said. 'Why didn't you tell me about this?'

'Mother, I hardly even understand what I've just read.'

'It's no wonder we've heard so much from Nobu Toshikazu these past few days. You must know he's proposed himself as your *danna*. I was thinking of turning him down. Who wants a man with an uncertain future? Now I can see why you've seemed so distracted these past few weeks! Well, you can relax now. It's finally happening. We all know how fond you've been of Nobu these many years.'

I went on gazing down at the table just like a proper daughter. But I'm sure I wore a pained expression on my face; because in a moment Mother went on:

'You mustn't be listless this way when Nobu wants you in his bed. Perhaps your health isn't what it should be. I'll send you to a doctor the moment you return from Amami.'

The only Amami I'd ever heard of was a little island not far from Okinawa; I couldn't imagine this was the place she meant. But in fact, as Mother went on to tell me, the mistress of the Ichiriki had received a telephone call that very morning from Iwamura Electric concerning a trip to the island of Amami the following weekend. I'd been asked to go, along with Mameha and Pumpkin, and also another geisha whose name Mother couldn't remember. We would leave the following Friday afternoon.

'But Mother . . . it makes no sense at all,' I said. 'A weekend trip as far as Amami? The boat ride alone will take all day.'

'Nothing of the sort. Iwamura Electric has arranged for all of you to travel there in an airplane.'

In an instant I forgot my worries about Nobu, and sat upright as quickly as if someone had poked me with a pin. 'Mother!' I said. 'I can't possibly fly on an airplane.'

'If you're sitting in one and the thing takes off, you won't be able to help it!' she replied. She must have thought her little joke was very funny because she gave one of her huffing laughs.

With gasoline so scarce, there couldn't possibly be an airplane, I decided, so I made up my mind not to worry – and this worked well for me until the following day, when I spoke with the mistress of the Ichiriki. It seemed that several American officers on the island of Okinawa traveled by air to Osaka several weekends a month. Normally the airplane flew home empty and returned a few days later to pick them up. Iwamura Electric had arranged for our group to ride on the return trips. We were going to Amami only because the empty airplane was available; otherwise we'd probably have been on our way to a hot-springs resort, and not fearing for our lives at all. The last thing the mistress said to me was, 'I'm just grateful it's you and not me flying in the thing.'

When Friday morning came, we set out for Osaka by train. In addition to Mr. Bekku, who came to help us with our trunks as far as the airport, the little group consisted of Mameha, Pumpkin, and me, as well as an elderly geisha named Shizue. Shizue was from the Pontocho district rather than Gion, and had unattractive glasses and silver hair that made her look even older than she really was. What was worse, her chin had a big cleft in the middle, like two breasts. Shizue seemed to view the rest of us as a cedar views the weeds growing beneath it. Mostly she stared out the window of the train; but every so often she opened the clasp of her orange and red handbag to take out a piece of candy, and looked at us as if she couldn't see why we had to trouble her with our presence.

From Osaka Station we traveled to the airport in a little bus not much larger than a car, which ran on coal and was very dirty. At last after an hour or so, we climbed down beside a silver airplane with two great big propellers on the wings. I wasn't at all reassured to see the tiny wheel on which the tail rested; and when we went inside, the aisle sloped downward so dramatically I felt sure the airplane was broken.

The men were onboard already, sitting in seats at the rear and talking business. In addition to the Chairman and Nobu, the Minister was there, as well as an elderly man who, as I later learned, was regional director of the Mitsubishi Bank. Seated beside him was a man in his thirties with a chin just like Shizue's, and glasses as thick as hers too. As it turned out, Shizue was the longtime mistress of the bank director, and this man was their son.

We sat toward the front of the airplane and left the men to their dull conversation. Soon I heard a coughing noise and the airplane trembled . . . and when I looked out the window, the giant propeller outside had begun to turn. In a matter of moments it was whirling its swordlike blades inches from my face, making the most desperate humming noise. I felt sure it would come tearing through the side of the airplane and slice me in half. Mameha had put me in a window seat thinking the view might calm me once we were airborne, but now that she saw what the propeller was doing, she refused to switch seats with me. The noise of the engines grew worse and the airplane began to bump along, turning here and there. Finally the noise reached its most terrifying volume yet, and the aisle tipped level. After another few moments we heard a thump and began to rise up into the air. Only when the ground was far below us did someone finally tell me the trip was seven hundred kilometers and would take nearly four hours. When I heard this, I'm afraid my eyes glazed over with tears, and everyone began to laugh at me.

451

I pulled the curtains over the window and tried to calm myself by reading a magazine. Quite some time later, after Mameha had fallen asleep in the seat beside me, I looked up to find Nobu standing in the aisle.

'Sayuri, are you well?' he said, speaking quietly so as not to wake Mameha.

'I don't think Nobu-san has ever asked me such a thing before,' I said. 'He must be in a very cheerful mood.'

'The future has never looked more promising!'

Mameha stirred at the sound of our talking, so Nobu said nothing further, and instead continued up the aisle to the toilet. Just before opening the door, he glanced back toward where the other men were seated. For an instant I saw him from an angle I'd rarely seen, which gave him a look of fierce concentration. When his glance flicked in my direction, I thought he might pick up some hint that I felt as worried about my future as he felt reassured about his. How strange it seemed, when I thought about it, that Nobu understood me so little. Of course, a geisha who expects understanding from her *danna* is like a mouse expecting sympathy from the snake. And in any case, how could Nobu possibly understand anything about me, when he'd seen me solely as a geisha keeping my true self carefully concealed? The Chairman was the only man I'd ever entertained as Sayuri the geisha who had also known me as Chiyo – though it was strange to think of it this way, for I'd never realized it before. What would Nobu have done if he had been the one to find me that day at the Shirakawa Stream? Surely he would have walked right past . . . and how much easier it might have been for me if he had. I wouldn't spend my nights yearning for the Chairman. I wouldn't stop in cosmetics shops from time to time, to smell the scent of talc in the air and remind myself of his skin. I wouldn't strain to picture his presence beside me in some imaginary place. If you'd asked me why I wanted these things, I would have answered, Why does a ripe persimmon taste delicious? Why does wood smell smoky when it burns?

But here I was again, like a girl trying to catch mice with her hands. Why couldn't I stop thinking about the Chairman?

I'm sure my anguish must have shown clearly on my face

when the door to the toilet opened a moment later, and the light snapped off. I couldn't bear for Nobu to see me this way, so I laid my head against the window, pretending to be asleep. After he passed by, I opened my eyes again. I found that the position of my head had caused the curtains to pull open, so that I was looking outside the airplane for the first time since shortly after we'd lifted off the runway. Spread out below was a broad vista of aqua blue ocean, mottled with the same jade green as a certain hair ornament Mameha sometimes wore. I'd never imagined the ocean with patches of green. From the sea cliffs in Yoroido, it had always looked the color of slate. Here the sea stretched all the way out to a single line pulled across like a wool thread where the sky began. This view wasn't frightening at all, but inexpressibly lovely. Even the hazy disk of the propeller was beautiful in its own way, and the silver wing had a kind of magnificence, and was decorated with those symbols that American warplanes have on them. How peculiar it was to see them there, considering the world only five years earlier. We had fought a brutal war as enemies; and now what? We had given up our past; this was something I understood fully, for I had done it myself once. If only I could find a way of giving up my future . . .

And then a frightening image came to mind: I saw myself cutting the bond of fate that held me to Nobu, and watching him fall all the long way into the ocean below.

I don't mean this was just an idea or some sort of daydream. I mean that all at once I understood exactly how to do it. Of course I wasn't really going to throw Nobu into the ocean, but I did have an understanding, just as clearly as if a window had been thrown open in my mind, of the one thing I could do to end my relationship with him forever. I didn't want to lose his friendship; but in my efforts to reach the Chairman, Nobu was an obstacle I'd found no way around. And yet I could cause him to be consumed by the flames of his own anger; Nobu himself had told me how to do it, just a moment after cutting his hand that night at the Ichiriki Teahouse only a few weeks earlier. If I was the sort of woman who would give myself to the Minister, he'd said, he wanted me to leave the room right then and would never speak to me again.

453

The feeling that came over me as I thought of this . . . it was like a fever breaking. I felt damp everywhere on my body. I was grateful Mameha remained asleep beside me; I'm sure she would have wondered what was the matter, to see me short of breath, wiping my forehead with my fingertips. This idea that had come to me, could I really do such a thing? I don't mean the act of seducing the Minister; I knew perfectly well I could do that. It would be like going to the doctor for a shot. I'd look the other way for a time, and it would be over. But could I do such a thing to Nobu? What a horrible way to repay his kindness. Compared with the sorts of men so many geisha had suffered through the years, Nobu was probably a very desirable *danna*. But could I bear to live a life in which my hopes had been extinguished forever? For weeks I'd been working to convince myself I could live it; but could I really? I thought perhaps I understood how Hatsumomo had come by her bitter cruelty, and Granny her meanness. Even Pumpkin, who was scarcely thirty, had worn a look of disappointment for many years. The only thing that had kept me from it was hope; and now to sustain my hopes, would I commit an abhorrent act? I'm not talking about seducing the Minister; I'm talking about betraying Nobu's trust.

During the rest of the flight, I struggled with these thoughts. I could never have imagined myself scheming in this way, but in time I began to imagine the steps involved just like in a board game: I would draw the Minister aside at the inn – no, not at the inn, at some other place – and I would trick Nobu into stumbling upon us . . . or perhaps it would be enough for him to hear it from someone else? You can imagine how exhausted I felt by the end of the trip. Even as we left the airplane, I must still have looked very worried, because Mameha kept reassuring me that the flight was over and I was safe at last.

We arrived at our inn about an hour before sunset. The others admired the room in which we would all be staying, but I felt so agitated I could only pretend to admire it. It was as spacious as the largest room at the Ichiriki Teahouse, and furnished beautifully in the Japanese style, with tatami mats and gleaming wood. One long wall was made entirely of glass doors, beyond which lay extraordinary tropical plants – some with leaves nearly as big as a man. A covered walkway led down through the leaves to the banks of a stream.

When the luggage was in order, we were all of us quite ready for a bath. The inn had provided folding screens, which we opened in the middle of the room for privacy. We changed into our cotton gowns and made our way along a succession of covered walkways, leading through the dense foliage to a luxurious hot-springs pool at the other end of the inn. The men's and women's entrances were shielded by partitions, and had separate tiled areas for washing. But once we were immersed in the dark water of the springs and moved out beyond the partition's edge, the men and women were together in the water. The bank director kept making jokes about Mameha and me, saying he wanted one of us to fetch a certain pebble, or twig, or something of the sort, from the woods at the edge of the springs – the joke being, of course, that he wanted to see us naked. All this while, his son was engrossed in conversation with Pumpkin; and it didn't take us long to understand why Pumpkin's bosoms, which were fairly large, kept floating up and exposing themselves on the surface while she jabbered away as always without noticing.

Perhaps it seems odd to you that we all bathed together, men and women, and that we planned to sleep in the same room later that night. But actually, geisha do this sort of thing all the time with their best customers – or at least they did in my day. A single geisha who values her reputation will certainly never be caught alone with a man who isn't her *danna*. But to bathe innocently in a group like this, with the murky water cloaking us . . . that's quite another matter. And as for sleeping in a group, we even have a word for it in Japanese – *zakone*, 'fish sleeping.' If you picture a bunch of mackerel thrown together into a basket, I suppose that's what it means.

Bathing in a group like this was innocent, as I say. But that doesn't mean a hand never strayed where it shouldn't, and this thought was very much on my mind as I soaked there in the hot springs. If Nobu had been the sort of man to tease, he might have drifted over toward me; and then after we'd chatted for a time he might suddenly have grabbed me by the hip, or . . . well, almost anywhere, to tell the truth. The proper next step would be for me to scream and Nobu to laugh, and that would be the end of it. But Nobu wasn't the sort of man to tease. He'd been immersed in the bath for a time, in conversation with the Chairman, but now he was sitting on a rock with only his legs in the water, and a small, wet towel draped across his hips; he wasn't paying attention to the rest of us, but rubbing at the stump of his arm absentmindedly and peering into the water. The sun had set by now, and the light faded almost to evening but Nobu sat in the brightness of a paper lantern. I'd never before seen him so exposed. The scarring that I thought was at its worst on one side of his face was every bit as bad on his damaged shoulder though his other shoulder was beautifully smooth like an egg. And now to think that I was considering betraying him . . . He would think I had done it for only one reason, and would never understand the truth. I couldn't bear the thought of hurting Nobu or of destroying his regard for me. I wasn't at all sure I could go through with it.

After breakfast the following morning, we all took a walk through the tropical forest to the sea cliffs nearby where the stream from our inn poured over a picturesque little waterfall into the ocean. We stood a long while admiring the view; even when we were all ready to leave, the Chairman could hardly tear himself away. On the return trip I walked beside Nobu, who was still as cheerful as I'd ever seen him. Afterward we toured the island in the back of a military truck fitted with benches, and saw bananas and pineapples growing on the trees, and beautiful birds. From the mountaintops, the ocean looked like a crumpled blanket in turquoise, with stains of dark blue.

That afternoon we wandered the dirt streets of the little village, and soon came upon an old wood building that looked like a warehouse, with a sloped roof of thatch. We ended up walking around to the back, where Nobu climbed stone steps to open a door at the corner of the building, and the sunlight fell across a dusty stage built out of planking.

Evidently it had at one time been a warehouse but was now the town's theater. When I first stepped inside I didn't think very much about it. But after the door banged shut and we'd made our way to the street again, I began to feel that same feeling of a fever breaking because in my mind I had an image of myself lying there on the rutted flooring with the Minister as the door creaked open and sunlight fell across us. We would have no place to hide; Nobu couldn't possibly fail to see us. In many ways I'm sure it was the very spot I'd half-hoped to find. But I wasn't thinking of these things; I wasn't really thinking at all, so much as struggling to put my thoughts into some kind of order. They felt to me like rice pouring from a torn sack.

As we walked back up the hill toward our inn, I had to fall back from the group to take my handkerchief from my sleeve. It was certainly very warm there on that road, with the afternoon sun shining full onto our faces. I wasn't the only one perspiring. But Nobu came walking back to ask if I was all right. When I couldn't manage to answer him right away, I hoped he would think it was the strain of walking up the hill.

'You haven't looked well all weekend, Sayuri. Perhaps you ought to have stayed in Kyoto.'

'But when would I have seen this beautiful island?'

'I'm sure this is the farthest you've ever been from your home. We're as far from Kyoto now as Hokkaido is.'

The others had walked around the bend ahead. Over Nobu's shoulder I could see the eaves of the inn protruding above the foliage. I wanted to reply to him, but I found myself consumed with the same thoughts that had troubled me on the airplane, that Nobu didn't understand me at all. Kyoto wasn't my home; not in the sense Nobu seemed to mean it, of a place where I'd been raised, a place I'd never strayed from. And in that instant, while I peered at him in the hot sun, I made up my mind that I would do this thing I had feared. I would betray Nobu, even though he stood there looking at me with kindness. I tucked away my handkerchief with trembling hands, and we continued up the hill, not speaking a word.

By the time I reached the room, the Chairman and Mamcha had already taken seats at the table to begin a game of go against the bank director, with Shizue and her son looking on. The glass doors along the far wall stood open; the Minister was propped on one elbow staring out, peeling the covering off a short stalk of cane he'd brought back with him. I was desperately afraid Nobu would engage me in a conversation I'd be unable to escape, but in fact, he went directly over to the table and began talking with Mameha. I had no idea as yet how I would lure the Minister to the theater with me, and even less idea how I would arrange for Nobu to find us there. Perhaps Pumpkin would take Nobu for a walk if I asked her to? I didn't feel I could ask such a thing of Mameha, but Pumpkin and I had been girls together; and though I won't call her crude, as Auntie had called her, Pumpkin did have a certain coarseness in her personality and would be less aghast at what I was planning. I would need to direct her explicitly to bring Nobu to the old theater; they wouldn't come upon us there purely by accident.

For a time I knelt gazing out at the sunlit leaves and wishing I could appreciate the beautiful tropical afternoon. I kept asking myself whether I was fully sane to be considering this plan; but whatever misgivings I may have felt, they weren't enough to stop me from going ahead with it. Clearly nothing would happen until I succeeded in drawing the Minister aside, and I couldn't afford to call attention to myself when I did it. Earlier he'd asked a maid to bring him a snack, and now he was sitting with his legs around a tray, pouring beer into his mouth and dropping in globs of salted squid guts with his chopsticks. This may seem like a nauseating idea for a dish, but I can assure you that you'll find salted squid guts in bars and restaurants here and there in Japan. It was a favorite of my father's, but I've never been able to stomach it. I couldn't even watch the Minister as he ate.

'Minister,' I said to him quietly, 'would you like me to find you something more appetizing?'

'No,' he said, 'I'm not hungry.' I must admit this raised in my mind the question of why he was eating in the first place. By now Mameha and Nobu had wandered out the back door in conversation, and the others, including Pumpkin, were gathered around the go board on the table. Apparently the

Chairman had just made a blunder, and they were laughing. It seemed to me my chance had come.

'If you're eating out of boredom, Minister,' I said, 'why don't you and I explore the inn? I've been eager to see it, and we haven't had the time.'

I didn't wait for him to reply but stood and walked from the room. I was relieved when he stepped out into the hallway a moment later to join me. We walked in silence down the corridor, until we came to a bend where I could see that no one was coming from either direction. I stopped.

'Minister, excuse me,' I said, 'but . . . shall we take a walk back down to the village together?'

He looked very confused by this.

'We have an hour or so left in the afternoon,' I went on, 'and I remember something I'd very much like to see again.'

After a long pause, the Minister said, 'I'll need to use the toilet first.'

'Yes, that's fine,' I told him. 'You go and use the toilet; and when you're finished, wait right here for me and we'll take a walk together. Don't go anywhere until I come and fetch you.'

The Minister seemed agreeable to this and continued up the corridor. I went back toward the room. And I felt so dazed – now that I was actually going through with my plan – that when I put my hand on the door to slide it open, I could scarcely feel my fingers touching anything at all.

Pumpkin was no longer at the table. She was looking through her travel trunk for something. At first when I tried to speak, nothing came out. I had to clear my throat and try again.

'Excuse me, Pumpkin,' I said. 'Just one moment of your time . . .'

She didn't look eager to stop what she was doing, but she left her trunk in disarray and came out into the hallway with me. I led her some distance down the corridor, and then turned to her and said:

'Pumpkin, I need to ask a favor.'

I waited for her to tell me she was happy to help, but she just stood with her eyes on me.

'I hope you won't mind my asking –'

'Ask,' she said.

'The Minister and I are about to go for a walk. I'm going to take him to the old theater, and –'

'Why?'

'So that he and I can be alone.'

'The Minister?' Pumpkin said incredulously.

'I'll explain some other time, but here's what I want you to do. I want you to bring Nobu there and . . . Pumpkin, this will sound very strange. I want you to discover us.'

'What do you mean, "discover" you?'

'I want you to find some way of bringing Nobu there and opening the back door we saw earlier, so that . . . he'll see us.'

While I was explaining this, Pumpkin had noticed the Minister waiting in another covered walkway through the foliage. Now she looked back at me.

'What are you up to, Sayuri?' she said.

'I don't have time to explain it now. But it's terribly important, Pumpkin. Truthfully, my entire future is in your hands. Just make sure it's no one but you and Nobu – not the Chairman, for heaven's sake, or anyone else. I'll repay you in any way you'd like.'

She looked at me for a long moment. 'So it's time for a favor from Pumpkin again, is it?' she said. I didn't feel certain what she meant by this, but rather than explaining it to me, she left.

I wasn't sure whether or not Pumpkin had agreed to help. But all I could do at this point was go to the doctor for my shot, so to speak, and hope that she and Nobu would appear. I joined the Minister in the corridor and we set out down the hill.

As we walked around the bend in the road and left the inn behind us, I couldn't help remembering the day Mameha had cut me on the leg and taken me to meet Dr. Crab. On that afternoon I'd felt myself in some sort of danger I couldn't fully understand, and I felt much the same way now. My face was as hot in the afternoon sun as if I'd sat too close to the hibachi; and when I looked at the Minister, sweat was running down his temple onto his neck. If all went well he would soon be pressing that neck against me . . . and at this thought I took my folding fan from my obi, and waved it until my arm was tired, trying to cool both myself and him. All the while, I kept up a flow of conversation, until a few minutes later, when we came to a stop before the old theater with its thatched roof. The Minister seemed puzzled. He cleared his throat and looked up at the sky.

'Will you come inside with me for a moment, Minister?' I said.

He didn't seem to know what to make of this, but when I walked down the path beside the building, he plodded along behind me. I climbed the stone steps and opened the door for him. He hesitated only a moment before walking inside. If he had frequented Gion all his life, he'd certainly have understood what I had in mind – because a geisha who lures a man to an isolated spot has certainly put her reputation at stake, and a first-class geisha will never do such a thing casually. But the Minister just stood inside the theater, in the patch of sunlight, like a man waiting for a bus. My hands were trembling so much as I folded my fan and tucked it into my obi again, I wasn't at all certain I could see my plan through to the end. The simple act of closing the door took all my strength; and then we were standing in the murky light filtering under the eaves. Still, the Minister stood inert, with his face pointed toward a stack of straw mats in the corner of the stage.

'Minister . . .' I said.

My voice echoed so much in the little hall, I spoke more quietly afterward.

'I understand you had a talk with the mistress of the Ichiriki about me. Isn't that so?'

He took in a deep breath, but ended up saying nothing.

'Minister, if I may,' I said, 'I'd like to tell you a story about a geisha named Kazuyo. She isn't in Gion any longer, but I knew her well at one time. A very important man – much like you, Minister – met Kazuyo one evening and enjoyed her company so much that he came back to Gion every night to see her. After a few months of this, he asked to be Kazuyo's *danna*, but the mistress of the teahouse apologized and said it

461

wouldn't be possible. The man was very disappointed; but then one afternoon Kazuyo took him to a quiet spot where they could be alone. Someplace very much like this empty theater. And she explained to him that . . . even though he couldn't be her *danna* –'

The moment I said these last words, the Minister's face changed like a valley when the clouds move away and sunlight rushes across it. He took a clumsy step toward me. At once my heart began to pound like drums in my ears. I couldn't help looking away from him and closing my eyes. When I opened them again, the Minister had come so close, we were nearly touching, and then I felt the damp fleshiness of his face against my cheek. Slowly he brought his body toward mine until we were pressed together. He took my arms, probably to pull me down onto the planking, but I stopped him.

'The stage is too dusty,' I said. 'You must bring over a mat from that stack.'

'We'll go over there,' the Minister replied.

If we had lain down upon the mats in the corner, Nobu wouldn't have seen us in the sunlight when he opened the door.

'No, we mustn't,' I said. 'Please bring a mat here.'

The Minister did as I asked, and then stood with his hands by his side, watching me. Until this moment I'd half-imagined something would stop us; but now I could see that nothing would. Time seemed to slow. My feet looked to me like someone else's when they stepped out of my lacquered zori and onto the mat.

Almost at once, the Minister kicked off his shoes and was against me, with his arms around me tugging at the knot in my obi. I didn't know what he was thinking, because I certainly wasn't prepared to take off my kimono. I reached back to stop him. When I'd dressed that morning, I still hadn't quite made up my mind; but in order to be prepared, I'd very deliberately put on a gray underrobe I didn't much like – thinking it might be stained before the end of the day – and a lavender and blue kimono of silk gauze, as well as a durable silver obi. As for my undergarments, I'd shortened my *koshimaki* – my 'hip wrap' – by rolling it at the waist, so that if I decided after all to seduce the Minister, he'd have no trouble finding his way inside it. Now, when I withdrew his hands from around me, he gave me a puzzled look. I think he believed I was stopping him, and he looked very relieved as I lay down on the mat. It wasn't a tatami, but a simple sheet of woven straw; I could feel the hard flooring beneath. With one hand I folded back my kimono and underrobe on one side so that my leg was exposed to the knee. The Minister was still fully dressed, but he lay down upon me at once, pressing the knot of my obi into my back so much, I had to raise one hip to make myself more comfortable. My head was turned to the side as well, because I was wearing my hair in a style known as *tsubushi shimada*, with a dramatic chignon looped in the back, which would have been ruined if I'd put any weight on it. It was certainly an uncomfortable arrangement, but my discomfort was nothing compared with the uneasiness and anxiety I felt. Suddenly I wondered if I'd been thinking at all clearly when I'd put myself in this predicament. The Minister raised himself on one arm and began fumbling inside the seam of my kimono with his hand, scratching my thighs with his fingernails. Without thinking about what I was doing, I brought my hands up to his shoulders to push him away . . . but then I imagined Nobu as my *danna*, and the life I would live without hope; and I took my hands away and settled them onto the mat again. The Minister's fingers were squirming higher and higher along the inside of my thigh; it was impossible not to feel them. I tried to distract myself by focusing on the door. Perhaps it would open even now, before the Minister had gone any further; but at that moment I heard the jingling of his belt, and then the zip of his pants and a moment later he was forcing himself inside me. Somehow I felt like a fifteen-year-old girl again, because the feeling was so strangely reminiscent of Dr. Crab. I even heard myself whimper. The Minister was holding himself up on his elbows with his face above mine I could see him out of only one corner of my eye. When viewed up close like this with his jaw protruding toward me he looked more like an animal than a human. And even this wasn't the worst part, for with his jaw jutted forward, the Minister's lower lip became like a cup in which his saliva began to pool. I don't know if it was the squid guts he'd eaten, but his saliva had a kind of gray thickness to it, which made me think of the residue left on the cutting board after fish have been cleaned.

When I'd dressed that morning, I'd tucked several sheets of a very absorbent rice paper into the back of my obi. I hadn't expected to need them until afterward, when the Minister would want them for wiping himself off – if I decided to go through with it, that is. Now it seemed I would need a sheet much sooner, to wipe my face when his saliva spilled onto me. With so much of his weight on my hips, however, I couldn't get my hand into the back of my obi. I let out several little gasps as I tried, and I'm afraid the Minister mistook them for excitement – for in any case, he suddenly grew even more energetic, and now the pool of saliva in his lip was being jostled with such violent shock waves I could hardly believe it held together rather than spilling out in a stream. All I could do was pinch my eyes shut and wait. I felt as sick as if I had been lying in the bottom of a little boat, tossed about on the waves, and with my head banging again and again against the side. Then all at once the Minister made a groaning noise, and held very still for a bit, and at the same time I felt his saliva spill onto my cheek.

I tried again to reach the rice paper in my obi, but now the Minister was lying collapsed upon me, breathing as heavily as if he'd just run a race. I was about to push him off when I heard a scraping sound outside. My feelings of disgust had been so loud within me, they'd nearly drowned out everything else. But now that I remembered Nobu, I could feel my heart pounding once again. I heard another scrape; it was the sound of someone on the stone steps. The Minister seemed to have no idea what was about to happen to him. He raised his head and pointed it toward the door with only the mildest interest, as if he expected to see a bird there. And then the door creaked open and the sunlight flooded over us. I had to squint, but I could make out two figures. There was

Pumpkin; she had come to the theater just as I'd hoped she would. But the man peering down from beside her wasn't Nobu at all. I had no notion of why she had done it, but Pumpkin had brought the Chairman instead.

34

I CAN SCARCELY REMEMBER anything after that door opened – for I think the blood may have drained out of me, I went so cold and numb. I know the Minister climbed off me, or perhaps I pushed him off. I do remember weeping and asking if he'd seen the same thing I had, whether it really had been the Chairman standing there in the doorway. I hadn't been able to make out anything of the Chairman's expression, with the late-afternoon sun behind him; and yet when the door closed again, I couldn't help imagining I'd seen on his face some of the shock I myself was feeling. I didn't know if the shock was really there – and I doubted it was. But when we feel pain, even the blossoming trees seem weighted with suffering to us; and in just the same way, after seeing the Chairman there . . . well, I would have found my own pain reflected on anything I'd looked at.

If you consider that I'd taken the Minister to that empty theater for the very purpose of putting myself in danger – so that the knife would come slamming down onto the chopping block, so to speak – I'm sure you'll understand that amid the worry, and fear, and disgust that almost overwhelmed me, I'd also been feeling a certain excitement. In the instant before that door opened, I could almost sense my life expanding just like a river whose waters have begun to swell; for I had never before taken such a drastic step to change the course of my own future. I was like a child tiptoeing along a precipice overlooking the sea. And yet somehow I hadn't imagined a great wave might come and strike me there, and wash everything away.

When the chaos of feelings receded, and I slowly became

aware of myself again, Mameha was kneeling above me. I was puzzled to find that I wasn't in the old theater at all any longer, but rather looking up from the tatami floor of a dark little room at the inn. I don't recall anything about leaving the theater, but I must have done it somehow. Later Mameha told me I'd gone to the proprietor to ask for a quiet place to rest; he'd recognized that I wasn't feeling well, and had gone to find Mameha soon afterward.

Fortunately Mameha seemed willing to believe I was truly ill, and left me there. Later, as I wandered back toward the room in a daze and with a terrible feeling of dread, I saw Pumpkin step out into the covered walkway ahead of me. She stopped when she caught sight of me; but rather than hurrying over to apologize as I half-expected she might, she turned her focus slowly toward me like a snake that had spotted a mouse.

'Pumpkin,' I said, 'I asked you to bring Nobu, not the Chairman. I don't understand –'

'Yes, it must be hard for you to understand, Sayuri, when life doesn't work out perfectly!'

'Perfectly? Nothing worse could have happened . . . did you misunderstand what I was asking you?'

'You really do think I'm stupid!' she said.

I was bewildered, and stood a long moment in silence. 'I thought you were my friend,' I said at last.

'I thought you were my friend too, once. But that was a long time ago.'

'You talk as if I've done something to harm you, Pumpkin, but –'

'No, you'd never do anything like that, would you? Not the perfect Miss Nitta Sayuri! I suppose it doesn't matter that you took my place as the daughter of the okiya? Do you remember that, Sayuri? After I'd gone out of my way to help you with that Doctor – whatever his name was. After I'd risked making Hatsumomo furious at me for helping you! Then you turned it all around and stole what was mine. I've been wondering all these months just why you brought me into this little gathering with the Minister. I'm sorry it wasn't so easy for you to take advantage of me this time –'

'But Pumpkin,' I interrupted, 'couldn't you just have refused to help me? Why did you have to bring the Chairman?'

She stood up to her full height. 'I know perfectly well how you feel about him,' she said. 'Whenever there's nobody looking, your eyes hang all over him like fur on a dog.'

She was so angry, she had bitten her lip; I could see a smudge of lipstick on her teeth. She'd set out to hurt me, I now realized, in the worst way she could.

'You took something from me a long time ago, Sayuri. How does it feel now?' she said. Her nostrils were flared, her face consumed with anger like a burning twig. It was as though the spirit of Hatsumomo had been living trapped inside her all these years, and had finally broken free.

During the rest of that evening, I remember nothing but a blur of events, and how much I dreaded every moment ahead of me. While the others sat around drinking and laughing, it was all I could do to pretend to laugh. I must have spent the entire night flushed red, because from time to time Mameha touched my neck to see if I was feverish. I'd seated myself as far away from the Chairman as I could, so that our eyes would never have to meet; and I did manage to make it through the evening without confronting him. But later, as we were all preparing for bed, I stepped into the hallway as he was coming back into the room. I ought to have moved out of his way, but I felt so ashamed, I gave a brief bow and hurried past him instead, making no effort to hide my unhappiness.

It was an evening of torment, and I remember only one other thing about it. At some point after everyone else was asleep, I wandered away from the inn in a daze and ended up on the sea cliffs, staring out into the darkness with the sound of the roaring water below me. The thundering of the ocean was like a bitter lament. I seemed to see beneath everything a layering of cruelty I'd never known was there – as though the trees and the wind, and even the rocks where I stood, were all in alliance with my old girlhood enemy Hatsumomo. The howling of the wind and the shaking of the trees seemed to mock me. Could it really be that the stream of my life had divided forever? I removed the Chairman's handkerchief from my sleeve, for I'd taken it to bed that evening to comfort myself one last time. I dried my face with it, and held it up into the wind. I was about to let it dance away into the darkness, when I thought of the tiny mortuary tablets that Mr. Tanaka had sent me so many years earlier. We must always keep something to remember those who have left us. The mortuary tablets back in the okiya were all that remained of my childhood. The Chairman's handkerchief would be what remained of the rest of my life.

Back in Kyoto, I was carried along in a current of activity over the next few days. I had no choice but to put on my makeup as usual, and attend engagements at the teahouses just as though nothing had changed in the world. I kept reminding myself what Mameha had once told me, that there was nothing like work for getting over a disappointment; but my work didn't seem to help me in any way. Every time I went into the Ichiriki Teahouse, I was reminded that one day soon Nobu would summon me there to tell me the arrangements had been settled at last. Considering how busy he'd been over the past few months, I didn't expect to hear from him for some time – a week or two, perhaps. But on Wednesday morning, three days after our return from Amami, I received word that Iwamura Electric had telephoned the Ichiriki Teahouse to request my presence that evening.

I dressed late in the afternoon in a yellow kimono of silk gauze with a green underrobe and a deep blue obi interwoven with gold threads. Auntie assured me I looked lovely but when I saw myself in the mirror, I seemed like a woman defeated. I'd certainly experienced moments in the past when I felt displeased with the way I looked before setting out from the okiya; but most often I managed to find at least one feature I could make use of during the course of the evening. A certain persimmon-colored underrobe, for example, always brought out the blue in my eyes, rather than the gray no matter how exhausted I felt. But this evening my face seemed utterly hollow beneath my cheekbones – although I'd put on Western-style makeup just as I usually did – and even my hairstyle seemed lopsided to me. I couldn't think of any way to improve my appearance, other than asking Mr. Bekku to retie my obi just a finger's-width higher, to take away some of my downcast look.

My first engagement was a banquet given by an American colonel to honor the new governor of Kyoto Prefecture. It was held at the former estate of the Sumitomo family, which was now the headquarters of the American army's seventh division. I was amazed to see that so many of the beautiful stones in the garden were painted white, and signs in English – which of course I couldn't read – were tacked to the trees here and there. After the party was over, I made my way to the Ichiriki and was shown upstairs by a maid, to the same peculiar little room where Nobu had met with me on the night Gion was closing. This was the very spot where I'd learned about the haven he'd found to keep me safe from the war; it seemed entirely appropriate that we should meet in this same room to celebrate his becoming my *danna* – though it would be anything but a celebration for me. I knelt at one end of the table, so that Nobu would sit facing the alcove. I was careful to position myself so he could pour sake using his one arm, without the table in his way; he would certainly want to pour a cup for me after telling me the arrangements had been finalized. It would be a fine night for Nobu. I would do my best not to spoil it.

With the dim lighting and the reddish cast from the tea-colored walls, the atmosphere was really quite pleasant. I'd forgotten the very particular scent of the room – a combination of dust and the oil used for polishing wood – but now that I smelled it again, I found myself remembering details about that evening with Nobu years earlier that I couldn't possibly have called to mind otherwise. He'd had holes in both of his socks, I remembered; through one a slender big toe had protruded, with the nail neatly groomed. Could it really be that only five and a half years had passed since that evening? It seemed an entire generation had come and gone; so many of the people I'd once known were dead. Was this the life I'd come back to Gion to lead? It was just as Mameha had once told me: we don't become geisha because we want our lives to be happy; we become geisha because we have no choice. If my mother had lived, I might be a wife and mother at the seashore myself, thinking of Kyoto as a faraway place where the fish were shipped – and would my life really be any worse? Nobu had once said to me, 'I'm a very easy man to understand, Sayuri. I don't like things held up before me that I cannot have.' Perhaps I was just the same; all my life in Gion, I'd imagined the Chairman before me, and now I could not have him.

After ten or fifteen minutes of waiting for Nobu, I began to wonder if he was really coming. I knew I shouldn't do it, but I laid my head down on the table to rest, for I'd slept poorly these past nights. I didn't fall asleep, but I did drift for a time in my general sense of misery. And then I seemed to have a most peculiar dream. I thought I heard the tapping sound of drums in the distance, and a hiss like water from a faucet, and then I felt the Chairman's hand touching my shoulder. I knew it was the Chairman's hand because when I lifted my head from the table to see who had touched me, he was there. The tapping had been his footsteps; the hissing was the door in its track. And now he stood above me with a maid waiting behind him. I bowed and apologized for falling asleep. I felt so confused that for a moment I wondered if I was really awake; but it wasn't a dream. The Chairman was seating himself on the very cushion where I'd expected Nobu to sit, and yet Nobu was nowhere to be seen. While the maid placed sake on the table, an awful thought began to take hold in my mind. Had the Chairman come to tell me Nobu had been in an accident, or that some other horrible thing had happened to him? Otherwise, why hadn't Nobu himself come? I was about to ask the Chairman, when the mistress of the teahouse peered into the room.

'Why, Chairman,' she said, 'we haven't seen you in weeks!'

The mistress was always pleasant in front of guests, but I could tell from the strain in her voice that she had something else on her mind. Probably she was wondering about Nobu, just as I was. While I poured sake for the Chairman, the mistress came and knelt at the table. She stopped his hand before he took a sip from his cup, and leaned toward him to breathe in the scent of the vapors.

'Really, Chairman, I'll never understand why you prefer this sake to others,' she said. 'We opened some this afternoon, the best we've had in years. I'm sure Nobu-san will appreciate it when he arrives.'

'I'm sure he would,' the Chairman said. 'Nobu appreciates fine things. But he won't be coming tonight.'

I was alarmed to hear this; but I kept my eyes to the table. I could see that the mistress was surprised too, because of how quickly she changed the subject.

'Oh, well,' she said, 'anyway, don't you think our Sayuri looks charming this evening!'

'Now, Mistress, when has Sayuri not looked charming?' said the Chairman. 'Which reminds me . . . let me show you something I've brought.'

The Chairman put onto the table a little bundle wrapped in blue silk; I hadn't noticed it in his hand when he'd entered the room. He untied it and took out a short, fat scroll, which he began to unroll. It was cracked with age and showed – in miniature – brilliantly colored scenes of the Imperial court. If you've ever seen this sort of scroll, you'll know that you can unroll it all the way across a room and survey the entire grounds of the Imperial compound, from the gates at one end to the palace at the other. The Chairman sat with it before him, unrolling it from one spindle to the other – past scenes of drinking parties, and aristocrats playing kickball with their kimonos cinched up between their legs – until he came to a young woman in her lovely twelve-layered robes, kneeling on the wood floor outside the Emperor's chambers.

'Now what do you think of that!' he said.

'It's quite a scroll,' the mistress said. 'Where did the Chairman find it?'

'Oh, I bought it years ago. But look at this woman right here. She's the reason I bought it. Don't you notice anything about her?'

The mistress peered at it; afterward the Chairman turned it for me to see. The image of the young woman, though no bigger than a large coin, was painted in exquisite detail. I didn't notice it at first, but her eyes were pale . . . and when I looked more closely I saw they were blue-gray. They made me think at once of the works Uchida had painted using me as a model. I blushed and muttered something about how beautiful the scroll was. The mistress admired it too for a moment, and then said:

'Well, I'll leave the two of you. I'm going to send up some of that fresh, chilled sake I mentioned. Unless you think I should save it for the next time Nobu-san comes?'

'Don't bother,' he said. 'We'll make do with the sake we have.'

'Nobu-san is . . . quite all right, isn't he?'

'Oh, yes,' said the Chairman. 'Quite all right.'

I was relieved to hear this; but at the same time I felt myself growing sick with shame. If the Chairman hadn't come to give me news about Nobu, he'd come for some other reason – probably to berate me for what I'd done. In the few days since returning to Kyoto, I'd tried not to imagine what he must have seen: the Minister with his pants undone, me with my bare legs protruding from my disordered kimono . . .

When the mistress left the room, the sound of the door closing behind her was like a sword being drawn from its sheath.

'May I please say, Chairman,' I began as steadily as I could, 'that my behavior on Amami –'

'I know what you're thinking, Sayuri. But I haven't come here to ask for your apology. Sit quietly a moment. I want to tell you about something that happened quite a number of years ago.'

'Chairman, I feel so confused,' I managed to say. 'Please forgive me, but –'

'Just listen. You'll understand soon enough why I'm telling it to you. Do you recall a restaurant named Tsumiyo? It closed toward the end of the Depression, but . . . well, never mind; you were very young at the time. In any case, one day quite some years ago – eighteen years ago, to be exact – I went there for lunch with several of my associates. We were accompanied by a certain geisha named Izuko, from the Pontocho district.'

I recognized Izuko's name at once.

'She was everybody's favorite back in those days,' the

Chairman went on. 'We happened to finish up our lunch a bit early, so I suggested we take a stroll by the Shirakawa Stream on our way to the theater.'

By this time I'd removed the Chairman's handkerchief from my obi; and now, silently, I spread it onto the table and smoothed it so that his monogram was clearly visible. Over the years the handkerchief had taken on a stain in one corner, and the linen had yellowed; but the Chairman seemed to recognize it at once. His words trailed off, and he picked it up.

'Where did you get this?'

'Chairman,' I said, 'all these years I've wondered if you knew I was the little girl you'd spoken to. You gave me your handkerchief that very afternoon, on your way to see the play Shibaraku. You also gave me a coin –'

'Do you mean to say . . . even when you were an apprentice, you knew that I was the man who'd spoken to you?'

'I recognized the Chairman the moment I saw him again, at the sumo tournament. To tell the truth, I'm amazed the Chairman remembered me.'

'Well, perhaps you ought to look at yourself in the mirror sometime, Sayuri. Particularly when your eyes are wet from crying, because they become . . . I can't explain it. I felt I was seeing right through them. You know, I spend so much of my time seated across from men who are never quite telling me the truth; and here was a girl who'd never laid eyes on me before, and yet was willing to let me see straight into her.'

And then the Chairman interrupted himself.

'Didn't you ever wonder why Mameha became your older sister?' he asked me.

'Mameha?' I said. 'I don't understand. What does Mameha have to do with it?'

'You really don't know, do you?'

'Know what, Chairman?'

'Sayuri, I am the one who asked Mameha to take you under her care. I told her about a beautiful young girl I'd met, with startling gray eyes, and asked that she help you if she ever came upon you in Gion. I said I would cover her expenses if necessary. And she did come upon you, only a few months later. From what she's told me over the years, you would

474

certainly never have become a geisha without her help.'

It's almost impossible to describe the effect the Chairman's words had on me. I'd always taken it for granted that Mameha's mission had been personal – to rid herself and Gion of Hatsumomo. Now that I understood her real motive, that I'd come under her tutelage because of the Chairman . . . well, I felt I would have to look back at all the comments she'd ever made to me and wonder about the real meaning behind them. And it wasn't just Mameha who'd suddenly been transformed in my eyes; even I seemed to myself to be a different woman. When my gaze fell upon my hands in my lap, I saw them as hands the Chairman had made. I felt exhilarated, and frightened, and grateful all at once. I moved away from the table to bow and express my gratitude to him; but before I could even do it, I had to say:

'Chairman, forgive me, but I so wish that at some time years ago, you could have told me about . . . all of this. I can't say how much it would have meant to me.'

'There's a reason why I never could, Sayuri, and why I had to insist that Mameha not tell you either. It has to do with Nobu.'

To hear mention of Nobu's name, all the feeling drained out of me – for I had the sudden notion that I understood where the Chairman had been leading all along.

'Chairman,' I said, 'I know I've been unworthy of your kindness. This past weekend, when I –'

'I confess, Sayuri,' he interrupted, 'that what happened on Amami has been very much on my mind.'

I could feel the Chairman looking at me; I couldn't possibly have looked back at him.

'There's something I want to discuss with you,' he went on. 'I've been wondering all day how to go about it. I keep thinking of something that happened many years ago. I'm sure there must be a better way to explain myself, but . . . I do hope you'll understand what I'm trying to say.'

Here he paused to take off his jacket and fold it on the mats beside him. I could smell the starch in his shirt, which made me think of visiting the General at the Suruya Inn and his room that often smelled of ironing.

'Back when Iwamura Electric was still a young company,' the Chairman began, 'I came to know a man named Ikeda, who worked for one of our suppliers on the other side of town. He was a genius at solving wiring problems. Sometimes when we had difficulty with an installation, we asked to borrow him for a day, and he straightened everything out for us. Then one afternoon when I was rushing home from work, I happened to run into him at the pharmacist. He told me he was feeling very relaxed, because he'd quit his job. When I asked him why he'd done it, he said, 'The time came to quit. So I quit!' Well, I hired him right there on the spot. Then a few weeks later I asked him again, 'Ikeda-san, why did you quit your job across town?' He said to me, 'Mr. Iwamura, for years I wanted to come and work for your company. But you never asked me. You always called on me when you had a problem, but you never asked me to work for you. Then one day I realized that you never *would* ask me, because you didn't want to hire me away from one of your suppliers and jeopardize your business relationship. Only if I quit my job first, would you then have the opportunity to hire me. So I quit.'

I knew the Chairman was waiting for me to respond, but I didn't dare speak.

'Now, I've been thinking,' he went on, 'that perhaps your encounter with the Minister was like Ikeda quitting his job. And I'll tell you why this thought has been on my mind. It's something Pumpkin said after she took me down to the theater. I was extremely angry with her, and I demanded she tell me why she'd done it. For the longest time she wouldn't even speak. Then she told me something that made no sense at first. She said you'd asked her to bring Nobu.'

'Chairman, please,' I began unsteadily, 'I made such a terrible mistake. . .'

'Before you say anything further, I only want to know why you did this thing. Perhaps you felt you were doing Iwamura Electric some sort of . . . favor. I don't know. Or maybe you owed the Minister something I'm unaware of.'

I must have given my head a little shake, because the Chairman stopped speaking at once.

'I'm deeply ashamed, Chairman,' I managed to say at last, 'but . . . my motives were purely personal.'

After a long moment he sighed and held out his sake cup. I poured for him, with the feeling that my hands were someone else's, and then he tossed the sake into his mouth and held it there before swallowing. Seeing him with his mouth momentarily full made me think of myself as an empty vessel swelled up with shame.

'All right, Sayuri,' he said, 'I'll tell you exactly why I'm asking. It will be impossible for you to grasp why I've come here tonight, or why I've treated you as I have over the years, if you don't understand the nature of my relationship with Nobu. Believe me, I'm more aware than anyone of how difficult he can sometimes be. But he is a genius; I value him more than an entire team of men combined.'

I couldn't think of what to do or say, so with trembling hands I picked up the vial to pour more sake for the Chairman. I took it as a very bad sign that he didn't lift his cup.

'One day when I'd known you only a short time,' he went on, 'Nobu brought you a gift of a comb, and gave it to you in front of everyone at the party. I hadn't realized how much affection he felt for you until that very moment. I'm sure there were other signs before, but somehow I must have overlooked them. And when I realized how he felt, the way he looked at you that evening . . . well, I knew in a moment that I couldn't possibly take away from him the thing he so clearly wanted. It never diminished my concern for your welfare. In fact, as the years have gone by, it has become increasingly difficult for me to listen dispassionately while Nobu talks about you.'

Here the Chairman paused and said, 'Sayuri, are you listening to me?'

'Yes, Chairman, of course.'

'There's no reason you would know this, but I owe Nobu a great debt. It's true I'm the founder of the company and his boss. But when Iwamura Electric was still quite young, we had a terrible problem with cash flow and very nearly went out of business. I wasn't willing to give up control of the company and I wouldn't listen to Nobu when he insisted on bringing in investors. He won in the end, even though it caused a rift between us for a time; he offered to resign, and I almost let him. But of course, he was completely right, and I was wrong. I'd have lost the company without him. How do you repay a man for something like that? Do you know why I'm called 'Chairman' and not 'President'? It's because I resigned the title so Nobu would take it – though he tried to refuse. This is why I made up my mind, the moment I became aware of his affection for you, that I would keep my interest in you hidden so that Nobu could have you. Life has been cruel to him, Sayuri. He's had too little kindness.'

In all my years as a geisha, I'd never been able to convince myself even for a moment that the Chairman felt any special regard for me. And now to know that he'd intended me for . . .

'I never meant to pay you so little attention,' he went on. 'But surely you realize that if he'd ever picked up the slightest hint of my feelings, he would have given you up in an instant.'

Since my girlhood, I'd dreamed that one day the Chairman would tell me he cared for me; and yet I'd never quite believed it would really happen. I certainly hadn't imagined he might tell me what I hoped to hear, and also that Nobu was my destiny. Perhaps the goal I'd sought in life would elude me, but at least during this one moment, it was within my power to sit in the room with the Chairman and tell him how deeply I felt.

'Please forgive me for what I am about to say,' I finally managed to begin.

I tried to continue, but somehow my throat made up its mind to swallow – though I can't think what I was swallowing, unless it was a little knot of emotion I pushed back down because there was no room in my face for any more.

'I have great affection for Nobu, but what I did on Amami . . .' Here I had to hold a burning in my throat a long moment before I could speak again. 'What I did on Amami, I did because of my feelings for you, Chairman. Every step I have taken in my life since I was a child in Gion, I have taken in the hope of bringing myself closer to you.'

When I said these words, all the heat in my body seemed to

rise to my face. I felt I might float up into the air, just like a piece of ash from a fire, unless I could focus on something in the room. I tried to find a smudge on the tabletop, but already the table itself was glazing over and disappearing in my vision.

'Look at me, Sayuri.'

I wanted to do as the Chairman asked, but I couldn't.

'How strange,' he went on quietly almost to himself, 'that the same woman who looked me so frankly in the eye as a girl, many years ago, can't bring herself to do it now.'

Perhaps it ought to have been a simple task to raise my eyes and look at the Chairman; and yet somehow I couldn't have felt more nervous if I'd stood alone on a stage with all of Kyoto watching. We were sitting at a corner of the table, so close that when at length I wiped my eyes and raised them to meet his, I could see the dark rings around his irises. I wondered if perhaps I should look away and make a little bow and then offer to pour him a cup of sake . . . but no gesture would have been enough to break the tension. As I was thinking these thoughts, the Chairman moved the vial of sake and the cup aside, and then reached out his hand and took the collar of my robe to draw me toward him. In a moment our faces were so close, I could feel the warmth of his skin. I was still struggling to understand what was happening to me – and what I ought to do or say. And then the Chairman pulled me closer, and he kissed me.

It may surprise you to hear that this was the first time in my life anyone had ever really kissed me. General Tottori had sometimes pressed his lips against mine when he was my *danna*; but it had been utterly passionless. I'd wondered at the time if he simply needed somewhere to rest his face. Even Yasuda Akira – the man who'd bought me a kimono, and whom I'd seduced one night at the Tatematsu Teahouse – must have kissed me dozens of times on my neck and face, but he never really touched my lips with his. And so you can imagine that this kiss, the first real one of my life, seemed to me more intimate than anything I'd ever experienced. I had the feeling I was taking something from the Chairman, and that he was giving something to me, something more private

479

than anyone had ever given me before. There was a certain very startling taste, as distinctive as any fruit or sweet, and when I tasted it, my shoulders sagged and my stomach swelled up; because for some reason it called to mind a dozen different scenes I couldn't think why I should remember. I thought of the head of steam when the cook lifted the lid from the rice cooker in the kitchen of our okiya. I saw a picture in my mind of the little alleyway that was the main thoroughfare of Pontocho, as I'd seen it one evening crowded with well-wishers after Kichisaburo's last performance, the day he'd retired from the Kabuki theater. I'm sure I might have thought of a hundred other things, for it was as if all the boundaries in my mind had broken down and my memories were running free. But then the Chairman leaned back away from me again, with one of his hands upon my neck. He was so close, I could see the moisture glistening on his lip, and still smell the kiss we'd just ended.

'Chairman,' I said, 'why?'

'Why what?'

'Why . . . everything? Why have you kissed me? You've just been speaking of me as a gift to Nobu-san.'

'Nobu gave you up, Sayuri. I've taken nothing away from him.'

In my confusion of feelings, I couldn't quite understand what he meant.

'When I saw you there with the Minister, you had a look in your eyes just like the one I saw so many years ago at the Shirakawa Stream,' he told me. 'You seemed so desperate, like you might drown if someone didn't save you. After Pumpkin told me you'd intended that encounter for Nobu's eyes, I made up my mind to tell him what I'd seen. And when he reacted so angrily. . . well, if he couldn't forgive you for what you'd done, it was clear to me he was never truly your destiny.'

One afternoon back when I was a child in Yoroido, a little boy named Gisuke climbed a tree to jump into the pond. He climbed much higher than he should have; the water wasn't deep enough. But when we told him not to jump, he was afraid to climb back down because of rocks under the tree. I ran to the village to find his father, Mr. Yamashita, who came walking so calmly up the hill, I wondered if he realized what danger his son was in. He stepped underneath the tree just as the boy – unaware of his father's presence – lost his grip and fell. Mr. Yamashita caught him as easily as if someone had dropped a sack into his arms, and set him upright. We all of us cried out in delight, and skipped around at the edge of the pond while Gisuke stood blinking his eyes very quickly, little tears of astonishment gathering on his lashes.

Now I knew exactly what Gisuke must have felt. I had been plummeting toward the rocks, and the Chairman had stepped out to catch me. I was so overcome with relief, I couldn't even wipe away the tears that spilled from the corners of my eyes. His shape was a blur before me, but I could see him moving closer, and in a moment he'd gathered me up in his arms just as if I were a blanket. His lips went straight for the little triangle of flesh where the edges of my kimono came together at my throat. And when I felt his breath on my neck, and the sense of urgency with which he almost consumed me, I couldn't help thinking of a moment years earlier, when I'd stepped into the kitchen of the okiya and found one of the maids leaning over the sink, trying to cover up the ripe pear she held to her mouth, its juices running down onto her neck. She'd had such a craving for it, she'd said and begged me not to tell Mother.

35

NOW, NEARLY FORTY years later, I sit here looking back on that evening with the Chairman as the moment when all the grieving voices within me fell silent. Since the day I'd left Yoroido, I'd done nothing but worry that every turn of life's wheel would bring yet another obstacle into my path; and of course, it was the worrying and the struggle that had always made life so vividly real to me. When we fight upstream against a rocky undercurrent, every foothold takes on a kind of urgency.

But life softened into something much more pleasant after the Chairman became my *danna*. I began to feel like a tree whose roots had at last broken into the rich, wet soil deep beneath the surface. I'd never before had occasion to think of myself as more fortunate than others, and yet now I was. Though I must say, I lived in that contented state a long while before I was finally able to look back and admit how desolate my life had once been. I'm sure I could never have told my story otherwise; I don't think any of us can speak frankly about pain until we are no longer enduring it.

On the afternoon when the Chairman and I drank sake together in a ceremony at the Ichiriki Teahouse, something peculiar happened. I don't know why, but when I sipped from the smallest of the three cups we used, I let the sake wash over my tongue, and a single drop of it spilled from the corner of my mouth. I was wearing a five-crested kimono of black, with a dragon woven in gold and red encircling the hem up to my thighs. I recall watching the drop fall beneath my arm and roll down the black silk on my thigh, until it came to a stop at the heavy silver threads of the dragon's teeth. I'm sure most geisha would call it a bad omen that I'd spilled sake; but to me, that droplet of moisture that had slipped from me like a tear seemed almost to tell the story of my life. It fell through empty space, with no control whatsoever over its destiny; rolled along a path of silk; and somehow came to rest there on the teeth of that dragon. I thought of the petals I'd thrown into the Kamo River shallows outside Mr. Arashino's workshop, imagining they might find their way to the Chairman. It seemed to me that, somehow, perhaps they had.

In the foolish hopes that had been so dear to me since girlhood, I'd always imagined my life would be perfect if I ever became the Chairman's mistress. It's a childish thought, and yet I'd carried it with me even as an adult. I ought to have known better: How many times already had I encountered the painful lesson that although we may wish for the barb to be pulled from our flesh, it leaves behind a welt that doesn't heal? In banishing Nobu from my life forever, it wasn't just that I lost his friendship; I also ended up banishing myself from Gion.

The reason is so simple, I ought to have known beforehand it would happen. A man who has won a prize coveted by his friend faces a difficult choice: he must either hide his prize away where the friend will never see it – if he can – or suffer damage to the friendship. This was the very problem that had arisen between Pumpkin and me: our friendship had never recovered after my adoption. So although the Chairman's negotiations with Mother to become my *danna* dragged out over several months, in the end it was agreed that I would no longer work as a geisha. I certainly wasn't the first geisha to leave Gion; besides those who ran away, some married and left as wives, others withdrew to set up teahouses or okiya of their own. In my case, however, I was trapped in a peculiar middle ground. The Chairman wanted me out of Gion to keep me out of sight of Nobu, but he certainly wasn't going to marry me, he was already married. Probably the perfect solution, and the one that the Chairman proposed, would have been to set me up with my own teahouse or inn – one that Nobu would never have visited. But Mother was unwilling to have me leave the okiya; she would have earned no revenues from my relationship with the Chairman if I had ceased to be a member of the Nitta family, you see. This is why in the end, the Chairman agreed to pay the okiya a very considerable sum each month on the condition that Mother permit me to end my career. I continued to live in the okiya, just as I had for so many years; but I no longer went to the little school in the mornings, or made the rounds of Gion to pay my respects on special occasions; and of course, I no longer entertained during the evenings.

Because I'd set my sights on becoming a geisha only to win the affections of the Chairman, probably I ought to have felt no sense of loss in withdrawing from Gion. And yet over the years I'd developed many rich friendships, not only with other geisha but with many of the men I'd come to know. I wasn't banished from the company of other women just because I'd ceased entertaining; but those who make a living in Gion have little time for socializing. I often felt jealous when I saw two geisha hurrying to their next engagement, laughing together over what had happened at the last one. I didn't envy them the uncertainty of their existence; but I did envy that sense of promise I could well remember, that the evening ahead might yet hold some mischievous pleasure.

I did see Mameha frequently. We had tea together at least several times a week. Considering all that she had done for me since childhood – and the special role she'd played in my life on the Chairman's behalf – you can imagine how much I felt myself in her debt. One day in a shop I came upon a silk painting from the eighteenth century showing a woman teaching a young girl calligraphy. The teacher had an exquisite oval face and watched over her pupil with such benevolence, it made me think of Mameha at once, and I bought it for her as a gift. On the rainy afternoon when she hung it on the wall of her dreary apartment, I found myself listening to the traffic that hissed by on Higashi-oji Avenue. I couldn't help remembering, with a terrible feeling of loss, her elegant apartment from years earlier, and the enchanting sound out those windows of water rushing over the knee-high cascade in the Shirakawa Stream. Gion itself had seemed to me like an exquisite piece of antique fabric back then; but so much had changed. Now Mameha's simple one-room apartment had mats the color of stale tea and smelled of herbal potions from the Chinese pharmacy below – so much so that her kimono themselves sometimes gave off a faint medicinal odor.

After she'd hung the ink painting on the wall and admired it for a while, she came back to the table. She sat with her hands around her steaming teacup, peering into it as though she expected to find the words she was looking for. I was surprised to see the tendons in her hands beginning to show themselves from age. At last, with a trace of sadness, she said:

'How curious it is, what the future brings us. You must take care, Sayuri, never to expect too much.'

I'm quite sure she was right. I'd have had an easier time over the following years if I hadn't gone on believing that Nobu would one day forgive me. In the end I had to give up questioning Mameha whether he'd asked about me; it pained me terribly to see her sigh and give me a long, sad look, as if to say she was sorry I hadn't known better than to hope for such a thing.

In the spring of the year after I became his mistress, the Chairman purchased a luxurious house in the northeast of Kyoto and named it *Eishin-an* – 'Prosperous Truth Retreat.' It was intended for guests of the company, but in fact the Chairman made more use of it than anyone. This was where he and I met to spend the evenings together three or four nights a week, sometimes even more. On his busiest days he arrived so late he wanted only to soak in a hot bath while I talked with him, and then afterward fall asleep. But most evenings he arrived around sunset, or soon after, and ate his dinner while we chatted and watched the servants light the lanterns in the garden.

Usually when he first came, the Chairman talked for a time about his workday. He might tell me about troubles with a new product, or about a traffic accident involving a truckload of pans, or some such thing. Of course I was happy to sit and listen, but I understood perfectly well that the Chairman wasn't telling these things to me because he wanted me to know them. He was clearing them from his mind, just like draining water from a bucket. So I listened closely not to his words, but to the tone of his voice, because in the same way that sound rises as a bucket is emptied, I could hear the Chairman's voice softening as he spoke. When the moment was right, I changed the subject, and soon we were talking about nothing so serious as business, but about everything else instead, such as what had happened to him that morning on the way to work, or something about the film we may have watched a few nights earlier there at the *Eishin-an*, or perhaps I told him a funny story I might have heard from Mameha, who on some evenings came to join us there. In any case, this simple process of first draining the Chairman's mind and then relaxing him with playful conversation had the same effect water has on a towel that has dried stiffly in the sun. When he first arrived and I washed his hands with a hot cloth, his fingers felt rigid, like heavy twigs. After we had talked for a time, they bent as gracefully as if he were sleeping.

I expected that this would be my life, entertaining the Chairman in the evenings and occupying myself during the daylight hours in any way I could. But in the fall of 1952, I accompanied the Chairman on his second trip to the United States. He'd traveled there the winter before, and no experience of his life had ever made such an impression on him; he said he felt he understood for the first time the true meaning of prosperity. Most Japanese at this time had electricity only during certain hours, for example, but the lights in American cities burned around the clock. And while we in Kyoto were proud that the floor of our new train station was constructed of concrete rather than old-fashioned wood, the floors of American train stations were made of solid marble. Even in small American towns, the movie theaters were as grand as our National Theater, said the Chairman, and the public bathrooms everywhere were spotlessly clean. What amazed him most of all was that every family in the United States owned a refrigerator, which could be purchased with the wages earned by an average worker in only a month's time. In Japan, a worker needed fifteen months' wages to buy such a thing; few families could afford it.

In any case, as I say, the Chairman permitted me to accompany him on his second trip to America. I traveled alone by rail to Tokyo, and from there we flew together on an airplane bound for Hawaii, where we spent a few remarkable days. The Chairman bought me a bathing suit – the first I'd ever owned – and I sat wearing it on the beach with my hair hanging neatly at my shoulders just like other women around me. Hawaii reminded me strangely of Amami; I worried that the same thought might occur to the Chairman, but if it did, he said nothing about it. From Hawaii, we continued to Los Angeles and finally to New York. I knew nothing about the United States except what I'd seen in movies; I don't think I quite believed that the great buildings of New York City really existed. And when I settled at last into my room at the Waldorf-Astoria Hotel, and looked out the window at the mountainous buildings around me and the smooth, clean streets below, I had the feeling I was seeing a world in which anything was possible. I confess I'd expected to feel like a baby who has been taken away from its mother; for I had never before left Japan, and couldn't imagine that a setting as alien as New York City would make me anything but fearful. Perhaps it was the Chairman's enthusiasm that helped me to approach my visit there with such goodwill. He'd taken a separate room, which he used mostly for business; but every night he came to stay with me in the suite he'd arranged. Often I awoke in that strange bed and turned to see him there in the dark, sitting in a chair by the window holding the sheer curtain open, staring at Park Avenue below. One time after two o'clock in the morning, he took me by the hand and pulled me to the window to see a young couple dressed as if they'd come from a ball, kissing under the street lamp on the corner.

Over the next three years I traveled with the Chairman twice more to the United States. While he attended to business during the day, my maid and I took in the museums and restaurants – and even a ballet, which I found breathtaking. Strangely, one of the few Japanese restaurants we were able to find in New York was now under the management of a chef

I'd known well in Gion before the war. During lunch one afternoon, I found myself in his private room in the back, entertaining a number of men I hadn't seen in years – the vice president of Nippon Telephone & Telegraph; the new Japanese Consul-General, who had formerly been mayor of Kobe; a professor of political science from Kyoto University. It was almost like being back in Gion once again.

In the summer of 1956, the Chairman – who had two daughters by his wife, but no son – arranged for his eldest daughter to marry a man named Nishioka Minoru. The Chairman's intention was that Mr. Nishioka take the family name of Iwamura and become his heir; but at the last moment, Mr. Nishioka had a change of heart, and informed the Chairman that he did not intend to go through with the wedding. He was a very temperamental young man, but in the Chairman's estimation, quite brilliant. For a week or more the Chairman was upset, and snapped at his servants and me without the least provocation. I'd never seen him so disturbed by anything.

No one ever told me why Nishioka Minoru changed his mind, but no one had to. During the previous summer, the founder of one of Japan's largest insurance companies had dismissed his son as president, and turned his company over instead to a much younger man – his illegitimate son by a Tokyo geisha. It caused quite a scandal at the time. Things of this sort had happened before in Japan, but usually on a much smaller scale, in family-owned kimono stores or sweets shops – businesses of that sort. The insurance company director described his firstborn in the newspapers as 'an earnest young man whose talents unfortunately can't be compared with' and here he named his illegitimate son, without ever giving any hint of their relationship. But it made no difference whether he gave a hint of it or not, everyone knew the truth soon enough.

Now, if you were to imagine that Nishioka Minoru, after already having agreed to become the Chairman's heir, had discovered some new bit of information – such as that the Chairman had recently fathered an illegitimate son . . . well,

I'm sure that in this case, his reluctance to go through with the marriage would probably seem quite understandable. It was widely known that the Chairman lamented having no son, and was deeply attached to his two daughters. Was there any reason to think he wouldn't become equally attached to an illegitimate son – enough, perhaps, to change his mind before death and turn over to him the company he'd built? As to the question of whether or not I really had given birth to a son of the Chairman's . . . if I had, I'd certainly be reluctant to talk too much about him, for fear that his identity might become publicly known. It would be in no one's best interest for such a thing to happen. The best course, I feel, is for me to say nothing at all; I'm sure you will understand.

A week or so after Nishioka Minoru's change of heart, I decided to raise a very delicate subject with the Chairman. We were at the *Eishin-an*, sitting outdoors after dinner on the veranda overlooking the moss garden. The Chairman was brooding, and hadn't spoken a word since before dinner was served.

'Have I mentioned to Danna-sama,' I began, 'that I've had the strangest feeling lately?'

I glanced at him, but I could see no sign that he was even listening.

'I keep thinking of the Ichiriki Teahouse,' I went on, 'and truthfully, I'm beginning to recognize how much I miss entertaining.'

The Chairman just took a bite of his ice cream, and then set his spoon down on the dish again.

'Of course, I can never go back to work in Gion; I know that perfectly well. And yet I wonder, Danna-sama . . . isn't there a place for a small teahouse in New York City?'

'I don't know what you're talking about,' he said. 'There's no reason why you should want to leave Japan.'

'Japanese businessmen and politicians are showing up in New York these days as commonly as turtles plopping into a pond,' I said. 'Most of them are men I've known already for years. It's true that leaving Japan would be an abrupt change. But considering that Danna-sama will be spending more and more of his time in the United States . . .' I knew this was true, because he'd already told me about his plan to open a branch of his company there.

'I'm in no mood for this, Sayuri,' he began. I think he intended to say something further, but I went on as though I hadn't heard him.

'They say that a child raised between two cultures often has a very difficult time,' I said. 'So naturally, a mother who moves with her child to a place like the United States would probably be wise to make it her permanent home.'

'Sayuri –'

'Which is to say,' I went on, 'that a woman who made such a choice would probably never bring her child back to Japan at all.'

By this time the Chairman must have understood what I was suggesting – that I remove from Japan the only obstacle in the way of Nishioka Minoru's adoption as his heir. He wore a startled look for an instant. And then, probably as the image formed in his mind of my leaving him, his peevish humor seemed to crack open like an egg, and out of the corner of his eye came a single tear, which he blinked away just as swiftly as swatting a fly.

In August of that same year, I moved to New York City to set up my own very small teahouse for Japanese businessmen and politicians traveling through the United States. Of course, Mother tried to ensure that any business I started in New York City would be an extension of the Nitta okiya, but the Chairman refused to consider any such arrangement. Mother had power over me as long as I remained in Gion; but I broke my ties with her by leaving. The Chairman sent in two of his accountants to ensure that Mother gave me every last yen to which I was entitled.

I can't pretend I didn't feel afraid so many years ago, when the door of my apartment here at the Waldorf Towers closed behind me for the first time. But New York is an exciting city. Before long it came to feel at least as much a home to me as Gion ever did. In fact, as I look back, the memories of many long weeks I've spent here with the Chairman have made my life in the United States even richer in some ways than it was in Japan. My little teahouse, on the second floor of an old club off Fifth Avenue, was modestly successful from the very beginning; a number of geisha have come from Gion to work with me there, and even Mameha sometimes visits. Nowadays I go there myself only when close friends or old acquaintances have come to town. I spend my time in a variety of other ways instead. In the mornings I often join a group of Japanese writers and artists from the area to study subjects that interest us – such as poetry or music or, during one month-long session, the history of New York City. I lunch with a friend most days. And in the afternoons I kneel before my makeup stand to prepare for one party or another – sometimes here in my very own apartment. When I lift the brocade cover on my mirror, I can't help but remember the milky odor of the white makeup I so often wore in Gion. I dearly wish I could go back there to visit; but on the other hand, I think I would be disturbed to see all the changes. When friends bring photographs from their trips to Kyoto, I often think that Gion has thinned out like a poorly kept garden, increasingly overrun with weeds. After Mother's death a number of years ago, for example, the Nitta okiya was torn down and replaced with a tiny concrete building housing a bookshop on the ground floor and two apartments overhead.

Eight hundred geisha worked in Gion when I first arrived there. Now the number is less than sixty, with only a handful of apprentices, and it dwindles further every day – because of course the pace of change never slows, even when we've convinced ourselves it will. On his last visit to New York City, the Chairman and I took a walk through Central Park. We happened to be talking about the past; and when we came to a path through pine trees, the Chairman stopped suddenly He'd often told me of the pines bordering the street outside Osaka on which he'd grown up; I knew as I watched him that he was remembering them. He stood with his two frail hands on his cane and his eyes closed, and breathed in deeply the scent of the past.

'Sometimes,' he sighed, 'I think the things I remember are more real than the things I see.'

As a younger woman I believed that passion must surely fade with age, just as a cup left standing in a room will gradually give up its contents to the air. But when the Chairman and I returned to my apartment, we drank each other up with so much yearning and need that afterward I felt myself drained of all the things the Chairman had taken from me, and yet filled with all that I had taken from him. I fell into a sound sleep and dreamed that I was at a banquet back in Gion, talking with an elderly man who was explaining to me that his wife, whom he'd cared for deeply, wasn't really dead because the pleasure of their time together lived on inside him. While he spoke these words, I drank from a bowl of the most extraordinary soup I'd ever tasted; every briny sip was a kind of ecstasy. I began to feel that all the people I'd ever known who had died or left me had not in fact gone away, but continued to live on inside me just as this man's wife lived on inside him. I felt as though I were drinking them all in – my sister, Satsu, who had run away and left me so young; my father and mother; Mr. Tanaka, with his perverse view of kindness; Nobu, who could never forgive me; even the Chairman. The soup was filled with all that I'd ever cared for in my life; and while I drank it, this man spoke his words right into my heart. I awoke with tears streaming down my temples, and I took the Chairman's hand, fearing that I would never be able to live without him when he died and left me. For he was so frail by then, even there in his sleep, that I couldn't help thinking of my mother back in Yoroido. And yet when his death happened only a few months later, I understood that he left me at the end of his long life just as naturally as the leaves fall from the trees.

I cannot tell you what it is that guides us in this life; but for me, I fell toward the Chairman just as a stone must fall toward the earth. When I cut my lip and met Mr. Tanaka, when my mother died and I was cruelly sold, it was all like a stream that falls over rocky cliffs before it can reach the ocean. Even now that he is gone I have him still, in the richness of my memories. I've lived my life again just telling it to you.

It's true that sometimes when I cross Park Avenue, I'm

struck with the peculiar sense of how exotic my surroundings are. The yellow taxicabs that go sweeping past, honking their horns; the women with their briefcases, who look so perplexed to see a little old Japanese woman standing on the street corner in kimono. But really, would Yoroido seem any less exotic if I went back there again? As a young girl I believed my life would never have been a struggle if Mr. Tanaka hadn't torn me away from my tipsy house. But now I know that our world is no more permanent than a wave rising on the ocean. Whatever our struggles and triumphs, however we may suffer them, all too soon they bleed into a wash, just like watery ink on paper.

ACKNOWLEDGMENTS

ALTHOUGH THE CHARACTER of Sayuri and her story are completely invented, the historical facts of a geisha's day-to-day life in the 1930s and 1940s are not. In the course of my extensive research I am indebted to one individual above all others. Mineko Iwasaki, one of Gion's top geisha in the 1960s and 1970s, opened her Kyoto home to me during May 1992, and corrected my every misconception about the life of a geisha – even though everyone I knew who had lived in Kyoto, or who lived there still, told me never to expect such candor. While brushing up my Japanese on the airplane, I worried that Mineko, whom I had not yet met, might talk with me for an hour about the weather and call it an interview. Instead she took me on an insider's tour of Gion, and together with her husband, Jin, and her sisters, Yaetchiyo and the late Kuniko, patiently answered all my questions about the ritual of a geisha's life in intimate detail. She became, and remains, a good friend. I have the fondest memories of her family's trip to visit us in Boston, and the otherworldly sense my wife and I felt while watching tennis on television in our living room with our new friend, a Japanese woman in her forties who also happened to be one of the last geisha trained in the old tradition.

To Mineko, thank you for everything.

I was introduced to Mineko by Mrs. Reiko Nagura, a long-time friend and a fiercely intelligent woman of my mother's generation, who speaks Japanese, English, and German with equal fluency. She won a prize for a short story she wrote in English while an undergraduate at Barnard, only a few years after first coming to the United States to study, and soon became a lifelong friend of my grandmother's. The affection between her family and mine is now in its fourth generation. Her home has been a regular haven on my visits to Tokyo; I owe her a greater debt than I can express. Along with every other kindness she has done for me, she read over my manuscript at various stages and offered a great many invaluable suggestions.

During the years I have worked on this novel, my wife, Trudy, has provided more help and support than I had any right to expect. Beyond her endless patience, her willingness to drop everything and read when I needed her eye, and her frankness and extreme thoughtfulness, she has given me that greatest of gifts: constancy and understanding.

Robin Desser of Knopf is the kind of editor every writer dreams about: passionate, insightful, committed, always helpful – and a load of fun besides.

For her warmth, her directness, her professionalism, and her charm, there's no one quite like Leigh Feldman. I am extremely lucky to have her for an agent.

Helen Bartlett, you know all you did to help me from early on. Thanks to you, and to Denise Stewart.

I'm very grateful to my good friend Sara Laschever, for her careful reading of the manuscript, her generous involvement, and her many thoughtful suggestions and ideas.

Teruko Craig was kind enough to spend hours talking with me about her life as a schoolgirl in Kyoto during the war. I am grateful also to Liza Dalby, the only American woman ever to become a geisha, and to her excellent book, *Geisha*, an anthropological study of geisha culture, which also recounts her experiences in the Pontocho district; she generously lent me a number of useful Japanese and English books from her personal collection.

Thanks also to Kiharu Nakamura, who has written about her experiences as a geisha in the Shimbashi district of Tokyo, and kindly spent an evening talking with me during the course of my research.

I am grateful, too, for the thoughtful insights and empathetic concern of my brother, Stephen.

Robert Singer, curator of Japanese art at the Los Angeles

County Museum of Art, went to considerable trouble while I was in Kyoto to show me firsthand how aristocrats there once lived.

Bowen Dees, whom I met on an airplane, permitted me to read his unpublished manuscript about his experiences in Japan during the Allied Occupation.

I'm thankful also to Allan Palmer for giving me the benefit of his extensive knowledge of tea ceremony and Japanese superstitions.

John Rosenfield taught me Japanese art history as no one else can, and made a university as gigantic as Harvard feel like a small college. I'm grateful to him for helpful advice all along the way.

I'm profoundly in Barry Minsky's debt, for the valuable role he played as I worked to bring this novel into being.

In addition, for their kindnesses too numerous to recount, thanks to David Kuhn, Merry White, Kazumi Aoki, Yasu Ikuma, Megumi Nakatani, David Sand, Yoshio Imakita, Mameve Medwed, the late Celia Millward, Camilla Trinchieri, Barbara Shapiro, Steve Weisman, Yoshikata Tsukamoto, Carol Janeway of Knopf, Lynn Pleshette, Denise Rusoff, David Schwab, Alison Tolman, Lidia Yagoda, Len Rosen and Diane Fader.

For my wife, Trudy,
and my children, Hays and Tess